Y0-CUL-108

I dedicate this book to my husband Ivan and my sons Jarrett and Justin.

Ivan and I were high school sweethearts. We married at the age of nineteen in 1985 and are now moving toward thirty-eight years together! It has been quite an adventure. He has always been my support system, protector, shoulder to lean on, and the first person I turn to for every single thing going on in my life.

His strong personality is what drives my dreamer personality to achieve the goals I desire.

Jarrett and Justin have given me more joy in my life than any one person deserves. Their laughter and sense of humor has always kept a smile on my face. They made it easy to be their mother!

Thank-you for being the men that you are.

I love you!

CHAPTER 1

ON THAT THURSDAY EVENING OF MARCH 5, 2016, TWO LITTLE BOYS BY THE names of Jarrett and Justin Chase were born. Jarrett arrived seven minutes before his brother. Both had entered the world with loud and healthy lungs.

Their father, Luke, proudly strolled down the hospital corridor to inform his impatiently waiting family of the fact that he was now a dad. He had entered the hospital's waiting room wearing his greens over his casual attire of jeans and a T-shirt. His blond hair was messy from continually running his hands through it, but it didn't take away from the pride that radiated from his bright blue eyes.

Nora, his girlfriend of five years, had been settled in her private room with the boys and sat anxiously waiting to introduce them to their grandparents, aunt, and uncle. Her long auburn hair had been brushed to a high silky sheen and lay fanned around her. She was anxious to have a shower and to change out of her hospital garb, but it would have to wait. She smiled as she heard the hushed tones of her family approaching the room.

Luke's younger brother, Jessie, asked, "Is it a boy or a girl?"

Luke had not answered him. Instead, he kept smiling and walking toward Nora's room.

Then, she heard his mother, Elle, ask, "Is Nora okay?"

Luke answered with, "She's great! Tired, but doing great."

Nora smiled to herself. She could only imagine the grumblings of Jessie because his question had been dismissed.

Once they had reached the door to her room, Luke slowly opened it and stuck his head in. Nora lay in the bed, propped up with a son in each arm, smiling proudly.

He opened the door wider to allow the group to enter, and then moved to Nora's side.

Elle had entered first and whispered, "Oh my goodness!" as she slowly approached the bed. Nora could see Jessie trying to vie for space to get a look.

Once he had entered, he whispered to Luke, "Are you kidding me right now?"

"I'm gonna cry!" said Jessie's wife, Ava, as she swiped at her tears. Her tiny, pixie-like frame moved lightning fast to push past her husband. Jessie smoothly let her by with a shake of his head and a smile on his face.

Elle's husband, Danny, grinned and said, "Congratulations!"

Tears of happiness ran down Elle's face. Walking into that hospital room to see her eldest son gazing at Nora and their two sons was heartwarming.

"Grandma, meet your grandsons, Jarrett and Justin."

Elle could hardly contain her excitement. She was overjoyed at being a grandmother. The fact that she was a grandmother to twin boys was incredible.

Elle approached the bed and gently ran her hand over Nora's hair. The smile on Elle's face and the tears in her eyes had Nora's eyes welling up.

She smiled down at her grandsons and placed her hands on their chests where their little hearts were beating. They were tightly wrapped in receiving blankets and wore tiny little cotton hats to help keep them warm.

Ava stood silently beside Elle to allow her this precious moment.

Elle smiled at Nora and then at Luke. "How am I supposed to tell them apart?" she asked happily.

"Jarrett's wearing the green hat and Justin's is blue."

Nora carefully handed Jarrett to Elle, and then Justin to Ava.

The three women smiled gently at each other. Nora adjusted her coral-colored gown, scooped her long auburn hair to lay it to one side of her neck, and settled back in her bed.

"Oh, Nora and Luke, they're perfect." Elle rubbed her finger along Jarrett's sweet little cheeks as he slept bundled up in her arms. She cradled him while swaying back and forth, as women always do when they're holding a child. She lifted the edge of his green hat to get a look at his hair. The blond fluffiness of it had her smiling.

"We think they're pretty cute," Luke answered, as he bent to kiss Nora's forehead.

Ava had fallen in love all over again. "Just look at their sweet little faces." She began opening the blanket to get a look at Justin's fingers and toes as she slowly walked toward Jessie.

"Look, honey. I want one, too," she said simply.

Jessie peeked at Justin and smiled. "How about we just enjoy these two for a little while." He wrapped his arm around

Ava's shoulder as he watched the baby work his little mouth. He checked under his blue hat, and sure enough, there was a light blond fluffiness that matched his brother's hair.

He turned to Luke. "Did you know you were having twins?"

Luke smiled. "We did. We wanted to surprise all of you."

"Well, you sure did!" exclaimed Danny. He walked over to Luke and shook his hand. "Congratulations again."

Next, he moved closer to Nora and took her gently by the hand.

"Congratulations, Nora. Your sons are beautiful."

She smiled broadly. "Thanks Danny."

She turned to Elle. "Doin' okay over there, Grandma?"

Elle was completely engrossed with Jarrett. She looked up and answered with a huge smile on her face, "Doin' just great."

Nora returned the smile and then said to Ava, "A baby in your arms suits you."

Ava had tears in her eyes when she answered. "I want one. They're just so precious."

Ava walked closer to Elle again. "Wanna switch for a bit? I need to hold him, too."

They smoothly exchanged babies.

Elle cooed at Justin. "Well, hi there, handsome." She rubbed her finger along his cheek and started swaying again.

She turned her attention to Nora. "Are you feeling okay?"

"I feel great! A little tired, maybe," she said quietly. "The doctor wants us to stay here at the hospital for a few days to keep an eye on the boys and me."

"That's a good idea. It'll be good to have the nurses here to help out for a bit." She turned her attention back to Justin. "And Grandma will be here to help, too," she whispered.

UNITY

"You won't be able to get rid of her," said Danny with a chuckle.

"I sure hope not!" exclaimed Nora.

Danny strode over to Elle and placed his arm around her shoulder and gazed at Justin. He was nearly a foot taller than his wife. Elle and Justin looked tiny next to him. "You two boys might get a little spoiled," he commented, and then kissed Elle's cheek.

Luke laughed when Elle nodded at the remark.

She looked up at Luke and smiled. "We'll need to get another set of everything made."

Luke turned to Nora. She nodded and smiled.

"That's not a problem. There are a couple of people who knew we were having twins."

"Who?" Jessie asked. He had been a little offended that Luke wouldn't answer his question back in the hallway about the gender. Now he was offended all over again because he wasn't one of the people who knew they would be having twins. Of course, once he had seen the babies, he'd gotten over the first part, but now he was seriously annoyed.

Luke smiled at his brother, knowing he was driving him crazy.

"When we found out, we asked Dave and Mike to make two extra cribs and rocking chairs."

Danny smiled. "That's so cool."

"They used your crib plans, Danny, and my rocking chair plans."

Luke turned to Elle with a smile. "Your extra set will likely be delivered this week, Mom."

Elle returned his smile. "That's perfect. We'll just rearrange the nursery." She played with Justin's chin as she spoke. "When are your parents coming in, Nora?"

"They're on their way home from their trip to Australia. I don't think we'll see them for a couple of days."

Just then, Nora's nurse quietly entered the room. She smiled at the group gathered around. "I see these two little boys are going to get lots of love."

The grouped turned to her and smiled back.

"They certainly are," replied Elle as she nuzzled Justin.

"I'm going to need you all to step out to the hall while I check Nora's vitals."

As Elle and Ava walked toward the door with the babies, the nurse cleared her throat. "Uh, ladies, I'll need to check the boys, too."

"Oh, yes, of course." Elle laughed. "Sorry."

The nurse smiled back. After all, she was a grandma, too, and knew how hard it was to hand back a grandchild.

The women returned Jarrett and Justin to Nora.

Danny suggested that they all head for home and let Nora get some rest.

"Okay, I'll see you guys tomorrow." Elle walked back to the bed and bent to kiss Nora on the cheek. Next, she kissed the twins and touched their tiny chests again.

She rounded the bed and gave Luke a big hug.

"Love you, sweetie. Congratulations."

"Love you too, Mom. Thanks," replied Luke. "See you tomorrow?"

"Absolutely!"

The group waved at the new parents as they left the room.

UNITY

Luke carefully took the boys from Nora and sat in the big comfortable chair in the corner of the room. The nurse would first check Nora and then the twins. He sat with a child cradled in each arm, dividing his attention between them both. Nora smiled sweetly at them.

Nurse Jane did her routine check of Nora. She had been pleased with the results. She made sure Nora was comfortable and then moved to retrieve Jarrett from his dad. His vital signs were perfect. She changed his diaper, traded babies with Luke, and did the same for Justin. All was well with him, too. They each fussed a little at the disturbance.

Jane had warmed up the bottles of formula earlier, and now handed one to Nora for Justin's feeding. While Luke sat cuddling Jarrett, she gave him the second bottle.

She excused herself and left the room.

"We're gonna have our hands full, Mommy," stated Luke as he watched his son drink.

Nora laughed. "We sure are, Daddy!"

They each sat and soaked in the atmosphere.

Luke looked up from Jarrett and said, "I'm going to meet with Gavin tonight after you and the boys are settled. I want to put him in charge of the jobs this week while I'm home with you. I think these two little munchkins are going to need all four of our hands." He smiled at Jarrett as he said the last sentence.

Nora smiled. "I'm glad you'll be home with us."

"I wouldn't have it any other way. I can manage the jobs from home if I need to. I'll be at home for as long as you need my help."

"I would imagine your mom will be around to help out, too."

"She sure will be. She'll be a huge help."

They both smiled at the memory of her reaction when she first saw the twins.

Nurse Jane came back in to check on the feeding process. She was pleased to see it was going well and that both Luke and Nora were relaxed and enjoying it.

"Do you want me to take the boys to the nursery tonight, Nora, or would you rather have them here in your room?"

"I think the nursery would be a good choice for tonight. I could use the sleep."

"Of course. No problem. You just give me a buzz when you're ready for me to come back." She smiled at them and left.

Luke and Nora finished feeding the boys, and then sat quietly to hold them a bit longer. Jarrett looked so tiny nestled in Luke's big arms.

It wasn't long before Nora started yawning. Luke buzzed Jane to come for the boys. They took turns kissing their little faces before she came back into the room. Once they were gone, Luke went to sit on the edge of the bed.

"You must be exhausted," he said as he ran his fingers through her hair.

"A little," she said around a yawn.

He smiled and then kissed her. "Okay. I'm gonna go and let you sleep. I'll be back in the morning. I love you."

"Love you, too. See you in the morning." She watched him leave and then turned on her side to curl up for the long-overdue sleep she craved.

CHAPTER 2

JESSIE AND AVA WALKED OUT OF THE HOSPITAL WITH DANNY AND ELLE. THEY had said their good nights in the parking lot and had agreed they would likely see each other at the hospital the following day.

Ava couldn't wait to get home. She was anxious to get started on "this baby-making." Jessie laughed when she told him exactly that. They made it back in record time.

Danny and Elle called Dave.

"You guys are great at keeping a secret!" exclaimed Elle when Dave answered his phone. Mike could be heard in the background, laughing.

"It wasn't easy," he said.

"Yeah, we had to make the furniture in the back corner of the warehouse in the evenings so Dad wouldn't find out," said Mike.

Danny laughed. "You hid it well."

"How are the twins and Nora doing?" asked Dave.

"Everyone is doing great!"

"Oh, good! We can deliver the crib and chair tomorrow if you are home, Elle."

"That would be great. I'll be at the hospital for a bit in the morning, but I'll be home in the afternoon if that works."

"Sounds good. See you then."

"Say hi to the girls for us!" said Danny.

"You bet," answered Dave.

Elle turned to face Danny. "Your boys are so sweet. That was really nice of them to build the furniture for Luke and Nora."

"Yeah, they like being involved in the family."

"Well, they're stuck with us. And new uncles now, too!"

Danny reached across the seat to hold her hand. "And how does it feel to be a grandma? You look too young to be one."

She smiled broadly. "It feels amazing! And how do you feel about being a grandpa?"

He grinned back at her. "So far, so good!"

"My God, they're adorable." Elle sighed as she lay her head back on the truck headrest, her long blond hair flowing down her shoulders.

"They sure are. Luke and Nora will need some help for the first few weeks," he commented as he turned to look at her. The smile on her face said it all.

"Well, Grandma is ready, willing, and able to help."

Danny laughed. "And she'll love every minute of it." He squeezed her hand gently.

When they arrived home, Elle went directly to the nursery. Danny followed.

"I think if we slide the crib farther along the wall, we can put the other one next to it." She pointed to the intended locations. "And I think the change table would fit perfectly along that wall, with the rocking chair right here." She continued pointing.

"Okay. Let's give it a try."

They pushed and shoved at the solid furniture until it had been placed where Elle wanted it. They stood back to view the room. It wasn't an overly large room, but it would certainly be big enough for the boys. The large windows made the room light and airy.

"Perfect! Dave and Mike can set the crib in its spot, and the other rocking chair out in the living room. What do you think?" she asked. Elle stood with her hands on her slim hips. Her tight T-shirt showed her curves.

"It's gonna work perfectly! Now let's go have a drink and celebrate our grandsons."

They left the nursery, smiling. Danny placed his hand on the small of her back and then slid it down a little farther to cup her butt.

"Easy, tiger!" She laughed as she said it.

He grinned and went to the kitchen to retrieve a beer for himself and a glass of red wine for Elle. He turned on the music system and went to join her. She had already settled on the sofa when he handed her the glass.

"Cheers," he said, once he had settled beside her.

"Cheers." They each took a sip and dreamt of what the future would hold for Jarrett and Justin.

"I love the names they chose for the babies. Now, I just have to find a way to tell the difference between the two!" Elle said with a laugh.

"Yeah, they probably won't dress them in green and blue forever," Danny said with a smirk.

Elle smiled. "It's incredible how identical they really are."

"It's crazy. Oh, by the way, I have a bunch of work to catch up on tomorrow, but I can go to the hospital for a little while with you in the morning if you want," he said, as he lightly rubbed her hand.

"That's okay, babe. I'll go for a visit and then be back here by lunchtime for when Dave and Mike come with the furniture. You'll have plenty of time to visit them once Nora comes home."

"Okay. I should be home by late afternoon, then."

They settled in with their drinks and listened to the country music playing softly in the room.

Luke met with Gavin at The Bar. They shook hands, and Gavin congratulated Luke as he sat across the table from him.

"Thanks. It'll be a big change in our lives," Luke said, smiling as he clinked his beer against Gavin's.

"So, did you want to go over the details of the jobs lined up for this week?"

"Yeah. I'd like to put you in charge of the men while I'm home with Nora. I may need you to take over for a couple of weeks, depending on how it goes with the babies. Is that okay with you?"

"For sure. No problem. I'm happy to help out. Thanks for the trust."

They settled in to go over the upcoming projects. Luke's company, "Chase Your Dreams Construction," was in the process of building a home and workshop for a young couple. The materials had already been ordered and were expected to be delivered to the site by the next day. It was a big job for

Luke and his men. He told Gavin to call him at any time if he had any questions.

Once they were finished with their beers, Luke stood and shook Gavin's hand again.

"Thanks for stepping in for me."

"Well, I hope I do a good job of it."

"I'm not the least bit worried. I'm a phone call away if you have any problems or questions."

They left The Bar feeling confident.

Luke went straight home to bed. He had thought of calling Nora to say goodnight, but figured she'd already be sound asleep. He crawled into bed with a huge smile on his face. 'I'm a daddy!' He slept for a solid six hours.

The following morning, he made himself a quick breakfast before driving to the hospital. He was anxious to see Nora and the boys.

Nora was already busy feeding Jarrett when Luke quietly opened the door. He stood there for a moment to gaze at them. He wanted to soak up the moment.

"Good morning," he whispered as he walked to the edge of the bed. He bent and kissed Nora gently on the lips. Next, he kissed Jarrett on the top of his head and then moved to kiss Justin, who was sound asleep in his little bed.

"Good morning," answered Nora.

"Has Justin been fed yet?" he asked as he watched his son sleep.

"No, not yet. You can feed him when he wakes up, though."

"Gladly." He smiled at Nora and took a seat in the chair across from her bed. "How are you feeling? Did you sleep okay?"

"I had a great sleep. I was exhausted. I feel pretty good, too. Jane brought the boys in about thirty minutes ago. She said they woke once during the night to be fed and went back to sleep immediately." She relayed the details as she ran her finger along Jarrett's cheek while he drank.

Luke jumped from his chair when he heard Justin grunt and groan. He went to his little bed and scooped him up. Nora laughed at how quickly he had reacted.

"Well, hi there, little guy." He nuzzled Justin's cheek. "Are you hungry?" Luke reached for the bottle from the side table and settled back in the chair to feed him.

Elle walked in a few minutes later. She smiled broadly at the scene before her. "You guys look great with those babies in your arms."

They returned the smile. "Hi, Mom," said Luke cheerfully.

"Good morning." She made her way over to him.

She touched Justin's head lightly and then went to Nora.

"Hi, Elle."

"Hi. How are you feeling?" Elle asked as she bent to kiss Nora's cheek. She lightly touched Jarrett's head as well.

"I'm feeling really good. The boys had a good night in the nursery, too. Jarrett's done eating if you want to hold him."

"Absolutely." She set her purse on the table and gently took him from Nora's arms.

"Well, hi there, handsome." She cooed at him while he held onto her finger. She looked up and smiled at Luke and Nora. "Oh my God, they are adorable!"

"Here, Mom. Have a seat. Justin's done eating as well." Luke stood so Elle could sit. He filled her empty arm with Justin.

She smiled broadly as Luke took photos of her and her grandsons. She sat with the sleeping boys in her arms for well over an hour as they chatted quietly.

Nora took a hot shower while Elle sat with the boys. She felt refreshed and ready for the day. She was sitting on the edge of the bed in leggings and an oversized shirt, chatting with Elle and Luke, when Jessie and Ava arrived.

Ava went straight to the babies and gently slid one of them from Elle's arm.

"Hi," she whispered to Elle.

Jessie was right behind her to take the other from Elle. "Hi," he repeated.

Elle smiled at how comfortable they already were with the boys.

Jessie and Ava turned to Luke and Nora. "Good morning."

Luke looked at Nora with a lopsided grin. "Guess we're third and fourth around here now."

"I'm okay with that," replied Nora with a smile on her face.

As Ava ran her fingers along Jarrett's cheek, she asked Nora how she was feeling.

"Great, now that I've showered. I had a great sleep last night while the boys slept in the nursery. I'll have them sleep in here tonight, though."

"I'm sure you needed the rest!" exclaimed Ava with a smile. "When do you think you'll be coming home?"

"I'm hoping they'll let me go home tomorrow. I'm anxious to start a routine with the boys."

Jessie laughed. "You may regret that decision," he said, as he played with Justin's tiny fingers.

Elle spoke up. "We'll all be there to help when you need it."

"Thanks, Elle. I'm sure we'll need lots of help for the first little while."

Nora gazed at her sons while they slept in the arms of her family.

Elle stayed a bit longer, and then said she needed to be home to meet Dave and Mike with the crib and rocking chair. She gave everyone in the room a kiss and headed out the door.

Ava and Jessie visited for a few more minutes before they had to leave for work.

"Is there a job site you need me to check on, Luke?" asked Jessie.

"No, that's okay. Gavin should be able to handle it. Thanks for the offer. If I need you, I'll definitely call."

Ava reluctantly handed over Jarrett. She kissed him and then Justin.

"I'm trying to find a difference between the two. How will I ever tell them apart?" Ava asked in a concerned voice.

Nora laughed. "It won't be easy. I've only found one little difference."

She gently turned Justin's left wrist over. There at the base of it, was a tiny birthmark that resembled the shape of a heart.

Ava moved a little closer. "Oh, my God! That is the sweetest thing I've ever seen. Her eyes instantly filled with tears.

Next, Nora held Jarrett a little further from her chest to get a better look at his face.

"If you look at Jarrett's hairline, you'll see a swirl in the hair."

Ava inspected him as well. "That's so cute! Okay, so wrist and hairline. I'm not giving up the clues. I want people to wonder how I know the difference," she said with a laugh.

Jessie checked out the differences as well. Mostly, so he could say the same as Ava. He gave Nora a kiss on the cheek and the boys a peck on the top of their heads. He shook Luke's hand and guided Ava toward the door after she had said her good byes.

"We'll probably be back tonight," Jessie stated.

"Okay, see you later, guys. Thanks for coming in."

They left, hand in hand.

"So, how soon do you have to be at work?" asked Ava while she waggled her eyebrows at him.

Jessie laughed. "You are unbelievable. Not that I'm complaining." He squeezed her hand.

Jessie led her to her car and kissed her. "Have a great day, babe. I'll see you tonight after work."

She tried to deepen the kiss, but he pulled back. "Don't start it, Ava!" he said jokingly.

"Fine. I'll see you tonight." She tried to sound upset, but couldn't pull it off. She waved and left the parking lot.

Jessie laughed at her as he climbed into his truck to head for the job site. He shook his head at the thought of how badly she now wanted a child. Well, he was happy to try to make that dream come true!

Elle arrived home about an hour before Dave and Mike showed up with the furniture.

"Hi, guys!" she said, as she hugged each of them.

"Hi, Elle. How are you?" asked Mike.

"Just fine, thanks."

"Can you show us where you want the crib? Then we can set it in place for you."

"Yep. The nursery is in the front spare room." She led them through the open kitchen and living area. She pointed to where she wanted it set.

The boys went back out to their work truck and carried the crib inside. They put it exactly where Elle had said she wanted it. Next, they brought in the rocking chair and set it in the living room for her.

"Oh, that's perfect! Thank-you so much."

"No problem. We'll get out of your way now," said Dave.

"Not before you have some lunch." She pointed to the kitchen table. "Have a seat, and I'll get you something cold to drink."

Mike nudged his brother. "See, Jessie was right. He knew Elle would make us lunch."

Elle laughed at his comment. "The boys are pros at timing their visits!"

They enjoyed lunch together as they chatted about what was going on in their lives and their new little nephews.

"We're going with Maggie and Emma tonight to visit," Dave said around a mouthful of food.

"Luke and Nora would love that!"

"We hear that they're identical!" commented Mike.

"They are. It's really hard to tell them apart. Maybe as they get older, it'll be easier."

They enjoyed the rest of their meal with Elle, then stood to clear the table.

"Don't worry about it, guys. Go back to work. I hear your boss is a real jerk about being late."

They both laughed out loud at that. "Thanks for lunch Elle."

"You're welcome. Thank-you for delivering the furniture." She hugged them before they headed out the door.

They climbed in their work truck and waved out the window to her.

"She's such a sweet lady. I'm glad she and Dad found each other," said Mike.

"Yeah, me too. Hey, do you ever think about Mom and where she might be?"

"Nope. Do you?" Mike asked, as he looked over at his brother sitting shotgun.

"Sometimes, but not very often."

Mike nodded in agreement.

They drove back to the warehouse in silence. Both were thinking of the day their mother had walked out the door. She had said that she wanted to travel around Europe, alone. She had packed her bags and told them she would be in touch. In the six years that she had been gone, they had not heard from her once.

Danny pulled into the yard at the same time as his sons.

"Hi, guys. Did you get the furniture to the house?"

"Yep. And we had lunch with Elle, too," said Dave, as he rubbed his full belly.

Danny laughed. "She loves to feed everyone who stops by."

"Just let us know when you need something else dropped off. We'd be glad to do it," said Mike.

Danny smiled. "I'm sure you would."

They strolled into the warehouse together to see how the set of cabinets for a new customer was coming along.

"What night are you guys available to come for dinner next week?" asked Danny, as they made their way through the maze of cabinets.

"We're all going to see the babies tonight, but other than that, I don't think there's much else going on. I'll ask Maggie about next week," answered Dave.

"Same here," stated Mike.

"Okay, I'll see what night works for us, and I'll let you know."

Danny was glad that his sons were comfortable around Elle and the rest of the family.

They had really gotten to know each other over the summer while building the cottages. Once the cabins had been completed, time had been spent together on the water, around the dinner tables, and the firepit. The kids had introduced each other to friends who had been invited up as well. It had been a fantastic summer and fall.

As Nora's belly had grown, the gang had slowed down on the cottage trips. They all wanted to be close by for when her due date came along. Now that the twins were here, it would only be a few more weeks before they all got back into the routine of cottaging again.

CHAPTER 3

NORA WAS RELEASED FROM THE HOSPITAL TWO DAYS LATER. THE DOCTOR HAD been pleased with her health and that of the boys.

Luke had made the doctor aware that he and his family would be with Nora, Jarrett, and Justin at all times for the next week or two while they adjusted to their new family life.

When Luke pulled in to their driveway, Elle's SUV and Ava's car were already there. Luke smiled at Nora.

"Help is here!"

They both laughed. Each of them was grateful for the support of their family.

Ava swung the front door open as soon as she had heard the crunching of tires on gravel.

"Welcome home!" she said excitedly.

Nora smiled. "Thanks for being here to greet us!"

Elle walked up to stand next to Ava. "What can we carry for you?"

"It's just the boys and my hospital bag. Luke brought home the rest of our stuff last night."

Ava went to grab the overnight bag as Luke and Nora unfastened the car seats. Each carried one into the house as Elle held the door open.

Nora's eyes grew large when she saw what sat on the kitchen table. Friends had stopped by with gift after gift for them. The table stood piled high.

"Oh, my goodness!" she said, as she set Jarrett on the kitchen island in his car seat. He was sound asleep. Luke set sleeping Justin right next to him.

"Your friends have been dropping these off at my place. Elle and I thought we'd bring them over for you." Ava spread her arms wide over the display of gifts.

"Thank-you!" Nora gave them each a hug.

Elle moved over to peek at the boys. She had already checked on the nursery, so she knew it was ready for them when she asked Luke if she should put the boys in their cribs.

"Sure, Mom. Thanks. I'll help," said Luke. They each unfastened the twins from their seats and carried them to their new room. Elle fussed over them after they had laid them down.

Luke smiled at her and put his arm across her shoulder. She lay her head on his shoulder.

"They're just so beautiful," she said, with tears in her eyes.

"They sure are. We'll need lots of help with them," he said, knowing it was exactly what she wanted to hear.

Elle lifted her head and smiled up at him. She turned and gave him a big hug. "I'll be right here whenever you need me."

"Yeah, I know it." He smiled again. "Should we go see what's in all those gift boxes?"

Elle turned on the baby monitor. They left the boys to sleep as they headed back to the kitchen.

UNITY

"Thanks for putting the boys to bed," said Nora.

"You don't have to thank me, honey. What have we got here?" Elle peeked at the opened gifts.

There were sleepers, cute little outfits, blankets, toys, and diapers, along with a whole assortment of other baby supplies.

Ava held up one of the sleepers and "oohed" over it. "This is so tiny!"

She carefully folded it and set it back on the pile of clothes.

"It's all so adorable!" exclaimed Elle. "Oh, how I remember those days."

Nora looked up at Luke. "It's hard to believe that you were once that tiny!"

He laughed. "Yeah, no kidding!"

Jessie walked in shortly after the gifts had been opened. He was loaded down with more. He set them on the floor and went back out to his truck. He carried in a huge box and then went back out to carry in a matching one.

He walked over to Nora and kissed her cheek. He shook Luke's hand, hugged his wife, and then his mom.

"I'm glad you're home!" he said excitedly.

"What is all of this?" asked Nora.

"Gifts for the boys from Ava and me."

Nora opened the gifts and fell in love with the little boy clothes. They had bought the tiniest of work boots, overalls, plaid shirts, onesies, socks, and just about anything else they could find for their nephews.

Luke eyed the two big boxes. "What the hell is in those?"

"A job for you and me," answered Jessie.

He pulled his jackknife from the front pocket of his jeans and sliced open the boxes. The sides fell away to reveal miniature ride-on trucks.

"Holy hell!" exclaimed Luke.

Both men knelt beside the boxes and pulled the trucks free.

"These are the coolest things ever!" Luke slapped Jessie on the back.

They started fidgeting with the buttons to see what noises would come from them. They spun the wheels and opened the tailgates. There were stickers to be attached, so they opened the packages and started affixing them to the trucks. They were smiling from ear to ear as they worked side by side.

Ava retrieved her camera from the counter and starting snapping pictures.

Elle nudged Nora and pointed at the men.

Nora burst out laughing. Ava joined in with the laughter.

Both men looked up to find themselves the center of attention.

"What? We have to make sure they're safe for the boys," Jessie said, a little chagrined.

"The stickers make them look cooler too." Luke smiled at his brother as they both went back to the job at hand.

Once they were satisfied, they rose and went to stand with the women, who were still fussing over the clothing.

"You guys are too much!" cried Nora. She hugged both Jessie and Ava.

"Thank-you for everything." Luke hugged Ava and shook Jessie's hand.

A soft knock on the door had each of them turning their heads.

Danny stood there with two small rocking horses in his hands. He had made them the day after the boys were born. One had green markings, and the other had blue markings.

"Hi. I just wanted to stop by and give these to my grandsons."

"How adorable are these? Did you make them?" asked Nora, as Danny set them on the floor.

"I did. I know the boys can't use them yet, but I couldn't help myself."

Nora gave him a hug and thanked him.

Luke stepped forward to do the same.

Danny walked to Elle and kissed her. "Hi."

"Hi. They really did turn out beautifully, Danny!"

He turned to look at the rocking horses and noticed the two trucks.

"Whoa! These are cool!" He dropped to his knees to inspect them and push the buttons.

The women laughed again.

Danny looked up. "What's so funny?"

"They did the same thing to us when we were checking them out," said Jessie with his hands on his hips. The girls laughed again.

The gifts were moved to the living room so Elle could set the table for the meal of spaghetti she had prepared. Ava helped her serve the food.

They sat around the table, talking about the babies. Everyone had agreed to help as much as they could. It would take a few weeks for a routine to settle in, but all were excited about the boys being home from the hospital.

And as if they knew they were being talked about, the boys started moaning and making soft noises. Everyone's attention turned to the monitor on the kitchen counter.

"Duty calls," announced Luke. He and Nora excused themselves from the table and went to the nursery.

The family could hear them gently speaking to the boys.

"Hi buddy," Luke said to Jarrett.

"Hey, you," Nora said to Justin.

They came back out to the kitchen once they had changed the diapers. Elle had warmed the bottles of formula while Luke and Nora were in the nursery.

"Thank-you, Elle," said Nora, as she reached for one of the bottles.

"I'll pull out the bottle warmer tonight once these guys are settled in," stated Luke.

Danny and Jessie cleared the table, while Elle and Ava washed and dried the dishes. The kitchen had been put back in order by the time the boys were fed.

Danny and Jessie had each claimed a child before Ava and Elle had the chance.

Ava scowled at her husband. "Not nice."

Jessie laughed as he gently turned over the baby's wrist. "You can have Justin in a minute."

"Smoothly done, Jessie. No one would even know that you checked his wrist," claimed Ava. He smiled back at her.

"So, I'm holding Jarrett?" asked Danny.

"Yep," Nora told him how to tell the difference. He was thankful for the tip.

UNITY

Elle walked into the living room. "Okay, you two, give them up for a few minutes, and then we'll let this little family be."

Ava smirked at Jessie. "My turn." He gave Justin over grudgingly.

Elle removed Jarrett from Danny's arm. "Thank-you," she said sweetly.

"Like I had a choice," grumbled Danny.

Nora and Luke laughed at the foursome.

The boys were handed back to their parents after a short while.

"Okay, so we're gonna head out of here. Now, please call if you need anything at all," announced Elle as she hugged them.

"Thank-you for everything, Mom."

"Yes, thank-you, Elle."

"I'll see you tomorrow unless you need me earlier."

She touched the babies' cheeks, and walked to the door.

Everyone said their good byes and left Luke and Nora alone for the first time in their home with their beautiful sons.

Once the house had emptied of their family, Luke and Nora sat comfortably on the sofa with their children.

"Can you believe the generosity of our friends and family?"

"They're all pretty amazing. I gotta say, my favorites are the trucks." He stole a look toward them.

Nora laughed at him. "Boys and their toys!"

They settled the twins into their cribs for the night. Nora headed for the shower, while Luke sat in the rocking chair in the nursery to gaze at his sons.

Once Nora had finished showering, they switched places.

Both were reluctant to leave the twins and go to bed, but, with the baby monitor turned on in their room, they would be able to hear the boys during the night. They were able to catch a few hours of sleep before Jarrett woke. Nora rose and went to change and feed him. Justin didn't wake until his brother was back in his crib, sleeping.

Nora fed and changed Justin and put him back to bed as well. She sat in the rocking chair for a few minutes to make sure they were asleep before she went back to bed herself.

She woke to the smell of bacon cooking and coffee brewing. She sniffed the air and smiled. It was going to be nice having Luke at home with her. She yawned, stretched, and pulled on a pair of yoga pants and one of Luke's T-shirts.

She went to the nursery to find that both of her sons were still sound asleep. She padded her way to the kitchen to find Luke filling his coffee mug. She walked up behind him and wrapped her arms around his waist.

"Mmmm, good morning."

He turned to kiss her. "Good morning. Did you sleep well?"

"I did. The boys only woke once, so I actually had quite a bit of sleep."

"Big help, I am. I didn't even hear them," Luke grumbled.

"That's okay. It was fine. I would have woken you if I needed you."

She kissed him again and went to fill her coffee mug. "Why are you up so early?" she asked.

"Habit, I guess. I've figured out the bottle warmer and set it up. The formula will be ready when we need it."

"Thanks, babe."

UNITY

They were able to enjoy about ten sips of coffee before the babies woke. They smiled at each other, set down their mugs, and went to the nursery.

Diapers had to be changed after the feeding. Nora came out from the nursery with Jarrett and went to trade with Luke so she could change Justin.

"No, I'll do it, babe. I've gotta get used to it." He kissed her cheek and lightly touched his son's toes as he walked by to take his turn in the nursery.

Nora laughed when she heard Luke gagging.

"Holy Christ, that's disgusting!" She heard him say over the monitor.

When he came back out to the living room, he was a little pale.

"You okay?" Nora asked while she tried to control her giggling.

"You don't have a problem changing those diapers?"

"Not in the least," she said easily.

"Wow. I hope it's not like that every time."

They were sitting watching the news on the television, cuddling their sons, when Elle arrived.

"Good morning. How'd the night go?" she asked.

"Hi. They only woke up once and went right back to sleep," answered Nora, smiling.

"Hi, Mom. They really don't do much except eat, sleep, and fill their diapers."

"Sounds about right," Elle said with a smile.

Luke rose and handed Justin to Elle. "Here you go. I'll go clean up the kitchen."

Nora relayed the story of Luke's gagging while she and Elle sat and chatted.

Elle laughed. "That sounds about right, too!"

Luke came back to the living room to sit with them. "All cleaned up."

"Thanks, babe."

"Luke, if you have work to do, go ahead. I can stay for as long as you want," said Elle, as she gave her attention to Justin.

"Thanks, Mom. I heard my phone go off earlier. Maybe I'll just go check my messages." He rose and went to his office.

Elle helped Nora bathe the boys and get them settled back in their cribs. They washed, dried, and folded the new clothing they had received as gifts, and then moved on to organize the dressers and change table to make things more accessible. They worked together for a couple of hours before the boys were awake again.

Luke didn't know what to do with himself. He wandered the house aimlessly.

Nora went to him and gave him a hug.

"Babe, why don't you go check on your job sites? Your mom and I have this covered."

He gave her a kiss. "Are you sure? I'm literally driving myself crazy with boredom."

She smiled. "Yes, I'm sure. Go have a coffee with Jessie."

"Okay. That sounds good. Thanks." And with that, he was out the door.

He called Jessie from his truck. "Hey, Jessie. How are ya?"

"Hey, Luke. I'm good. What are you up to? Bored with being at home yet?" he asked jokingly.

"Actually, yeah. Do you have time for a coffee?"

UNITY

"You buyin'?"

Luke rolled his eyes. "Yes, ya cheap bastard."

Jessie laughed out loud. "Perfect. Give me twenty minutes and I'll meet you at Ruby's."

Luke had sounded a little lost. Jessie could certainly spare the time to sit and listen to whatever his brother had on his mind.

As promised, Jessie arrived twenty minutes later. Luke was already seated at a table. He had been scrolling through his phone, looking at text messages. Most of them were to congratulate him on the arrival of his sons. He was smiling as Jessie approached him.

"Hey, Luke."

"Hey, how are ya? I ordered us coffee and pie."

"Perfect. How's it going with the boys?"

"Really well, actually. I'm just bored at home. They don't do much, you know. They sleep most of the time. I was going crazy by ten o'clock this morning. Nora politely asked me to leave. She suggested coffee with you," he said with a weak smile.

"I don't imagine you'll be bored for long. Before you know it, they'll be growing and doing much more in a day."

"You sound pretty wise for a guy who doesn't have kids yet."

The server arrived with their coffee and pie. "Here you go, guys. Enjoy."

They thanked her as she walked away.

"Ever since we found out you two were expecting, Ava's been filling our house with baby books. She reads them constantly. At first, it was so she could learn how to take care of your kids if you needed her. But now, she's pretty intent on becoming a mom herself," Jessie stated before he took a sip of coffee.

Luke set his mug down. "You guys are trying to get pregnant?"

Jessie smiled. "Every night of the week! I'm not complaining."

Luke smiled back. "Wouldn't it be amazing to have our kids so close in age?"

"That's what we were thinking. Imagine the fun they would have together. Especially up at the cottages!" exclaimed Jessie.

They sat and talked for half an hour. Unfortunately, Jessie needed to get back to work. "So, everything's okay then?" he asked, as they stood to leave.

"Everything's good. Thanks for coming for coffee."

"Any time. Especially when you're paying," Jessie said with a chuckle.

Luke paid the bill, and they walked out together.

"Ava and I will pick up dinner tomorrow night and bring it over to your place. She needs another baby fix."

"Sounds good. I'll let Nora know. Talk to you then."

"You bet." They each climbed into their trucks. Jessie headed back to the job site, and Luke headed to the flower shop up the street.

Luke always felt better when he talked to Jessie. It would be amazing if Ava were to get pregnant soon. Their children would grow up to be the best of friends, just as he and Jessie were.

He walked into the house to find it very quiet. He went to the nursery and found his mom sitting in the rocking chair, reading a book. Both boys were sound asleep. She smiled when he walked in.

UNITY

"Nora's taking a nap," she whispered. "Are you okay, honey?"

"I'm fine, Mom. I just don't know what to do around here all day long."

"Well, you were never one to sit for long. Talk to Nora. If you want to go back to work, Luke, I can certainly be here during the day. It's not a problem at all. I would love it. You know that."

He smiled at her. "Maybe I'll do that. I had coffee with Jessie. Did you know that they're trying to have a baby, too?"

"I didn't think they'd be far behind you guys." She smiled. "Good for them."

Luke moved closer to the cribs to peek at his sleeping sons. He smiled proudly.

"They're pretty cute," said Elle, as she rose and moved to stand beside him.

Luke nodded in agreement.

He hugged Elle and said he was going to his office to price out some new jobs. She gladly went back to the rocking chair to sit and wait for her grandchildren to wake up again.

Nora came into the room an hour later, feeling refreshed after her nap.

"I'm amazed at how tired I am," she said. "Thank-you for watching over the boys, Elle."

Elle smiled back at her. "It was pretty easy. They've barely moved. Oh, and Luke is in his office."

"Okay. I'll go say hi to him. Did he seem alright?" There was concern in her voice.

"He's fine. He's just not used to sitting idle for very long. I think he's already itching to get back to work," Elle said gently.

"That's what I thought." She left the nursery to go find him in his office.

"Hi, babe. Did you have coffee with Jessie?" she asked, as she moved closer to kiss him on the cheek.

"Hi. I did. He and Ava want to bring dinner over tomorrow night if that's okay with you."

"Sure. Sounds good. You okay?" she inquired.

"Yeah, I'm fine. I just don't know what to do with the spare time on my hands."

"I think you should go back to work, then," she said simply.

"No. That's not fair to you. I said I'd stay home with you." He rose from his office chair.

"Luke, your mom is having the time of her life being here with the boys. It won't be a problem. Really." She said the words sincerely.

"Yeah, Mom's already told me the same. I feel bad, though."

She wrapped her arms around him. "Don't feel bad. It's fine. I know how quickly you get antsy."

"Okay. I'll think about it. For now, I'll go start dinner." He kissed her on the cheek, and went to the nursery.

Elle was picking up Jarrett when Luke walked in. She turned and smiled at him. "They're just waking up."

"I was just going to start getting dinner together. Did you want to call Danny and join us?"

"I have dinner pulled out at home but, thanks anyway. Can you have Nora warm up their bottles? I can feed the boys and sit with each of them for a while."

"Okay, and thanks for the offer of coming over during the day. Nora and I just talked about it. I think I might go back to work."

UNITY

"Sure. No problem."

He left to warm the bottles, and let Nora know that the boys were awake. He found her in the laundry room, folding clothes and singing to herself. He smiled at her sweetness.

"Nice tune you're humming. I've started the bottle warmer. The boys are just waking up. Mom's already changing Jarrett."

"Okay. Thanks. I'll be right there. Thank-you for the flowers!"

She kissed him as she walked out.

Elle and Nora fed the boys while Luke made dinner. Jarrett and Justin were set in their seats, so Luke and Nora could enjoy their meal without babies in their arms.

They thanked Elle for her help as she headed out the door to have dinner with Danny. She had had a wonderful day with Nora and the boys. She knew Luke would be fine. He just needed to keep busy.

Elle arrived home twenty minutes later. Danny's truck was already parked in the laneway. She walked into the house to the smell of something delicious filling the air.

"Wow! Something sure smells great." She walked to Danny and gave him a hug and kiss. "I'm sorry I wasn't home in time to make dinner."

"No worries. I actually got home early, so I just added spice to the meat you had pulled out and, voila!" He pointed to the small roast he had just removed from the oven. "We all need to help Luke and Nora right now. This is my way of helping." He smiled.

"Well, thank-you. This is a huge help."

He grabbed plates from the cupboard and filled them with the roast, potatoes, and vegetables.

"Do you want to eat outside?" he asked.

"Sure. That would be nice."

"Great! You can grab the wine and beer."

They enjoyed their meal out on the deck, sipping their drinks and catching up on each other's day.

"So, how did it go today with the little ones?" Danny asked.

Elle went on to tell him about her day and how Luke was likely going to go back to work in the next day or two.

"Why's he going back so soon?"

"Boredom," she said simply.

"Well, I guess the kids don't do much right now, except sleep and eat."

"And fill their diapers, according to Luke." She retold the story that Nora had told her of Luke gagging.

Danny roared with laughter. "I was no better."

Elle joined in on his laughter.

"How was your day?"

"We have lots of new clients, so that's good. The house building industry is booming. Funnily enough, we're putting cabinets into the homes that Luke is building." His smile showed his pride in Luke.

"It sure is a small world."

They finished their drinks and went to the bedroom.

Elle started to undress. Danny chose to help. He slowly lifted her shirt over her head and began raining kisses down her neck to her breasts. She ran her hands across his back and then removed his shirt. His hands were busy trying to unsnap her jeans. She quickly lowered her hands to help move the process along. Next, she unsnapped and unzipped his jeans.

UNITY

They fell onto the bed together. Their hands ran wild over each other's bodies.

Danny covered her body with his and entered her smoothly. He slowed his pace after a moment. They made love slowly and leisurely, enjoying every minute of it. Once the release enveloped them, they lay quietly, holding each other.

Danny rolled to his side of the bed, bringing Elle with him. She curled into his arm.

"Not too bad for a couple of old grandparents," Danny joked.

"Not too bad at all," replied Elle, with a smile on her face.

They drifted off to sleep peacefully.

The following morning, Elle had coffee brewing when Danny came into the kitchen.

"What a great smell and view to wake up to." He walked toward her, bare-chested, wearing a pair of jeans with the snap and zipper undone. His light hair was messy from sleep.

When he reached her backside, he started pulling up on the hem of the t-shirt she was wearing.

She tugged it back down and gave him a playful swat.

"What? That's my shirt. I was gonna wear that today!" he said, smiling.

"Go get another one! This one's in use."

He marched off, pretending to be in a huff. Elle laughed at his foolishness.

After breakfast, Danny headed out the door for work.

"Have a great day, babe." She stood on her tiptoes and kissed him.

"Oh, so now you want a kiss." He ran his thumb across her lower lip.

She giggled and backed up. "See you tonight."

He went through the door and waited for her to lock it. Once he heard the click of the lock, he smiled and headed for his truck.

Even after all this time had passed since Max's death, he still wanted her to keep the doors locked. It was a habit that Elle had grown used to doing.

She made her way to the bedroom to make the bed, have a shower, and then she planned to head over to see Nora and the boys.

Her phone rang just as she was about to turn on the shower. Jillian Martin's number popped up.

She and Elle had been keeping in contact once a month. Ever since Jillian and Max's son, Chase, had confronted Elle about wanting his share of Max's inheritance, he had kept to the contract that Elle had asked the lawyer to write up.

Chase was to be admitted to a rehabilitation center for his drug addiction. Once the doctors had decided that he could control his addiction, he would be able to move home and have access once a month to a small portion of the one and a half million dollars, which Elle, Jessie, and Luke had graciously allotted him. Max had left behind a very large sum of money for his family.

Elle looked forward to the monthly calls from Jillian to receive the updates. She wanted Chase to clean himself up and live a better life. He had been on a downward spiral when Elle had first met him nearly six months before. The initial meeting had not gone well. Elle remembered it very clearly.

She had contacted Chase, and they had decided to meet at Ruby's, the local restaurant in town. Danny, Jessie, and Luke had accompanied her. Chase had arrived drunk and high. He had been rude to both Jessie and Elle. His defiant attitude had pissed her off. She had told Chase exactly what she thought of him and said that if he wished to speak with them again, he could do it through her lawyer. With that said, she and her family left him sitting at the table as they walked out the door.

Jillian had contacted Elle later that afternoon to apologize for her son's behavior. The two women met the following day for lunch. Once Elle had explained the money situation and the plan she and her sons had come up with for Chase, Jillian returned home to talk with her son about the amazing opportunity he was being given. Chase had listened intently and agreed to the terms. He would be a very wealthy man if he could kick his addiction.

"Good morning, Jillian. How are you?"

"Hi, Elle. I'm doing okay. Chase, on the other hand, is not."

"Oh, no! What's happened?"

"Well, as you know, the center gave Chase the clearance to leave two weeks ago."

"Yes."

"He took his first withdrawal from the bank and went straight to the liquor store and then to his drug dealer."

"Oh, Jillian. That's terrible news!"

"Yeah, he came stumbling into the house and passed out. He's been going back to the bank every day trying to get more money out."

"The bank isn't giving it to him, are they? Because if they are, I'll contact them immediately."

"No, they're not. That's the problem. Chase is getting angrier by the day. I don't know what to do."

"Maybe you should show him the contract again. Let him know that he's about to toss away over a million dollars because of a bottle of scotch and a line of cocaine."

"I've tried that. He threw the contract in my face."

"I'm not sure what you want me to do. He knows the consequences, Jillian."

"Do you think I should contact the lawyer? Maybe he can talk some sense into him."

"That may be the best option. Let me know what happens. Good luck."

"Thanks, Elle. I'm sorry about this. I had really hoped he was cured."

"There is no cure for alcoholism or drug abuse. It will have to be a new way of life for him. Maybe you should call the doctors at the rehab center as well."

"I will. I'll let you know what they say."

"Okay. Thanks for the call."

Elle was so disappointed in Chase. He had been given every opportunity to better his life, and yet here he was, throwing it all away. What an idiot!

Elle arrived at Luke and Nora's an hour later.

"I'm sorry that I'm late, Nora. I had to take a call this morning."

"It's not a problem. Is everything okay?" Nora sat cuddling Jarrett while Justin slept.

"Jillian called with news about Chase." She told her the situation while she sat next to her on the sofa.

"Well, that's too bad. He had a good thing going," Nora said sadly.

"Jillian will let me know what's happening over the next couple of days. How'd the boys do last night?"

"They were each up a couple of times, but Luke helped out, so it was fine."

"Was Luke happy to get back to work?"

"I think so. I think it's best for him."

The women went about their day with the twins.

CHAPTER 4

JESSIE AND HIS CREW OF MEN WERE HARD AT WORK ON A NEW LANDSCAPING job. Rock walls were being erected along the front of the property. Topsoil had been hauled in to level the existing lawn. Within the next day or two, sod would be delivered to finish the project.

Jessie had been giving hand signals to Adam, who was placing the stones with the excavator, when he heard his name called.

"Jessie!"

He turned to see who had bellowed his name. Chase stood thirty yards away with his hands stuffed in his jacket pockets.

Jessie gave the stop signal to Adam, and made his way over to Chase. He wiped his hands on his filthy jeans and then ran them across his forehead. He stomped his work boots to relieve them of some of the dust that had built up. It was a warm day. Jessie found it odd that Chase would be wearing a jacket.

He stuck out his hand to shake Chase's.

"Hey, how's it goin'?"

Chase didn't bother to shake Jessie's hand. Instead, he said sharply, "I need money."

Jessie scowled. "I heard you had succeeded at rehab, so go to the bank and get some. You have access to it, Chase."

"They won't give me any more," he said crossly.

Jessie furrowed his brow again. "Why? Did you already take this month's allotment?"

"Yeah, but I need more."

Jessie looked a little closer at him. "Are you high?"

"Yeah, so what?"

"Well, then I guess you won't be getting any more money now. You know the rules, Chase. They were made pretty clear to you."

By now, Jessie had his arms folded across his broad chest. He wasn't impressed with Chase's attitude.

"I just need a quick fix. Can you lend me some?"

"Absolutely not! I'm not feeding your fucking addiction."

"Now you sound just like my mother," Chase said angrily.

Jessie shrugged and turned to walk away.

Chase reached out and grabbed him by the arm. Jessie looked down at his hand and then back up to his face.

"You're startin' to piss me off. Get your fuckin' hand off me." Jessie's voice was low and deep.

Chase pulled his right hand from his jacket pocket and produced a handgun. "I told you, I need some money."

By now, Jessie's crew had started to move in a little closer to see what was happening. The boss didn't usually take so long talking to anyone unless it was the client or his brother.

"What the fuck?"

"I need some money," he repeated.

UNITY

"You're gonna want to put that gun away," Jessie said, as he turned to his men. He needed to get them away from the situation.

"Get back to work. I don't pay you to stand around!"

They scowled at his abruptness, then turned to walk back to their previous positions. Adam had turned off the excavator to wait for Jessie. He was the only one to give him instructions on the stone placement. He leaned over the steering wheel and rested his arms on it.

Jessie turned his attention back to Chase. "Relax, Chase. I don't have any cash on me, but I'll call the bank and tell them to release a thousand dollars for you, okay?"

"Hurry the fuck up."

Jessie reached into the front pocket of his jeans to retrieve his phone.

Luke answered on the second ring.

"Hey, Jessie."

"Hello? Yes, this is Jessie Chase. I'm here with Chase Martin. I would have come into the bank personally, but I'm across town on a job site at Heather's Crossing. Anyway, I'm calling because Chase needs money. I'd like you to release a thousand dollars. Yes, I'm aware he's already taken this month's allotment." He paused. "Yeah, I'm sure. He'll be leaving here shortly."

"What the hell? Shit, I'm on my way," was Luke's quick answer.

"Uh-huh. Yep. Okay, great. Thanks very much."

Jessie disconnected and slowly returned his phone to his jeans pocket. He knew that Luke would be arriving shortly. He and his crew were building a new home just three streets over.

Chase hadn't lowered the gun during the phone conversation. He held it low and close to his belly. It was pointed directly at Jessie's stomach.

"So they're gonna give it to me?"

"Yeah, they are. Just give them a few minutes, and they'll have it ready."

He looked at the gun pointed at his stomach and then back up to Chase's face. He could hear Luke's truck coming around the corner. He was moving quickly. As soon as the truck came to a stop, Luke threw it into park. The look on Jessie's face told him to play it cool. He slowly slid from his truck and slammed the door shut.

"Hey! What are you two slackers up to?" he called out jokingly.

Chase turned his head toward the distraction. Jessie took the opportunity to grab him by the wrist. He yanked it downward and cranked it to the right. He could hear the bones snap. Chase cried out in pain and fell to his knees. Jessie bent at the waist to lower himself with him. The gun fell to the ground. Luke ran up and kicked it out of Chase's reach.

"What the fuck just happened?" yelled Luke.

Jessie's knees hit the ground. He roughly flipped Chase so that his back lay on the dirt. He slammed his knee into Chase's chest. His hand shot out and wrapped around Chase's neck. He pressed and squeezed hard. His eyes never left Chase's face. Jessie's entire six-foot-two, one-hundred-and-ninety-pound frame vibrated with anger.

Luke yelled, "Jessie! Stop!" He grabbed at Jessie's shirt to pull him off of Chase.

Jessie released his hold on Chase's throat. He grabbed him by the front of his shirt and hauled him to his feet. He pulled him in closer and growled, "You are the second person to point a gun at me. It didn't turn out so well for your father. It's not going to turn out so well for you, either." He pulled back his arm and drove Chase in the side of the head so hard Luke could hear his jaw crack. He winced at the sound.

Jessie released him and let him fall to the ground in a heap. He turned to Luke. "Call the police."

By now, the crew of men had made their way over to Jessie and Luke. Adam looked at the gun on the ground and then to Jessie.

"Jesus! He pulled a gun on you?"

Jessie nodded as he stood over Chase. His fists were still clenched.

One of the other men said, "Why the fuck did you send us back to work then?"

"Because I didn't want him to start shooting at any of you." He said it simply. His eyes never left Chase's crumpled body.

His men shook their heads in disbelief at what had just taken place.

The police arrived within five minutes of Luke's call. Officer Jake Riley was the first to step from his SUV. An ambulance pulled in right behind him.

Jessie stepped away from Chase and moved forward with his hands held out in front of him to show he didn't have a weapon. Luke moved to stand by his side.

Jake nodded at the two men and approached the injured Chase. He kept his right hand on his holster. There wasn't any need to unsnap it. He lowered himself to Chase's level.

His breathing was ragged, but he'd be okay eventually. Jake recalled the damage that Jessie could inflict. He remembered it clearly from when he had knocked the teeth out of his father's mouth.

He walked over to the discarded weapon on the ground and picked it up with a clear plastic bag he had retrieved from his back pocket. Once it was placed in the bag, he turned to the ambulance attendants.

"He's all yours, boys. Go ahead and take him to the County Hospital. I'll interrogate him there." The attendants nodded and went to work on Chase. They splinted his broken wrist, secured his neck in a brace, and carefully lay him on their gurney.

Officer Riley kept a careful watch while they loaded him in the ambulance. His hand still rested on the butt of his gun. Once Chase had been loaded in the ambulance and the doors were closed, Jake stepped forward to speak with Jessie and Luke.

"You boys okay?" he asked.

They both nodded in agreement.

"Okay then. I'm gonna need you to come to the station and give me your side of the story."

"It'll just be me. I'm the one Chase came after, and I'm the one who did the damage to him."

Jake nodded. He turned to look at Jessie's employees and then back at Jessie. "Come down as soon as you can."

"I'll be there in an hour."

Jake climbed in his cruiser and headed back to the police station.

Jessie ran his fingers through his hair, wiped his hand on the thigh of his jeans, and then shook Luke's hand.

"Thanks for getting here so quickly. I wasn't sure what his next move was going to be. He's pretty stoned on something."

"No worries. It took me a second to figure out what the hell you were trying to tell me." Luke ran his fingers through his thick blond hair as well. "I hear his drug of choice is cocaine. They'll find out at the hospital when they take his blood samples. I'm glad you're okay."

"Give me a minute with the guys, will ya?"

Jessie walked back to his crew to instruct them to take the rest of the day off. He planned to do exactly the same thing. They loaded their trucks with their tools and promised to see him in the morning at the same site.

Jessie waved to them, and then returned to Luke. "Wanna go for a cold beer?"

"Don't you need to go to the police station?"

"Yeah, as soon as I have a damn beer."

They climbed into their separate trucks and drove straight to The Bar.

As they walked in, Jessie said, "You didn't call Mom, did you?"

"No. I didn't call anyone. This is your story to tell."

"I'll go see her when I'm finished at the station, and then go home to Ava. Guess we won't be bringing over dinner tonight."

Luke nodded and ordered two beers as they sat on the barstools.

Jessie told him the complete story and ended with, "Crazy bastard!

"You know, Luke, that's the second time that you've stepped in when I've had a gun pointed at me." He angled his beer bottle and tapped it against his brother's.

Luke smiled and said, "Let's hope there's not a third fuckin' time."

Jessie chuckled.

They went their separate ways after a couple of beers. Luke went back to his building site and Jessie to see Jake.

Jessie walked up to the attractive receptionist wearing his filthy jeans, T-shirt, and dusty work boots from his workday.

"Excuse me," he said. "I'm here to see Officer Riley, please."

She smiled sweetly at him. "Just a moment, please. I'll see if he's in." She eyed him up and down as she dialed Jake's number. Jessie didn't pay any further attention to her. He wanted to get this over with, talk to his mother, and then hold his wife tight.

Officer Riley walked out of his office and asked Jessie to follow him to an interrogation room.

"Doin' okay, Jessie?" he asked.

"Yeah, doing fine."

"How's your Mom and Danny doing?"

"Pretty good. They're grandparents now. Luke and Nora had twin boys a week ago."

"Hey, that's great news! Say hi to them for me."

Jessie nodded.

"Okay, so let's get this over with. I just need to go over a few details with you, and then you can be on your way."

Jessie took the vacant chair across from the officer.

"How well do you know Chase Martin?"

"He's my half-brother."

Jake's head snapped up a notch higher. "He's your half-brother? And he came after you with a gun?"

Jessie settled in his chair. He slouched a little and crossed his ankles.

He replayed the day of his father's death in his mind. It was still as clear as if it had happened yesterday.

Max had kidnapped Elle and taken her to his cottage, where he had proceeded to threaten her mentally and physically. Danny, Luke, and Jessie were able to find her with the help of Jake. Jake had used his resources and had tracked her cell phone. Jessie had nearly run Elle over when she had come running out of the forest. She had escaped the clutches of Max and had run for her life. She had been cut and scraped from running through the brush and trees. Jessie could still see the fear in her eyes and the bruised cheek from the slap she had received from Max. When Luke and Danny arrived seconds later, they had placed Elle in Jessie's truck. Danny stayed with her while her sons tore off for the cottage to confront their father. They'd found him lying on the floor, moaning in pain. Elle had done quite a number on him. His leg had been rebroken from the forceful kick she'd given him.

Luke and Jessie had taken turns at Max. His face had been mangled by Luke's fists, and four of his teeth had been smashed out by Jessie's. By the time they had dragged his unconscious body out the front door of the cottage, Officer Jake Riley had been pulling into the yard with lights flashing and sirens blaring. He had found Max lying on the front porch. Luke and Jessie had walked away, and were standing by Luke's truck when Max had regained consciousness. He had grabbed Jake's unholstered service pistol and pointed it at his sons. Luke had shoved Jessie behind himself to protect him. Before Jessie could react, Max had turned the gun on himself and took his own life.

"Jessie?" Jake interrupted his train of thought.

"Sorry, I just remembered the last time a gun was pointed at me."

"Yeah, I think about that day often."

Jake knew it had been his fault that fateful day that Max had taken his own life. If he hadn't unholstered his weapon before approaching Max, the man would have never gotten a hold of Jake's gun.

Jessie nodded and told Jake the story about his father having a son with Jillian. He added how they had come to meet him.

"So, he was drunk and probably high when we met for the first time in that restaurant. We eventually came up with a plan to help him. All he had to do was go to rehab, get clean, and he'd have access to a monthly sum of money. Apparently, the rehabilitation didn't work so well. He was high when he confronted me today. He was desperate for drug money, and when I refused to give it to him, he pulled the gun out."

"And then you broke his wrist and smashed his jaw," Jake said, matter-of-factly.

"Yep, that's pretty much it. Can I go now? I need to get home to my wife."

"That's it for now. Once Chase can speak, we'll get his side of the story. If we need you for any further questioning, we'll contact you."

"Sounds good. Thanks." He shook Jake's hand and left a business card on his desk.

Jake added, "By the way, Chase has been nothing but a pain in our asses around here for years. I wasn't sorry to see the damage you did to him." He smiled and released Jessie's hand. He searched his desk for a few seconds until he found a business card of his own to give to Jessie.

Jessie left the police station and drove straight to Elle's.

She saw him coming up the drive while she was finishing the dishes. She dried her hands on her jeans, and went to greet him at the door.

"Hi, Jessie! This is a nice surprise. How are you?"

"Alive."

"Okay," she said warily, with a small twitch of her head.

"Guess who showed up at my job site today?"

"I have no idea. Who?"

"Chase. He came demanding money from me, and when I told him I wasn't going to support his drug addiction, he pulled a gun on me."

"Oh, my God! Are you alright?" She moved closer to inspect him.

"Yeah, he didn't get the chance to fire it." He went on to re-tell the events.

Elle listened intently as they stood there just inside the entranceway.

"Jesus, come and sit down. I have to tell you about the conversation I had with his mother this morning."

Jessie left shortly after to get home to Ava.

He pulled into his laneway and walked quickly toward the door. Ava had heard his truck pull up and went to meet him.

"Hi babe, dinner is almost ready. How was your day?" she asked as she greeted him with a kiss and a hug.

He hugged her back and then held on for a moment longer. "Well, this is nice."

"I love you, Ava," he mumbled into her hair.

"I love you, too. Are you okay?"

He released her and slid his hands down her arms to hold her hands. "I had a bitch of a day."

He told the same story once again. Ava cried until there weren't any tears left in her.

Once she had settled, she asked, "So, now what happens to him?"

"I'm not too sure. I guess Chase could possibly get charged with assault with a deadly weapon or something," Jessie said tiredly.

"The bastard deserves to spend a long fuckin' time in jail," she said angrily.

"He will. I'm gonna go take a hot shower." He made his way up the stairs.

As he stood under the hot spray, he felt Ava's arms come around him. He turned to face her. She kissed him tenderly at first, and then the passion took over. It wasn't long before he had her pinned against the shower wall. She wrapped her legs around him to allow him entrance. He held her tightly with one arm around her waist while his other hand steadied him on the shower wall.

She slid down his body once he had finally released her. She reached for the bar of soap and proceeded to wash his entire body. She noticed his swollen hand and kissed it. They dried each other off and went directly to their bed, where they made love again before falling asleep. The thought of dinner never entered their minds.

UNITY

They woke the following morning to Ava's phone ringing. She groaned as she reached for it. The hour on the clock read five.

"Hello?" she said in a groggy voice.

"Ava, it's Nora. Luke wouldn't let me call last night. Is Jessie okay?"

"Yeah, he's okay, Nora. Can I call you back in an hour when I'm awake?"

"Sorry! I've been up with the boys for a while already. I didn't realize the time. Okay, I'll call later. Bye."

Ava rolled over to curl up with Jessie. He pulled her close and nuzzled at her neck.

"I think we should try a little harder for that baby," he suggested.

"I think that's a great idea." She smiled and slid closer.

CHAPTER 5

JESSIE AND HIS CREW OF MEN WERE BACK ON SITE THE FOLLOWING MORNING by six o'clock.

Each of his employees had asked after his health.

"I'm fine, guys. Chase is the one who ended up in the hospital with a broken wrist and jaw. I've been to the police station, and they'll contact me once they've heard his side of the story."

The men nodded and offered to speak on his behalf if needed. They knew Jessie was tough and incredibly strong, so they weren't surprised to hear the outcome of Chase's act of stupidity the day before.

Jessie gave his orders for the day, knowing it was going to be a scorcher. The temperatures were expected to reach high degrees. He was hoping to have everyone home at a decent hour to avoid the worst of the heat.

He smiled when his phone rang, and his wife's name popped up on the screen.

"Hi, babe."

"Hi. Sorry to bug you at work, but I was wondering if you'd like to have the family over for dinner tonight?"

"Sure. Is there something going on? I thought we were bringing dinner to Luke's since we didn't make it there last night." He smiled at the memory of the hot sex they'd had.

"No, nothing is going on, I just wanted to have everyone here."

"You want to cuddle the twins, don't you?" He smiled and laughed.

"Maybe."

He laughed out loud. "I should be home by five. Do you need me to pick up anything for dinner?"

"Nope. I'll grab what I need on my way home from work. See you later. Try to stay out of trouble today. I love you."

Jessie smiled again as he disconnected.

"Okay, guys, let's get this job wrapped up today!"

He got the thumbs-up from his men as they put their backs into the strenuous work.

Adam revved up the excavator and awaited hand signals from Jessie.

Luke arrived at his own job site shortly after six o'clock. He gathered his men around to make the plan for the day.

"How's Jessie?" asked Rob.

"He's a tough bastard. He's more pissed off than anything else."

Rob nodded. He knew all too well just how angry Jessie could get. He had been on the receiving end of a punch to the stomach when he had made a remark about how attractive Elle was. He had only been teasing, but Jessie didn't find it funny. Rob had put it down to bad timing, as Elle and Max hadn't been divorced for long.

"Let's get to work guys," said Luke, before he could be asked any further questions.

He hadn't slept well the night before. He had kept thinking "what if" all night. He couldn't bear it if something happened to his brother. Plus, the boys had woken a few times, too.

Now, he worked beside his men. His tool belt hung low on his hips as he swung his hammer. He tried to concentrate on the task at hand. They were erecting the walls of a new home. His heart wasn't in it today.

Luke normally loved his career choice. His company, Chase Your Dreams Construction, had been booming since he had started it the year before. He had more than enough work lined up for his men. His home life with Nora and the twins was amazing. He loved being a dad. But the thought of almost losing Jessie kept creeping into his mind.

His thought process was interrupted by his ringing cell phone. He holstered his hammer and looked at the screen. He smiled when Nora's name appeared.

"Hi," he said happily.

"Hi, babe. Hot enough for you?"

"Jesus! I think we'll work a shorter day today. How are the boys?"

"They're just waking up again now."

"It'd be nice if they slept a little more during the night."

Nora laughed at him. "I'm glad you'll have a shorter day. Ava called and invited us for dinner."

"I thought they were coming to our place."

"Change of plans, I guess."

"Our first night out for dinner with the kids!"

"Yep!"

"I'll see you later this afternoon."

Luke pocketed his phone and grabbed his hammer again. Nora disconnected and went to the nursery.

Elle arrived a few minutes later. "Good morning!" she said happily.

"Hi, Grandma!" said Nora as she handed over Justin.

"And the day starts. Well hello, handsome." She kissed Justin's cheek.

"Did they sleep well last night?" she called after Nora as she returned to the nursery for Jarrett.

"They were up a couple of times. It was Luke who had a terrible sleep. He tossed and turned all night."

Elle walked toward the nursery with Justin cradled in her arm. She bent to kiss Jarrett as Nora came out with him.

"Hey, you!" she said sweetly, and then added, "Luke never was able to handle anything happening to Jessie. He takes the big brother job to a whole new level."

"You know, it still amazes me how close they are," replied Nora, as she made her way to the kitchen to retrieve the baby bottles.

The two women moved to the living room to settle on the sofas for feeding the boys.

Elle smiled at her. "Growing up, they spent very little time apart. You know, at one point, Luke did most of Jessie's talking for him. Jessie would point at something, and there stood Luke, telling me what it was he wanted." Elle laughed at the memory.

"I love hearing these stories." Nora sat stroking Jarrett's soft blond hair as she spoke.

"I have a million more, but you'll likely go through all the same phases with these two little ones." She played with Justin's pudgy little fingers as she said the words.

"I bet we will. Are you and Danny going to Jessie and Ava's tonight?"

"Yes. I got the call earlier this morning. I think after what happened yesterday, she just wants us all close. Mike, Dave, Emma, and Maggie are coming as well."

"Oh, that's wonderful! I love spending time with them. They're so comfortable around the boys."

"We sure lucked out with this family of ours!" Elle exclaimed.

Justin had finished his bottle and was ready to be burped. Jarrett wasn't far behind. Once the boys had their clothes and diapers changed, Elle lay each of them in the playpen so they could amuse themselves with the bright lights and noise of the toys hanging above their heads.

She had just gotten them settled when her phone rang. She retrieved it from the kitchen island. Jillian's name showed on the screen.

"Hello, Jillian," she said as she tucked her hair behind her ear.

"Elle! Oh my God, I can't believe Chase pulled a gun on Jessie."

"I'm glad he was disarmed before he got the chance to use it," she said angrily.

"I am so sorry. I don't know what the hell was going through his head! Is Jessie okay?"

"He's fine. Chase has some serious problems, Jillian."

"I know." She sighed loudly.

"Have you spoken to the doctors or the police?"

"I just got home from the hospital. They thought they would have to wire his mouth shut. The damage wasn't as serious as they had originally believed. They've wrapped cloth around his head and under his jaw to keep him from opening it. I imagine the police will speak to him as soon as he's able to talk. Jessie did quite a number on him," she said quietly.

"Do you think he deserved anything less?"

"No, I don't. I actually think he deserves much more."

"Are you prepared for the much more, Jillian?"

"What do you mean?"

"I mean, Chase will probably spend some time in jail for what he's done."

"It may be the best thing for him, Elle."

"I have no idea what will happen next, but I hope he pays dearly for threatening Jessie's life. And just so you know, I'll be contacting our lawyer this afternoon to dissolve the contract we have with Chase. He hasn't got a hope in hell of getting one more penny from Max's estate. He's fucked up and needs serious help." Elle disconnected and turned to Nora.

"What's happening?" Nora asked.

"I don't know what will happen next, but it sounds like Jillian is kind of hoping Chase goes to jail. At least there, he'll possibly get over his addictions."

"Do you think Jessie will press charges?"

"It probably won't matter. It was assault with a weapon." Elle was starting to become upset all over again.

Nora walked toward her and gave her a hug. "I'm sorry for all that's happened. Maybe you should go home and rest for the day."

UNITY

"I'd rather be here with you and the boys, if you don't mind. Just give me a job to do, and I'll be fine."

"Your strength continues to amaze me." Nora squeezed Elle a little tighter. She released her, took a step back, and said, "Ava and I have been talking. Do you give courses on how to be so emotionally strong? And, how do you get your sons to do exactly as you want?"

Elle laughed out loud. "Believe me, with those two little boys, you won't need lessons!" She thumbed towards Jarrett and Justin with a huge grin on her face. "They'll have you wrapped around those pudgy little fingers in no time."

"It's already happened!"

Elle watched over the boys while Nora showered. She started laundry and tidied up the kitchen, just to have something to keep her mind occupied. She headed for home after feeding and settling the boys. Luke had promised to be home early, so Nora nudged her out the door and told her to go home and relax before dinner.

Elle arrived home to soft music playing and a glass of red wine on the table. Rose petals led her to the bedroom. She smiled to herself as she started to drop her clothing. By the time she had reached the bedroom, she was down to her lacy pale blue bra and matching panties.

Danny lay sprawled out on the bed, stark naked.

"Well, isn't this a nice surprise to come home to!"

He smiled devilishly. "I've missed you."

"I'm sorry I've been so busy with the twins."

"Don't be sorry. Just come over here."

"Gladly!" She dove onto the bed and landed squarely on him.

The breath left his body briefly, but he recovered quickly enough to roll her under himself and ravage her beautiful body.

He growled as he attacked her neck with his lips. His hands took every liberty with the rest of her body.

"Mmmm," was all she could manage.

She couldn't handle much more. Elle took her own tour of his body until they climaxed together.

They lay entwined and exhausted.

"We have dinner in an hour," said Elle.

"Shit, I forgot about that! Any chance we can cancel and go another round?" He began nibbling on her neck.

"Can't cancel, but we can pick up again when we get home."

"Deal!"

They showered and arrived at Jessie and Ava's an hour later with huge smiles on their faces.

Jessie had arrived just a few minutes before them, full of apologies for being late. Ava smiled and shook her head. She pointed up the stairs and told him to hurry with his shower.

Ava took one look at Danny and Elle when they arrived and grinned. She gave Danny a hug and moved on to Elle.

"You had a fun afternoon," she whispered.

"I did." Elle wrapped her in a hug and squeezed hard.

"You guys kill me!" She released Elle and went to greet her nephews. Luke and Nora were an afterthought. They were getting accustomed to the greetings, and smiled at the love.

Ava scooped both boys in each arm once they were released from their car seats. She moved to her rocking chair and sat.

"I'll serve you all dinner when I'm done loving up on these two!" she exclaimed.

UNITY

The group was still laughing when Danny's boys and their girlfriends arrived."

"What's so funny?" asked Mike.

"I imagine my wife is being a baby hog!" replied Jessie as he came down the stairs, dressed in shorts and a T-shirt. He shook Mike's hand.

"Ohhh, where are they?" asked Emma.

"Just follow the racket in the living room." He hugged Emma as she pushed past him.

"Hi, Jessie. We heard about what happened yesterday. Are you alright?"

"Hi, Maggie. Yeah, I'm okay. Thanks." He hugged her and pointed to the living room. "The babies are that way."

Dave walked through the door with an armful of wine and beer. Jessie pointed again, but this time to the island in the kitchen.

"I lost the help of the girls as soon as I put the truck in park." He scowled at his brother and said, "Thanks for all your help."

"No problem." Mike laughed as he grabbed a beer and made his way toward the oohing and aahing in the next room.

"You doin' okay, Jessie?" asked Dave.

"Yep. Thanks for asking. Now let's go see those two little guys." He rested his hand on Dave's shoulder and led him to the living room.

Nora made her way from the group and approached Jessie. She wrapped him in a huge hug and kissed his cheek. She looked him in the eyes and nodded. "We'll talk later. I'm so relieved to see you." She smiled and moved back to the crowd surrounding her children.

Jessie smiled back at her and glanced around the room.

Everyone vied for shoulder room to get a glance at the boys.

Ava reluctantly gave them up. "I'll get dinner ready, I guess," she said with a soft laugh.

Elle rose from her seat to help. She quietly asked Ava if she was okay.

Ava turned and wrapped Elle in a huge hug. She cried silently in the safety of her arms. "I could have lost him!"

Elle rubbed her back as she returned the hug.

"I know honey, but we didn't."

"How do you cope?" she asked as she pulled away.

"I don't have an answer for that. I just do."

"I love you, Elle."

"And I love you, Ava." She took a step back and held Ava by the shoulders. "You sure you're okay?"

"I guess so."

"Okay, let's buck up and get dinner going." Elle smiled as she brushed Ava's blond hair from her face.

The clan had been enjoying an amazing meal of chicken, salad, potatoes, and vegetables when Danny spoke up.

"I would like to raise a toast," he said. "First off, I'd like to thank Jessie and Ava for opening their home to us once again. The meal is delicious! And secondly, I just want to say to you, Jessie, that the minute I heard about your altercation yesterday, I wanted to run to wherever you were at." He cleared his throat as his eyes began to glisten with tears. "I guess I'm just trying to say that I feel you are like one of my sons, and I'm grateful that you're safe."

All glasses were raised, and "cheers" resounded around the table.

Jessie nodded at Danny and then thanked him.

Luke stood and said, "I would like to add to that toast."

All eyes turned to Luke.

Luke faced Jessie and said, "Yesterday was too damn close a call for me. I don't know where I would be without you in my life. You're my brother, and I love you." It was said simply and honestly.

"I love you too, Luke." And then he added as he looked around the table at his family, "I'm fine, everyone, so please stop worrying about me." Ava leaned over and kissed his cheek. Her eyes filled with tears.

Luke nodded, as brothers do when nothing else needs to be said.

"Okay, so the other thing I wanted to say is that I'm going to need all of you to save the date of June twentieth this summer."

The gang looked at him curiously. Nora had no idea what he was talking about. "Why? What's going on?"

He turned to Nora. "Well, I don't know what I would do without you in my life, either. You have made us a beautiful home and have given me the two most beautiful boys." He glanced at his sleeping sons. He slid his chair out of the way and knelt on one knee.

Nora clapped her hands over her mouth.

"Will you please do me the honor of being my wife?" He produced a gorgeous one-carat diamond ring from his pocket.

Ava burst into tears.

"Yes, yes, yes!"

Nora jumped from her chair to wrap Luke in a hug and smother his face in kisses.

The group cheered and applauded. The twins woke from their sleep in squeals.

Elle rose quickly from her chair to reach them. She hugged Luke and Nora on her way past them. "Just give me a minute, and I'll congratulate you properly!"

She scooped up screaming Justin and walked back to Danny to hand him off. He gladly took him into his arms. She walked back to the playpen to pick up Jarrett. She cooed softly to him as she made her way back to her chair. She peeked over at Justin. He was settling down again in Danny's arms as he cooed and rocked him.

The rest of the family had risen from their seats to congratulate the newly engaged couple. Hugs, kisses, and handshakes were exchanged excitedly.

Ava gave Luke and Nora one final squeeze and then went to relieve Danny and Elle of the babies.

Elle thanked her and rose with Danny to congratulate the happy couple.

With tears in her eyes, she clung to Luke. "I am so happy for you, honey."

He hugged her hard and lifted Elle off her feet to swing her around.

"This family has sure kept you busy over the last little while," he said with a chuckle.

She laughed back as he set her on her feet again.

Danny shook his hand and gave him a guy hug. "Congratulations!"

Elle moved to Nora and took her by the hands. "This is the best news! Congratulations!" The two women hugged each other tightly. Nora released her and showed Elle the ring. Elle whistled and wiggled her eyebrows.

"It's beautiful, Nora."

Danny moved closer to take a look. "Wow! That's some rock!"

The group settled back into their seats and chatted about the exciting news. Nora knelt in front of Ava to kiss her sons.

"Did you hear that, boys? Mommy and Daddy are getting married!"

She looked up to Ava and said, "I hope you'll be my maid of honor."

Ava's tears had just dried, and now her eyes welled up again. She smiled broadly. "Yes, of course, I will." Nora rose slightly and gently hugged her while Ava sat cradling Jarrett and Justin.

Next, she moved to Maggie and Emma. "It would make me so happy to have you two girls as my bridesmaids."

"We'd love to!"

Luke walked over to Jessie and said, "Mom said I had to ask you to be my best man."

Jessie scowled and then smiled when Luke broke into laughter. "You should see your face right now!" He was shaking his head from side to side as he said it.

"Yeah, you're fuckin' hilarious."

Luke smiled at him. "I couldn't get married without you by my side."

"Then that's where I'll be."

They swatted each other on the back and moved apart.

Luke approached Mike and Dave. "Will you stand by my side as well?"

"We'd be honored," said Mike.

"You bet," replied Dave.

Elle made her way over to Ava. She smoothly removed Justin from her arms and gave the head motion for her to follow. The two women took the boys up to Ava and Jessie's bedroom to lay them down in the quiet for a bit. They placed pillows all around the king-size bed for safety's sake.

As they walked back to the living room, Elle announced that each should refill their glasses for a toast. Danny went to the kitchen to start pouring.

Once the drinks were handed out, the conversation lit up again.

"So, June twentieth, eh? That's not so far off," Elle remarked.

Nora started wringing her hands. "I hope it's enough time."

Ava spoke up. "I think this entire group has proven that we can accomplish just about anything on a timeline." She smiled at her family.

They all remembered how they had put together Elle and Danny's wedding in one quick week, and then Ava and Jessie's a month later. Both had gone off without a hitch.

"I'll have to start making a list of what has to be done," worried Nora.

Luke chuckled. "Honey, who are you trying to fool? You have a complete book filled with ideas for your wedding day!"

"Ooh, and you have that tablet with the fancy app on it that you used for my wedding!" exclaimed Ava.

Nora put up her hands in defeat. "Okay, okay. So, I have a few ideas."

Maggie chimed in. "I'd be happy to do hair and makeup."

Nora smiled at her. "Thank-you, Maggie."

"I can pitch in wherever needed," said Emma.

Nora smiled and thanked her, as well.

"Just give me a job!" exclaimed Mike.

"Ready, willing, and able to help!" chirped Dave.

Elle and Danny sat side by side, holding hands and smiling at their kids. He leaned into her and whispered, "Here we go again!"

Elle squeezed his hand and rested her head on his shoulder. "Life is beautiful."

"Any idea of where you'll have this shindig?" asked Jessie.

"Well, we obviously haven't had time to discuss anything, but I was thinking about a small wedding at the cottages." Nora looked at Luke as she said the words.

"That's a great idea!" he exclaimed.

"And just like that, there's the first checkmark on your list!" Ava yelped.

Conversation continued for another hour before they all disbanded and headed for home.

Luke and Nora arrived home with the boys sound asleep in their car seats. They carried the seats in, and unbuckled them in the house.

Once they had them settled in their cribs, they stood back and looped their arms around each other's waists.

"My God, they are adorable." Nora sighed.

Luke smiled down at them. "Of course, they are. Look who their mama is."

Nora raised her head and turned. She wrapped him in a hug and then stood on her tiptoes to give him a kiss. When she broke the kiss, she said, "I love you."

"Well, that's perfect, considering you agreed to be my wife."

She snickered and led him from the nursery.

When they reached their bedroom, she went straight to the bathroom. Luke stripped off his clothing, checked the baby monitor, and climbed into bed.

Nora came out wearing a skimpy little lace negligee. She smiled sweetly as she padded to her side of the king-size bed.

Luke's eyes followed her closely as she made her way across the room. He wore a devilish grin.

She slid smoothly into the bed, snuggled in close, and placed her hands on either side of his face. She kissed him gently, pulled her head back, and said, "Good night, Luke. I love you."

"Good night? Are you kidding me right now? You can't come to bed looking like that and just say good night." He was dumbfounded.

"Four more weeks, babe." And with that, she slid to her side of the bed and curled up on her side to go to sleep.

He moved with her and whispered in her ear, "You are a tease."

"Yes, I am." She smiled into the darkness.

Luke moved back to his side of the bed with a huge sigh and mumbled, "Four weeks." It took him a little time to settle his heart rate, and was finally able to doze off.

CHAPTER 6

JESSIE CRACKED OPEN ANOTHER BEER AND OFFERED WINE TO AVA.

"I think I'll pass on the wine and just have some water."

Jessie looked down at her with concern on his face. "Why? What's wrong? Are you not feeling well tonight?"

"Oh no, I feel fine … just six weeks pregnant is all." She shrugged her shoulders and smiled sweetly.

Jessie set his beer on the counter and scooped her up. He swung her around in a big circle and then set her down gently.

"Seriously?"

She smiled broadly at him. "Yep."

He took her face in his hands and kissed her squarely on the mouth.

"When did you find out?"

"I kind of suspected it, so I went to the doctor this morning, and he confirmed it."

"This is amazing. So, when is our baby due?"

"Early August."

"I can't wait to spread the news!"

Ava laughed at him. "I think you'd better hold off until tomorrow. It's getting late." She started to make her way up the staircase.

He caught up to her and asked, "Did the doctor happen to say how many babies are in there?" He eyed her tiny belly.

She saw the panic on his face. She paused a moment for drama and then smiled sweetly back at him. She burst out laughing at the expression of horror on his face.

"There's only one in here." She rubbed her little bump as she said it.

The relief on his face said it all. He took a long swig of his beer and wiped his mouth with the back of his hand.

"Okay. Only one." He nodded his head.

"Relax, Jessie. It's all going to be fine." She kissed him and continued to make her way up the stairs, giggling to herself.

He walked back to the kitchen to set his beer on the counter.

"Me, a daddy. Damn!" He grinned to himself and climbed the stairs to their bedroom.

Ava had just come out of the bathroom wearing a midnight blue negligee that barely reached her thighs.

Jessie scooped her up and spun her around again. "You have no idea how happy I am right now!"

"I would imagine you're just as happy as I am!"

He set her down again. She pulled at the hem of her negligee to settle it back into place.

He tried to shimmy it back up again. He waggled his eyebrows at her and said, "Maybe we should make extra sure there's a baby in there."

"Then, you'd better hurry up and get into bed. This girl is tired." She had barely slid under the covers before he had stripped naked and began pulling back the blankets.

She giggled as he pulled her close.

He slid his strong hands up her body and began moulding her left breast to his hand. He moved to her right breast and then began to suckle them. He slowly made his way down her body. His hands wandered lower until he reached exactly where he wanted to be. He easily spread her legs and slipped his fingers inside her.

Ava couldn't get enough of him. She ran her hands down his back and then around to the front of him so she could cup him. He slowly moved to roll on top of her. He entered her easily. They both sighed deeply and climaxed together a few minutes later.

Jessie lay atop her for a few seconds and then rolled to his back, bringing her with him. She kissed him and then moved to lie beside him. She curled tightly to him, resting her hand on his broad chest and her head on his shoulder.

As they lay, sated, Jessie smiled and said, "Well, after that, I think we've just ensured your pregnancy."

She gave him a light slap. "I love you."

"Love you too, babe." He released his hold on her. "Have a good sleep."

"Mmm ... hmm." She was asleep within seconds.

The next morning, Jessie had coffee brewing when Ava came down the stairs. She wore black leggings and a flowy blue top.

"Oh, that coffee smells great!"

Jessie filled a mug with the coffee and topped it off with cream. He handed it to her with a kiss. "Good morning."

"Good morning." She kissed him back, sniffed the coffee, and took a big gulp.

"Do we have plans for tonight?" he asked.

Ava was thoroughly enjoying her coffee. "Nope."

"Do you want to go over to Mom and Danny's tonight and give them the news?" He smiled sheepishly.

She grinned back at him. "Sure!"

"Great! I'll call her this morning." He tucked his gray T-shirt into the waistband of his jeans. Next, he bent to put on his work boots, tied them, and straightened. He grabbed his lunch from the refrigerator, ball cap from the hook, and walked toward the door. He stopped, backed up, and kissed her. "Have a great day. Love you."

"Love you, too. Give me a call later."

Ava finished her coffee and then filled a travel mug for the drive to work. She counted herself lucky that she only had a fifteen-minute drive. Jessie, on the other hand, drove all over the place to job sites.

He called his mother on his way to meet his crew at the job site.

"Hi, Jessie."

"Hi, Mom. How are you?"

"Just waking up, so I'm not too sure yet." She laughed.

"Oh, sorry. I was just calling to see if you guys would be home tonight."

"As far as I know, we are. What's up?"

"Not much. I just wanted to run something by you."

"Everything okay?" she asked, with worry in her voice.

"Yep. I'll see you later on."

"Do you want to come for dinner?"

"Can't tonight. We're trying to finish up a job. But I should be there by seven."

"Okay, see you then."

After they had disconnected, Elle went to shower. She couldn't help but wonder what was on Jessie's mind. For now, she needed to shower and head to Nora's.

She arrived an hour later to find Nora frazzled and trying to appease two screaming boys.

"Ohh, what's going on here?" Elle dropped her purse on the counter and hurried to take one of the boys from Nora.

She handed Justin to Elle with a sigh and blew the hair from her eyes. "I don't know what happened. They had a good night's sleep, and then when Luke left this morning for work, all hell broke loose." Nora was swaying and lightly bouncing Jarrett as she spoke. Her hair was a mess, and she still wore her pajamas.

Elle listened as she tried to calm Justin down. She swayed back and forth while she rubbed his back.

"Okay, let's try to eliminate a few things. What time did they wake up this morning?"

"About two hours ago." Nora continued to sway with Jarrett. He was starting to settle down.

"Diapers have been changed?"

"Yes."

"They've been fed?"

"Yes."

Elle began walking the floors with Justin. "This little guy feels a little warm." She stepped closer to Nora and placed her wrist on Jarrett's forehead. "And you feel a little bit warm too, buddy." She spoke to him in the way everyone speaks to babies.

Nora placed her wrist on his forehead as well. "Okay, so I don't know that trick."

"You'll get used to what their normal temperature should be. It doesn't really seem like a fever to me, though. I think they're just warm because they've been crying and gotten themselves all worked up."

That calmed Nora down a bit. "So, now what?"

"Well, why don't you give me Jarrett for a minute and go start a lukewarm bath for them."

Nora handed over Jarrett, and Elle moved to the rocking chair with the boys. Nora rushed to the nursery and brought out the two little plastic tubs she used for bathing them. She quickly filled them with lukewarm water.

Elle continued to rock and coo to her grandsons.

"Okay, I think we're ready," said Nora. She took Jarrett back and moved to the island in the kitchen. Elle rose from the rocking chair and followed. They undressed the babies and set them in their baths. It didn't seem to calm them down much. The women spoke softly to the boys as they gently ran the little facecloths over their warm skin.

They wrapped them in soft fluffy towels and moved to the nursery to dress them in new sleepers. Once the boys were dressed, Elle and Nora went back to the living room to sit with them. They were still fussing after twenty minutes.

"This may sound crazy, Nora, but I'd like to try something."

"Of course, anything."

"I read somewhere that twins feel calmer when they're really close to each other. Let's set them in the same crib and see what happens."

"It's worth a try." The women carried the boys to the nursery. Nora placed Jarrett in his crib. Elle put Justin right next to him so they would be touching. Their little hands instinctively moved toward each other. Within a minute, they had both settled and fallen asleep. Elle smiled broadly.

"Are you kidding me?" Nora whispered.

They stood over the crib for another few minutes, then quietly left the room.

Elle made coffee while Nora cleaned the tubs and set them to the side.

"I can't believe that actually worked!"

Elle smiled. "When Luke and Jessie were small, they spent all of their time together. Max and I seldom took them anywhere separately. They just seemed happier being together."

The women had coffee together, and then Elle sent Nora to have her shower. She sat quietly in the nursery, reading a book, as her grandsons slept peacefully.

They were preparing lunch when the boys finally woke three hours later, with smiles on their faces.

Elle could hear Nora talking with them through the baby monitor. "So, that's all you guys needed, huh? Well, guess how the rest of your naps and bedtimes will be spent." She smiled at them and gently touched their cheeks.

Elle entered the room quietly and went to stand beside Nora. She peered at the boys and said, "Well, you two seem a lot happier!"

"Thank-you, Elle. I have lots to learn about being a mother."

"Oh, honey, it'll all come to you. I'm glad this little experiment worked, though." Elle smiled and gave her a quick squeeze. "Should we get these two changed and fed?" They each reached into the crib and picked up the boys.

"I may have to try this when my mom and dad get here!" Nora exclaimed as they left the nursery.

"I completely forgot they were coming in tonight. Is there something else I can do to help you get ready?"

Nora looked at her sweetly and tilted her head. "Elle, I think you've gone way above and beyond with help. I don't know how Luke and I can ever thank you enough."

"Believe me, it's been amazing for me to be able to be here." Elle reached for a warmed bottle of formula and handed it to Nora, and then took the other for Jarrett. "I can stop by tomorrow if you want, or I can stay away and let your parents enjoy these two boys." She settled in the rocking chair and tilted the bottle to Jarrett's mouth.

Nora sat on the sofa and did the same with Justin. "Oh, I'd like you to stop by and say hi to my parents! They'd love to see you."

"Okay, I'll come by in the morning for a bit, and then I'll stay out of the way so they can enjoy some grandparent time." She bent to kiss Jarrett's cheek and said, "You guys are about to get spoiled some more!"

Once the boys were fed, the two women sat and chatted a bit more.

"What are you and Danny up to tonight?"

"Well, Jessie called this morning and said he wanted to stop by."

Nora smiled. "And what are you making him for dinner?"

Elle laughed. "I offered him dinner but, I guess he has a job on the go that he's hoping to finish up today."

"Do you think he's doing okay after that day with Chase?"

"He hasn't really talked about it much." The concern could be heard in her voice.

"Jessie knows you'll be there when he needs you."

"Yeah, I guess so. Maybe that's why he's stopping by tonight." Her voice lightened a little at the thought of being able to help him work through this.

"Maybe."

The twins had started to fuss again. Elle and Nora glanced at them and then at each other. They both stood and walked back to the nursery. The boys were set closely together in one crib. Once again, their little hands found each other. The women smiled broadly at the cuteness of it and left the room grinning.

"Can I help with laundry, or dinner?" Elle offered.

"No, that's okay, Elle. You can go ahead home if you want. Thanks for your expertise today!"

Elle smiled. "Trial and error. Just enjoy them while they're small. Before you know it, they'll be teenagers and talking back to you."

"I imagine that'll come long before they're teenagers!" remarked Nora as she walked Elle to the door. Elle retrieved her purse from where she had left it on the counter, and slipped on her sandals.

"Okay, so, I'll see you in the morning. Enjoy the evening with your parents."

"See you tomorrow, Elle." Nora closed the door behind her and then flopped onto the couch. She just needed a small rest before the boys woke up, her parents arrived, and Luke returned home from work.

CHAPTER 7

AVA SAT AT HER DESK IN HER CUBICLE, GOING OVER LEDGERS. SHE WASN'T really interested in the columns of numbers on her computer screen. Instead, she dreamed of the future. She was incredibly happy about being pregnant. She rested her hand on her tummy and smiled. Jessie was going to be the best dad.

She daydreamed of going for walks around their property, pushing a stroller, and enjoying a sunny day. Then she switched gears to when their child would be older, and he or she would be riding on Jessie's shoulders as they roamed their twenty-five acres. She could picture their little one running wild with Jarrett and Justin. It didn't matter if she had a boy or a girl. A boy would be rough and tough. She smiled to herself. If she had a girl, she would have to be rough and tough as well if she wanted to keep up with her cousins! There would be no little princess in her household.

She thought of the lazy weekends they would all spend up at the cottages. The kids would splash and swim in the lake. She could already hear the laughter in the air. Parents and grandparents would be chasing them around, trying to corral them. The easy, quiet nights by the campfire was something else she was looking forward to. She pictured the little ones asleep on an adult's lap. She hoped Luke would teach the kids how to play the guitar someday. Jessie would be building sandcastles and forts with them. She could picture Mike and Dave pushing them around on toy tractors. Emma and Maggie would certainly be fussing over them. She smiled again as she thought of Elle cooking whatever the kids asked for. Danny would be playing hide and seek with them.

Ava started thinking of the nursery they would prepare for the newcomer. It would be directly across the hall from the master bedroom. She didn't want to find out the gender until the day of the birth, so she had decided on neutral tones for the walls of the room. Splashes of color would be everywhere. She would save an entire wall just for framed photos. Every stage of her child's life would be right there for all to see.

During all this daydreaming, Ava hadn't realized the time. She and Jessie were planning to go over to Elle and Danny's to share the news. She packed up her things and pushed in her chair. She waved to her co-workers as she exited the building.

The heat of the day hit her like a brick wall. She became light-headed instantly. She reached out to grasp onto anything to keep herself from falling. She thought she had lightly touched something on her way to the ground as she fainted.

She had actually touched the sleeve of an elderly gentleman's shirt as he was passing by. She had caught him by surprise, and unfortunately, he wasn't quick enough to stop her from falling. He slowly lowered his arthritic body to the ground.

"Miss? Are you okay?" He turned his head from side to side, seeking help. Another gentleman had seen what had taken place and quickened his pace. He knelt beside Ava and touched her cheek.

"I'll call an ambulance." He pulled his cell phone from his pocket and dialed.

The elderly gentleman tried to bring her around by lightly tapping the back of her hand. The man who had called for the ambulance sat on the concrete sidewalk and carefully sat Ava up to let her rest against his chest while he waited for the ambulance to arrive.

Sirens could be heard coming up the street. The attendants quickly moved to Ava. One of them pulled a blanket from his pack and proceeded to lift her head from the man's chest to lay her flat. They politely asked the two gentlemen to move aside to give them room. They had just begun to check her vitals when she came to. She lightly touched her head and looked around in confusion.

"What happened?" she asked, as she looked at the unfamiliar faces surrounding her.

"You just kinda fell," said the older man. "Are you okay?"

"I'm not sure. I just fell?"

"You did, and I'm sorry I wasn't quick enough to catch you."

She smiled weakly at him and then at the attendants.

"Miss? What's your name?"

"Ava. Ava Chase."

"Do you know where you are right now?"

She looked around. "Outside my office building. Is my baby okay?" she asked as she lay a hand on her stomach.

"You're pregnant?"

Ava nodded as tears filled her eyes.

"Okay. We're going to take you to the hospital and have you checked out."

"I have a bump on my head," she said as she rubbed at the sore spot.

Once she had been loaded into the ambulance, the attendants thanked the two men and told them they were taking her to the County Hospital. The men nodded and watched them drive off.

The older gentleman turned to the younger man and said, "I'm sure glad you came along when you did." He rubbed the whiskers on his chin and added, "I really should get me one of those cell phones."

The younger man smiled and shook his hand. "I'm glad I could be of help. I hope she'll be okay. And the baby, too. I'm Shawn, by the way."

"Nice to meet you. I'm Samuel."

"Well, you did something good today, Samuel, so don't beat yourself up about not being able to stop the fall." They nodded to each other. "See you around." And, with that, the men went their separate ways.

The ambulance arrived at the hospital with the sirens blaring. Ava was quickly unloaded and wheeled in. The on-duty doctor stopped the gurney and asked the usual questions.

The questions were answered quickly and precisely by the lead paramedic. He had added that Ava was pregnant. She was instantly taken to an examination room where an ultrasound was ordered.

Ava lay in the bed with tears running down her face. "Can you please contact my husband?"

The nurse continued with the ultrasound as she spoke. "You can give me his number in a moment. I just want to finish with the ultrasound first." A moment later, she wiped the jelly from Ava's belly and smiled. "The doctor will be in shortly to speak with you. I can take that number now if you like."

Ava gave her Jessie's cell number and lay back on the bed to wait for the doctor.

Within a few moments, Dr. Evans arrived. She had a kind smile on her face as she approached the bed.

"Hi, Ava. I'm Dr. Evans. How are you feeling?"

"Is my baby going to be okay?"

"You gave us quite a scare, but yes, it seems like everything is just fine. They have lots of protection in there." She lay her hand on Ava's belly. The monitor beside her beeped with a steady rhythm. The leads attached to her belly kept the doctor and nurses aware of what was happening with the baby.

The tears continued to run down Ava's face. "Thank God," she whispered.

"How were you feeling before fainting?"

"I felt fine. Maybe it was the heat. I had been in air conditioning all day."

"It's possible. The nurse is contacting your husband as we speak. So, you just lie back and relax. We'll get you some juice and a light snack."

"Thank-you, Dr. Evans."

"You're quite welcome. I'll be back once your husband arrives." She quietly left the room.

Ava had fallen into a light sleep and was resting peacefully when she heard the door swish open. There stood Jessie, with fear in his eyes. He was filthy from work. He placed his black ball cap on the chair and cautiously went to her side.

"Babe, are you okay?" He kissed her forehead and ran his hand across her hair.

She burst into tears. "Oh, Jessie. I don't know what happened! I walked out the door and woke up to a bunch of faces staring at me."

"Shh. It's okay. They're gonna take good care of you here." He wrapped her in a hug.

Dr. Evans knocked on the door and entered. She introduced herself to Jessie.

"Your wife is a tough little thing." She smiled as she moved toward the bed. She checked Ava's eyes with her tiny flashlight and checked her pulse. She placed the flashlight back in the pocket of her lab coat and looked up at Jessie.

"Ava hit her head on the concrete when she fell, but I don't believe she has a concussion. A nasty bump back there, but she'll be just fine. As for the baby, the little one is not showing any signs of stress, so no need to worry."

The tension lightened a bit for Jessie. "What do you think caused her to faint?"

"In my professional opinion, I would say it had a bit to do with the extreme change in temperature from inside to outside. Plus, Ava's blood pressure is a little lower than I'd like to see."

Ava lay quietly, listening to the conversation. Her voice was soft when she spoke. "So, can I go home now?"

The doctor looked at her and tilted her head to the side. "I'd like to monitor you and the baby here in the hospital tonight."

"Then we'll stay here. Right, Ava?" questioned Jessie.

Ava nodded.

"Alright, then. You can have a few visitors tonight, but I'd like you to get plenty of rest as well."

Jessie put his hand out to shake with Dr. Evans. "Thank-you for all your help."

She smiled back at him. "You're welcome. Everything will be just fine." She smiled at Ava and left the room.

Jessie settled on the bed beside her and held her hand. He picked it up and gently kissed it. "Is there someone you'd like to see tonight, or would you rather rest?"

Ava's eyes filled with tears once more. "I'd like to see your mom."

Jessie pulled out his phone and dialed Elle's number.

"Hey, Jessie. On your way over?"

"Sorry, Mom, change of plans. Can you come to the hospital, though?"

"The hospital? What's wrong? What happened?" she asked desperately.

"Ava fainted today and was brought to the County Hospital by ambulance. She'd really like to see you."

"Jesus Christ! Is she alright?"

"Yeah, she just wants to see you."

"Tell her we're on our way and give her a kiss for me."

Jessie did exactly as he was told.

"I'm going to get you some ice water. Are you hungry?"

Ava shook her head in answer.

Jessie left the room and pulled his phone from his pocket once more. He dialed his brother this time.

"Hey, Jessie."

"Hey, Luke. I need you at the hospital."

"What's wrong? Are you okay?"

"It's Ava. She had a scare today, and they've admitted her for the night."

"We're on our way. Room number?"

Danny, Elle, Luke, and Nora arrived within thirty minutes. Dave, Mike, Emma, and Maggie weren't far behind.

Luke led the troop to the room number Jessie had supplied him with. He quietly opened the door and stuck his head in. Ava lay propped up on the bed. Jessie sat in the chair next to her. He held her hand as they talked in hushed tones.

"Hi. Can we come in?"

They both turned their heads and smiled. Jessie released Ava's hand and went to greet his family.

Elle pushed past the group to reach Ava. "Oh, honey. Are you okay? What happened?" She stooped over her to kiss her cheek. Next, she stroked her hair gently and then wrapped her arms around her.

Ava burst into tears again. She let the love from Elle surround her.

"It's okay. I'm here now." Elle pulled back a bit to get a closer look at her.

The rest of the family stood back and watched the scene unfold. They all knew that Ava thought of Elle as her mother. She had lost her own a few years before. Elle had been her rock and support system. They were incredibly close.

Ava pulled her emotions in and peered around the room. She felt a little embarrassed about breaking down in front of them all.

UNITY

Nora crept a little closer and smiled weakly. "Can I give you a hug, too?" Ava nodded. Elle moved to the side to allow Nora space to come closer. Nora wrapped her arms around Ava and held on. She kissed the top of her head before she let go.

"Where are the boys?" she asked.

Luke spoke up from where he stood next to Jessie. "We kissed them, told them to behave, walked out the door, and locked it. They'll be fine." He casually shrugged his shoulders.

Ava's mouth dropped, and the monitor beside her sped up.

Nora scowled at him and said, "Fuck, you're an idiot." She turned her attention back to Ava and the monitor. "My parents arrived in town today. They're watching the kids while we're here."

Ava relaxed again and said, "You didn't have to come."

"Of course we did." She ran her hand along Ava's blond hair once more.

Danny stepped forward. He lay his hand on Ava's and then ran his thumb across her eyebrow. "You okay, honey?"

Ava closed her eyes at his gentleness and kindness. She nodded.

Next, Luke came forward. He sat on the edge of the bed, right beside her. She lifted her head from the pillow so he could place his arm there. He gave her a hug and kissed the top of her head.

"So, want to tell us what's going on?" he prodded.

She retold the story again of how she had fainted and fallen. She instinctively slid her hand over the blanket to touch her stomach.

"I'm just thankful that the baby is fine."

Every mouth in the room dropped, eyes widened, and then the smiles lit their faces.

Ava faced Jessie with a look of apology. She hadn't meant to let that piece of information slip. He simply smiled from where he stood.

Elle moved forward again with the broadest of smiles on her face. "Pregnant! This is wonderful news! Ohh, congratulations!" She bent at the waist to embrace her daughter-in-law again.

Luke squeezed her once more from where he sat. He glanced at his brother and smiled.

Danny stood at the foot of the bed, grinning from ear to ear. His sons and their girlfriends stood at the back of the room, smiling.

Nora jockeyed for Elle's space. She wrapped Ava in a huge hug. "I am so happy for you! Our kids will grow up to be the best of friends and cousins."

Ava had tears of joy running down her face.

"This is amazing news!" Luke started counting on his fingers. "Hey, our kids will only be, what? Like five or six months apart in age!"

Jessie started counting on his fingers too. He grinned broadly. He cleared his throat and said, "Uh, father-to-be, standing right here." He pointed his thumbs at himself.

Danny laughed out loud and pushed away from the bed. He walked toward Jessie with his hand out. They shook hands and did the quick guy hug. "The women get all the credit, right?"

Jessie laughed as Danny swatted him on the back in congratulations.

UNITY

Elle moved away from Ava and stepped around the bed to Jessie. She placed her hands on either side of his handsome face, smiled broadly, and then wrapped her arms around him. She whispered in his ear, "Congratulations, son." Jessie hugged her a little tighter, so, she hung on. Once he released her, she kissed his cheek.

Luke removed his arm from behind Ava's head and heaved himself up to a standing position. He shook Jessie's hand and gave him a swat on the back. "Congratulations, man!"

Jessie smiled broadly. "Our kids will get into so much trouble together!" They both laughed loudly.

Nora came around the bed and hugged Jessie as well. "If they get into half the mischief you two did, we're all in for one hell of a ride!"

The group giggled at that, especially Elle. She remembered exactly how much harmless mischief her two sons had gotten into.

A quiet knock came at the door. Jessie left his position and walked toward it to allow the visitor entrance.

An elderly gentleman stood in the doorway with a bouquet of flowers in his arms. His clothing hung loosely on his body. It seemed as if he had been a robust man at one time and had just never bothered to buy clothes to fit his now smaller frame.

"Hello. Can I help you?" asked Jessie.

"Is this the room of Ava Chase?"

"It sure is. And you are?"

The man shifted the bouquet to his left hand and stuck out his right hand. "I'm Samuel. I was there when Ava fell." He lowered his head. "My old body just wasn't quick enough to catch her."

Jessie felt bad for the older gentleman. He shook his hand and smiled. "Thank-you for being there, Samuel. I'm Ava's husband, Jessie."

Ava sat, smiling from her bed. "Yes, thank-you, Samuel."

He nodded at Jessie and approached the bed. The family members moved out of his way. He handed the flowers to Ava.

"How are you feeling?"

"I'm okay. Thank-you for the flowers. They're beautiful." She bent her head to sniff them.

"I'm glad you like them." He cleared his throat. "I bought a cell phone this afternoon, too."

The crew looked confused at his statement.

He looked around. "Sorry. I should explain myself. I've never owned a cell phone. The other gentleman who helped, Shawn, had a phone and called for the ambulance. I thought it best if I had one, too. You know, just in case." He lowered his head again in embarrassment.

Elle stepped forward and shook his hand. "Well, we're very appreciative of your help, Samuel." She motioned to a chair. "Please, have a seat. We're all Ava's family." She swept her arm around the room to include everyone.

He nodded. "It's nice to meet you all. I should be going, though."

He turned his attention back to Ava. "I hope everything is okay with the baby."

"The baby is just fine." She gently lay her hand on his. "Thank-you, Samuel."

He smiled and slid his hand out from under hers. He moved from the side of the bed and headed for the door.

UNITY

Jessie followed him. He opened it for the elderly gentleman and placed the palm of his hand on his shoulder. "Thanks for coming to see Ava."

He nodded once again. "Take care of her and that baby."

He walked out the door without looking back.

The family looked at each other and smiled.

"What a nice man!" Nora exclaimed.

"It was so kind of him to come by and check on you. Plus, the flowers are beautiful." Elle reached for them. She would hunt down a makeshift vase.

The nurse entered the room to check on Ava. She had settled back into a comfortable position in her bed and was enjoying the conversation going on around her. The nurse smiled at the happy faces in the room.

"How are you feeling, Ava?"

"I'm doing okay. I have a mother of a headache, though." She rubbed her head as she spoke.

"I imagine you do. I'll ask the doctor about medication for you. We don't want to give you anything that could harm the baby." She checked Ava's pulse and listened to her heartbeat. The family quietly moved out of her way as she moved to the wall to make notations on the chart.

"I'll be back shortly with something for that headache." She glanced at the clock on the wall and said, "Sorry, folks, but you only have about five more minutes before visiting hours are over." She smiled and silently left the room.

The group assembled around the bed once more. Each one of them took their turn touching, kissing, and hugging Ava. She thanked each of them for coming to see her. Jessie was hugged, and good nights were said.

"I'll be home tomorrow, guys," announced Ava. Jessie stood beside her and smiled.

"I'll be there waiting for you, Ava," said Elle with a small smile.

"We'll see you tomorrow, Ava. Get some rest. And congratulations!" Nora said.

They left with a wave and a smile.

The nurse returned with two pills in a tiny paper cup and a glass of water. "Here you go, Ava. This should alleviate the pain and help you get some rest." She turned her attention to Jessie. "Will you be staying for the evening, or going home?"

"I'd like to stay if I could."

"Okay, I'll have a cot brought in for you."

"No worries. I'm just going to lie right here beside Ava." He patted the space beside her on the bed.

Ava rolled her eyes. "He's just teasing you. He'll be going home to shower."

Jessie sniffed his shirt and nodded. "Yep, that sounds like a better plan." He smiled sheepishly.

The nurse laughed and left the room.

Jessie crawled onto the bed and set Ava's head on his shoulder. He stroked her hair. "I love you, Ava."

"I love you too, Jessie." She lifted her head from his shoulder and said, "You really need to go have that shower."

He laughed, kissed the top of her head, and rose from the bed. "Get some rest, babe, and I'll be here tomorrow morning. We'll see what the doctor has to say about you coming home and go from there, okay?"

She nodded with a sad smile. "I guess so."

He lifted her chin with his index finger. "You are just as bad of a patient as my mother." He kissed her nose and grinned.

UNITY

She grinned back at him. He pulled the blankets up on her and left the room.

He stopped at the nurses' station and lay his business card on the desk. "Please call me at any hour if I'm needed."

The receptionist smiled and said, "Of course, Mr. Chase."

He patted the desk, grinned, and walked away.

The woman watched him walk away until she couldn't see him any longer. She had thoroughly enjoyed the view.

CHAPTER 8

THE FAMILY SAID THEIR GOOD BYES IN THE PARKING LOT OF THE HOSPITAL.

"We'd better get home to the kids," Nora said as she hugged Elle and then Danny.

"I hope they behaved while they were left on their own!" Danny laughed at his own remark. His laughter was followed by Luke's.

The two women rolled their eyes and exchanged a smile.

They climbed in their vehicles, waved out the windows, and headed for home.

Luke and Nora arrived home in record time. They had never left the boys with anyone, and Nora was a little antsy about it.

"Honey, the boys were sleeping when we left. They'll be fine with your parents."

"I know, but I forgot to tell Mom that if the boys wake up, she needs to put them close together when she lays them down again."

"They probably didn't wake up. We haven't been gone for very long."

"I'll just be glad to be home with them."

Luke took her by the hand. "Well, we're here now." He threw the truck into park and stepped out. He went around to the other side to help Nora down.

They entered the house to hear two wailing children.

Nora grimaced and went to relieve her mother of Justin.

Luke took Jarrett from his grandfather, Frank.

Alice happily handed over Justin. "I don't know what's wrong! They've been fed, changed, and burped. We can't seem to settle them down."

Nora consoled Justin as she gave Luke "the look" to follow her to the nursery. He walked two steps behind her, lightly jiggling Jarrett.

"We're sorry!"

"It's okay, Mom. We'll be back out in a minute."

Luke and Nora could be heard talking quietly to their sons through the baby monitor.

"What's going on, buddy?"

"You're okay. Mommy's got you."

Once the boys had settled, they were placed close together in the crib. Nora and Luke watched as their eyes closed, and their little mouths made happy mewling sounds.

They walked back into the kitchen to sit with Nora's parents.

Frank smiled and said, "That was quick."

"Yeah." Luke chuckled. He went on to explain how Elle had come up with the sleeping plan for the boys.

Alice had a scowl on her face as she shook her head. "You'll spoil those two." Luke didn't like her tone of voice.

"Well, they're only a couple of weeks old, and if it makes them happy and we can get some sleep, we're good with it,"

Luke stated, as he sat back in his chair and crossed his arms across his broad chest.

Nora placed her hand on Luke's knee. His temper always rose quickly when her parents were around. Her mother never treated either of them with respect. She seemed to forget the fact that they were adults and were capable of taking care of themselves. Now that they had two children of their own, Luke was not likely to sit back and take any rude remarks from Alice for very long.

"How often does Elle come over here?" Alice demanded.

"She's been here every day since the twins were born." Nora smiled at Luke as she said it. She wanted this situation defused.

"And you're okay with her being in your home every day, taking care of—and apparently raising—your children?"

Frank shook his head at his wife. "Alice." He said it sternly.

"What?" She snapped the exclamation at her husband.

"Luke and Nora are doing a fine job of parenting, and it's none of your business."

Luke uncrossed his arms and sat up a little straighter. He rested his elbows on the kitchen table and looked directly at Alice. He spoke very clearly as he addressed her.

"My mother does not come here to take care of or raise our sons. She comes here to lend a helping hand, which she offered, and we gladly accepted. She is a huge help to Nora while I run our company and provide for our family. I'm sorry if you don't agree with our parenting practices. Wait, actually. I'm not sorry at all. I really don't care what you think. Elle has been more of a mother and friend to your daughter than you have ever been. She has been here for every up and down in her life since they met. You, on the other hand, have been traveling the world and barely keeping in contact."

Three sets of eyes were staring at him as he pushed away from the table. He set his chair back in its place and added, "Thank-you for watching the boys while we dealt with a family emergency. Ava is fine. Thanks for asking," he said sarcastically. He kissed Nora on the top of her head. "I'm going to bed." He turned his attention back to his in-laws. "You are welcome to stay in our home, but you are not to berate, belittle, or disrespect my wife or my mother again."

Alice looked at Frank for support. He shrugged his shoulders and said, "You had it coming."

He pushed away from the table and walked to Nora to place his hand on her shoulder. "I'm sorry, sweetie. We'll be leaving tomorrow morning."

"Dad, you don't have to leave," she said sadly.

"Yes, we do. It was wonderful to see you and to meet our grandsons, but Luke is right. You guys have everything under control here, and your mother has no right to speak to you like that." He looked directly at his wife and said, "Good night."

Alice sat speechless once again.

Nora rose. "Good night, Mom." She left her mother sitting alone at the table and went to check on her sons. Next, she went to find Luke.

She found him sitting on the edge of their bed, removing his clothing. She walked toward him.

He raised his head when he heard her enter the bedroom. "I'm sorry about that, babe. I just can't stand the way your mother talks to you. She hasn't changed a bit. When she started to cut us down yet again, I had to say something."

Nora knelt in front of him and took him by the hands. She rose a bit and wrapped her arms around him. "Thank-you. I wish I had the balls to speak to her that way." She kissed him and stood to her full height. He rose with her.

He rubbed her back and slid his hands down her back. "I'm glad you don't have any balls."

They both burst out laughing. The tension of the evening had eased.

They finished undressing and slid into bed. Luke pulled her toward him and held on tight.

They would see what tomorrow would bring.

Danny and Elle were driving home when he reached over and placed his hand on her left knee. "That must have been awfully scary for Jessie and Ava." He gently squeezed her knee. "You okay?"

She covered his hand with hers and let out a sigh of relief. "I'm just glad that Ava's okay." She lay her head back on the truck headrest and closed her eyes.

She smiled, opened her eyes, and turned to face Danny. "We're going to be grandparents again!"

"We sure are!"

"So, I think I'll go spend the day with Ava tomorrow."

"I know you will. She needs you right now." He smiled at her kindness and huge heart.

"I just need to make sure she gets her rest. She should probably take the rest of the week off, too."

"If anyone can talk her into that, it would be you."

He put the truck into park when they arrived home and unsnapped his seat belt. He slid a little closer to Elle to run his thumb across her lower lip. "You are the kindest person

I know. You always have been. Guess that's why I fell in love with you so many years ago." He replaced his thumb with his lips.

She unlocked herself from the restraining seatbelt and fell into the kiss. She whispered against his lips, "We should take this inside."

"Mm-hmm."

They ended the kiss and smiled. Each climbed out their doors and met at the front of the truck to reach for each other's hands. Danny's jean-clad legs took long strides to reach the house in a hurry. Elle's shorter legs tried to keep pace.

He dug into his front pocket for the house key when they reached the door. He put the key into the lock and found no resistance. He stopped and looked at Elle with raised eyebrows. Her eyes widened as she took a step backward.

He released her hand and gently moved her to stand behind him. He cautiously opened the door and stepped inside. He slowly climbed the three steps and looked around the open concept kitchen and living area. Nothing was amiss. He turned to let Elle know that everything was okay. She was so close to him that his shoulder bumped her.

"You never listen." He growled the words at her.

She simply shrugged her shoulders. He shook his head at her and stepped to the side to allow her in. She walked in and took a look around for herself. She had sworn to herself that fear would no longer rule her life after her dealings with Max.

She smiled to herself, and then turned to face him. She placed her hands on her hips. "Do you remember that time we put new locks on the doors and how we both promised to use them at all times?" She was the one to raise her eyebrows this time.

He smacked himself on the forehead. "Dammit! We left in such a rush to get to Ava that I forgot to lock the door."

She nodded, smiled, and then laughed.

"Sorry. It won't happen again," Danny said.

"And now you sound just like I did when I used to forget."

Danny walked back to the door and flipped the lock. He climbed the steps once more and took her by the hand. He pulled her to their bedroom. "Now, Miss Smartass, let's get back to what we started in the truck."

Elle gave him a sinful look and started to strip.

Danny hopped around on one foot as he struggled out of his jeans. He yanked his T-shirt over his head and tossed it to the floor. His black boxers weren't far behind.

Elle had been a little quicker. Her shorts, tank top, bra, and panties lay in a pile on the floor beside the bed. She lay sprawled out, waiting for him.

He growled as he crawled across the bed to reach her. He captured her mouth with his. Elle flung a leg over one of his. She ground her body against him. He reached behind her to squeeze and massage her ass. She raced her hands down his back. He entered her quickly. Elle had no problem keeping pace with him. Both raced to the finish line. They climaxed at the same time and collapsed. Danny lay atop her, trying to catch his breath. Both were panting.

Danny mumbled into her hair, "I can't quite move yet."

"Good."

They lay entwined for a few moments before he finally rolled to the side, pulling her with him. She gladly curled into him. She rested her hand on his chest and kissed his ear.

"I love you," she whispered.

"I love you too, babe." They fell into a sound sleep exactly as they lay.

The following morning, Elle called Jessie as soon as she had finished her breakfast with Danny.

"Hi, Mom."

"Good morning! How's Ava this morning?"

"I spoke with her a few minutes ago. She's just waiting for the doctor to come in to see her."

"Okay. I'll head over to your place shortly."

"Thanks, Mom. And, thanks for coming in last night. Ava really needed to see you."

Elle's eyes filled with tears. "Your welcome, honey. I wouldn't have wanted to be anywhere else. You know, I'm pretty excited about being a grandma again!"

Jessie chuckled. "I'll let you know when you can expect her home."

They disconnected just as Danny came into the kitchen.

"Was that Jessie?"

"Yep. Ava's just waiting to see the doctor."

"Are you heading over there?"

"Shortly. I'll give you a call later and let you know what's going on." She reached up to give him a kiss. "Have a great day."

"You bet. Say hi to Ava for me." She watched him walk to the door with the swagger she adored.

"Enjoying the view?" he called over his shoulder.

Elle laughed. "I certainly am!" She laughed and moved toward the bedroom to make their bed and get ready for the day.

Her agent, Kim, called as she finished fluffing the pillows.

"Kim! Hi. How are you?"

"Hi, doll! I'm good. What's new with you, Grandma?"

Elle chuckled. "I'm enjoying every minute of it! We are going to be grandparents again in August. Jessie and Ava are expecting."

"Oh, how wonderful! I wish my daughter would get busy and make me a grandma soon."

Elle laughed at her sweet friend. "What have you been up to? It's been a while since we last talked."

"Same shit, just a different pile. How's that handsome husband of yours?"

"Still as handsome as ever! He loves being a grandpa. But, like you, he'd love for his sons to get busy in the baby-making department, too."

"Say hi to him for me. Listen, I was wondering if you would be interested in another showing of your artwork."

"I haven't had much time to draw lately. I've been helping out over at Luke and Nora's with the twins. I have quite a few drawings put away, though. They just need to be framed. What were you thinking?"

"I'd love to have a show a couple of months from now. Back at The Studio again. We could meet for lunch and go over some details if you're interested."

"Sounds good to me. I'd love to meet for lunch! How about next week?"

"Perfect, I'll check in with you on Monday, and we'll make a plan."

"Great talking to you, Kim. I've missed you."

"I've missed you too, doll. We'll chat again on Monday."

Once they had disconnected, Elle started thinking back to her last showing at The Studio. The place had been packed with potential buyers. It was where she had had yet another confrontation with Max and Susan. It was where her sons had told their father and new wife to 'get out,' and it was where she had reunited with Danny. They had gone to The Bar for drinks after the showing and caught up with each other's lives. They had met a few times after that for dinner and drinks. The next thing she knew, she had fallen in love all over again!

The ringing of her cell phone ended her reminiscing. Luke's number popped up on the screen.

"Good morning, Luke!"

"Hi, Mom. How are you?"

"I'm good. I just got off the phone with Kim. She wants me to have another showing! How are you?"

"Hey, that's great news! Uh, are you going to be with Ava for the day?"

"Okay, spit it out. What's wrong?"

"Nora's parents got here yesterday afternoon and have just left for home."

"What? Why?"

"I got into it last night with Alice about sticking her damn nose in where it doesn't belong. She was rude to Nora and disrespectful of you."

"Well then, she probably deserved everything you said to her." Elle had always been disappointed in the relationship Nora had with her parents. She had only met them a handful of times, and never really thought much of Alice. Frank, on the other hand, was a very nice man.

"Yeah, but the problem is, I have to leave for a couple of hours to set the guys up on the job sites. Are you able to come over for a bit, or are you on your way to see Ava now?"

"Of course, I can come over. Jessie's going to call me when Ava is released. I'll slip over to your place to help Nora, and then go over to help Ava."

"You really are the best! Thanks, Mom."

"No worries. Let Nora know that I'm on my way."

Elle smiled to herself and thought, You never really stop worrying about your family.

She grabbed her purse and truck keys, locked the door behind her, and headed for Luke and Nora's.

She dialed Danny's number, but couldn't reach him, so she called his office.

"Dan's Designs. How can I help you?"

"It's nice to hear your voice, Lois!"

"Hello, Elle! How are you?"

"Just fine, thanks. And you?"

"Trying to keep that husband of yours in line."

"It's a full-time job, isn't it?" Elle laughed.

Lois joined in on the laughter. "Are you looking for him?"

"I am. Is he around? I tried his cell phone, but he didn't pick up."

"He's just in a meeting right now. I can interrupt him if it's important."

"No, no, that's okay. Can you just have him give me a call later, though?"

"I sure will. Have a great day!" Lois hung up and jotted down a note for Danny.

Danny had hired Lois once he'd realized he no longer had the time to take care of the bookwork or scheduling. She was a gentle soul. She had a sweet round face, gray hair, and a stout body that shouted "grandmother." Lois took her job seriously when it came to keeping Danny organized, and the rest of the employees as well. Danny adored her.

Elle let herself in at Nora's, and dropped her purse on the counter.

"Nora, it's just me!" she called out.

"In here, Elle."

Elle made her way to the nursery to find Nora with a baby in each arm, rocking gently in the chair.

"Good morning," Nora said tiredly.

"Hi." Elle stroked the back of her hair. "Hello, my handsome little men." She bent to kiss each of them.

Elle straightened and said, "It doesn't sound like you guys had much of a visit with your parents. Are you okay? You look tired."

"Yeah. More frustrated with my parents than anything else. I didn't sleep very well last night."

"Parents say some stupid things sometimes." She bent to relieve Nora of Jarrett. Justin was sound asleep.

"Well, mine do anyway. Just my mom, really." She said it sadly.

"Don't you let it get to you. Did Luke go a little too far with the discussion last night?"

"No. He said exactly what needed to be said. I was happy that he did, too."

"Okay then. Well, what have we got planned for today?"

"I need to strip the beds and tidy up the house. Mom didn't do a thing to help. I don't think they even had time to unpack. They were up and out the door by six o'clock this morning."

Elle's expression was pure sadness for Nora. "I'm sorry it turned out this way." Nora nodded. "Do you want me to do the housework or watch the boys?"

"Let's get the boys changed and ready for their nap. We can do the housework together."

The twins made sweet little noises to each other once they were settled in the crib. Their hands were lightly touching each other as they drifted off to sleep.

Elle cleaned up the kitchen while Nora stripped the beds and started laundry. They sat at the table an hour later, enjoying a cup of coffee, when Elle's phone rang.

"Hi, Jessie."

"Hi, Mom. I just wanted to let you know that Ava will be coming home in a couple of hours."

"Great! I'm just at Luke and Nora's, but can be at your place before you guys get home."

"Sounds good. How's Nora? I was talking with Luke earlier, and he said it didn't go very well with her parents."

"No, it didn't." She smiled at Nora. "I'll see you in a little while."

As they disconnected, Elle said to Nora, "Ava will be home in a couple of hours. I'll have to leave in a bit, but I can help with whatever else you need done."

"How is she feeling?"

"Health-wise, she must be okay. I'd like to see her stay home for the rest of the week, though."

Nora smiled and covered Elle's hand with her own. "You care so much about everyone. You are an incredibly giving person."

Elle returned the smile. "I love all of you guys and would do anything for any one of you."

Jarrett and Justin were making their voices heard through the monitor. Elle and Nora carried the coffee mugs to the sink, then made their way to the nursery.

Once the boys were fed and changed, the women sat with them for a bit before Elle had to leave for Ava and Jessie's.

"Are you sure there's nothing more I can do before I leave?"

"Nope, I think we've done it all. Thank-you so much for coming over today, Elle. And, please say hi to Ava for me. I'll give her a call tonight."

"You bet. I'll see you tomorrow."

CHAPTER 9

MIKE AND DAVE HAD BEEN BUSY IN THE WAREHOUSE ASSEMBLING CABINETS when Danny entered the building. His long strides had him reaching their workspace in short time.

The guys lifted their heads from their work when he stopped beside them.

"Hey, Dad. How's it goin'?" inquired Mike.

"Hey, Dad," Dave repeated.

"Hard at work, I see." He glanced around at the stack of cabinet pieces. The light oak would look fabulous in the Gibson's home. "These look great, guys!"

"Thanks. What are you up to?" asked Dave.

"Just wanted to let you know that Ava is coming home today."

"Oh, good. That's some scary shit for them. Thank God the baby is okay." said Mike.

"The four of us will head over to their place tomorrow night for a visit. We'll let Ava get some rest before we swoop in on her," said Dave.

"I'm sure they would love that. Elle is on her way over now to help out." Danny shook his head and smiled. "That woman never tires. She's already been helping out with the twins this morning!"

Dave smiled. "You found a keeper in her, Dad."

Danny smiled again. He stuffed his hands in the front pockets of his jeans. "Listen, I'm sorry we haven't had much time to get together with you guys. The babies keep Elle pretty busy, and now Ava as well."

Mike slapped Danny on the back. "We're not little kids who need attention all the time. We're okay with all of it. Wouldn't mind getting together for a beer sometime, though."

"Let's go tonight after work!"

"Sound good to me," said Dave.

"Great! Meet me in my office when you're done, and we'll go for dinner and grab that beer."

Danny left them to their work and headed for his office. He knew that Lois had left a stack of paperwork on his desk. She had threatened him with his life if he didn't "make that pile disappear."

He strolled into the building with a smile on his face and a wave for Lois.

She watched him coming through the door. "What's with the stupid look on your face?" she joked. "Did you ...?"

He stopped at her desk and said, "Before you even ask, no, I did not just get laid."

She laughed out loud. Danny was using the exact words she had said to him when he had first reunited with Elle.

"I was just out at the warehouse and made plans with my sons for the evening. We're going for dinner and beers."

"Good for you, boy! It's good to spend time together away from this place." She swooped an arm to encompass the room.

"Yep! I'll get that pile of shit you put on my desk cleared off first."

She chuckled and set her hands back on her keyboard.

Danny closed his office door behind him and pulled out his cell phone.

Elle answered on the first ring. "Hi, babe."

"Hi. You sound tired." He frowned into the phone.

"I'm okay. I just left Nora's and went to the grocery store. Now I'm on my way to Ava. I'm not sure what time I'll be home."

"Okay. Well, I was calling to let you know that I won't be home for dinner tonight. I'm taking Dave and Mike out."

"Oh, that's nice. Say hi to them for me and enjoy your evening! Love you."

"Love you, too. Don't overwork yourself. You need to take care of you."

"Yes, Mom."

"Christ, you're stubborn."

She laughed. "See you at home later."

They disconnected as Elle pulled into Ava and Jessie's laneway. She unlocked the house with her key and then retrieved the groceries from the cargo space of her truck.

She had just started preparing lasagna when she heard the crunching of tires on the gravel of the laneway.

She smiled and wiped her hands on the towel she had slung over her shoulder. Jessie gave her a hug when he entered the house and whispered, "Thanks for being here, Mom." Elle gave him an extra squeeze and released him so she could get to Ava. She hugged her and then slid her hands down Ava's arms so she could hold her hands.

"How are you feeling?"

"I actually feel fine. My head still hurts like a bastard, but the doctor said the headache would subside over the next day or two." Ava set her purse on the counter and added, "They did another ultrasound on the baby, and all is good." She rested her hands on her belly as if to protect it from any further harm.

Jessie sniffed the air. "Ahh, lasagna." He closed his eyes and took another big sniff.

Elle laughed at him. "It seems to be all I make for you. I just figured the leftovers would be easy to heat up tomorrow."

"Thank-you, Elle." Ava removed her light jacket and hung it on the back of one of the kitchen chairs. She pulled the chair out to sit.

Jessie caught her by the elbows before her butt hit the seat. "You are supposed to be resting." He gently guided her toward the staircase.

Ava rolled her eyes. "Ugh. You should go back to work."

"Your stubborn attitude will get you nowhere. It rolls right off of me." He continued to lead her to the stairs. "By the way, when I go back to work, Mom will be in charge. And, believe me, you won't get away with a thing."

"Elle, help!" Ava pleaded jokingly.

"Sorry, Ava. I have my instructions." She laughed as Ava stomped up the stairs.

Jessie settled Ava in their bed and came back down to the kitchen. "The doctor wants her to get lots of rest this week."

"Got it. She's on my watch during the day, so rest is what she'll get."

Jessie hugged her. "Thanks, Mom."

When he released her, she asked, "Are you okay, Jessie?"

He ran his hands through his thick blond hair. "Yeah. It really scared the hell out of me. We could have lost the baby, Mom." His eyes filled with tears.

She embraced him again. "I know, honey. But you know what, Ava's fine, and so is the baby. I'll be here for the week and longer if you want. She'll get all the love and care she needs from this family."

She pulled back and rested her forehead against his.

"You're going to be an amazing dad."

He smiled at that and lifted his head.

"How are you going to be here and with Nora too?"

"You just leave that to me. I'll figure it out."

He shook his head in wonder. "Luke and I will figure out our work schedules to lighten the load."

Elle shrugged her shoulders. "No worries. Now, go do something while I make dinner." She shooed him away.

"Is Danny coming for dinner?"

"No. He's having dinner with Dave and Mike."

"Nice. Okay, I'll be in the office if you need anything."

"Got it." She moved back to the stove.

Jessie called his brother the minute he entered his office.

"Hey, Jessie. How's Ava?"

"Hi, Luke. We're home now, and she's resting. Mom is here making dinner."

"Oh, good. What are you up to?"

"I was thinking that you and I should figure out our days so Mom won't be so overwhelmed with the girls and the twins."

"Absolutely! I can get the guys set up by the end of each day and show up later in the morning. Mom can be with

Ava in the morning and then Nora in the afternoons. Does that work?"

"Yep. That should work. I'll get to my job sites early and then leave early."

"Good plan. Anything else?"

"Nope. We can figure out meals. Mom shouldn't have to do all the cooking."

"Yep. And, when Ava's feeling stronger, we'll take Mom out for a nice evening."

"Sounds good. Talk to ya later."

"See ya."

Jessie disconnected, feeling a little better about alleviating the load for his mother. He rifled through his contracts and started calling his employees. He would need them at work by five on Monday morning.

Luke arrived home a little earlier than he had expected. He found Nora and the boys in the family room. She had spread out a big comforter and lay on her stomach, playing with the kids. She babbled away in baby talk to them. All they wore were their diapers. Their little smiles lit up the room.

He pulled out his phone and snapped a few photos of them. He got a great one of Nora smiling at the camera while her hands held the boys' toes. He moved closer and lay beside Nora. She smiled and kissed him.

"Hi."

"Hi. You're home early."

"We're waiting on supplies." He turned his attention to his sons. "Hi, guys! Are you having fun with Mommy?" He tweaked their toes and ran his hands over their bellies. In return, he got some cooing out of them. He smiled broadly.

"How was your day?"

"Good. Your mom came over for the morning, and then she went to help Ava. The boys have been amazing all day." She took Justin by the hand and then Jarrett. "Weren't you?"

"You're so great with them!"

She giggled and continued to play with their pudgy hands.

"I was talking to Jessie earlier today."

"How is he? I was planning on calling them later tonight once we get the boys to bed."

He went on to tell her of their plan for work schedules.

"What a great idea! I feel like I have a pretty good routine with the boys now. So, it's actually perfect timing to ease Elle out of the workload."

"Mom loves to be here, and she would never say so but, I think she could use some time to herself and Danny again. Poor guy." He chuckled.

"For sure. Plus, we'll all be opening up the cottages again soon to spend time up there."

He kissed her cheek. "Should I start dinner?"

"It's ready to go. I made stew while the boys napped."

"Okay. I'll set the table." He tweaked the boy's toes again and rose to get the table ready for dinner. He hummed to himself as he set about the work and thought to himself how life has a way of working out.

Jarrett and Justin had already been bathed, so Nora dressed them in their pajamas and carried them one by one to the kitchen to set them in their playpen. She loved the time that the four of them spent together, and she was looking forward to Luke being around a little longer in the mornings.

Dave and Mike put their tools away and dusted themselves off as they made their way to the office. They stopped at Lois's desk to say hello.

"I hear you guys are having dinner with your dad tonight."

"We are. It's been a while since the three of us hung out," replied Mike.

"Well, enjoy your evening and make sure your old man pays your bill." She chuckled as she rose from her chair. She tidied her desk and reached for her purse.

"You have a good night too, Lois. See you Monday," said Dave.

They tapped on Danny's door when they reached it.

"Come on in, guys!" he called from the other side.

"Ready to go, Dad?"

"Yep." He closed the file he had been going over and stood. "Lois will be shocked that I got her pile finished." He scooped up the stack of papers and carried it out to her desk. He left it neatly stacked in the center of it. He grabbed a piece of notepaper and wrote, "Got it done – happy now?" He chuckled to himself.

"Let's go."

The three men left the building together and climbed into Danny's truck.

"Where do you want to go?" he asked as he put the truck in gear.

"Why don't we just go to The Bar?"

"Perfect."

They arrived a few minutes later and found a table in the corner of the room.

The server approached the table. "What'll it be, guys?"

"Three beers and menus, please," Mike replied.

As she walked away, Danny asked, "So, what's new with you guys? How are Emma and Maggie? We didn't get much of a chance to talk at the hospital."

"Everything's good. Maggie's been busy at the hospital."

"Is she still enjoying the administrative side of it?" asked Danny.

"Yeah, I think so; she misses the interaction with the patients, though."

"And how's Emma?" Danny asked Mike.

"Good! The shop is going to implement her idea of the hair and makeup for weddings, so she's pretty excited about that."

Danny smiled at his sons. They had come a long way since their mother walked out the door years before.

"How are the twins?" asked Mike.

"Growing fast!"

The server returned with their beer and menus. "Let me know when you're ready to order."

The three men clinked bottles and took a swig.

"Maggie and I were talking the other night. We thought that when everything settles down with the twins and Ava, we'd have everyone over for dinner."

"Hey, that sounds great! I look forward to it," Danny answered.

"When do you think you'll be heading back up the cottages, Dad?" asked Mike.

"Hopefully, over the next couple of weeks. You guys?"

"The four of us were thinking we'd go up next weekend. We'll check on everyone's cottages for them while we're there."

"That would be great. It's been too long since we all sat around the campfire and had a few drinks together." Danny was looking forward to some time away.

Mike smiled. "It'll be so much fun next year with Jarrett and Justin. I can't wait to take them fishing!"

Danny smiled back and asked hopefully, "So, no wedding or baby plans for you yet?"

Mike laughed. "Not yet!"

Dave held up his hands. "Us neither!"

They spent the next couple of hours catching up. Work never came up once, and they were all glad for it.

Danny drove the boys back to the warehouse for their vehicles.

"Thanks for dinner, Dad." Mike stuck his hand out to shake.

Danny pulled him in for a hug. "My pleasure. I really enjoyed myself."

He released Mike and hugged Dave. "Glad we got out tonight."

"Me too. Thanks."

Danny climbed back into his truck. "See you guys next week. Have a good weekend. Say hi to the girls for me." He stuck his arm out the window and waved.

The boys stood smiling at him as they waved back.

Ava woke after a couple of hours of sleep feeling refreshed and energized. She came down the stairs and found Elle setting the table for dinner.

Elle turned and smiled when she saw Ava. "How was your nap?"

"Jesus, how long did I sleep for?" She looked a little chagrined.

UNITY

"A couple of hours. That's good. Your body must have needed it." Elle pulled out a kitchen chair. "Come and have a seat. Dinner is almost ready."

"Thanks, Elle. You didn't need to go to the trouble. I could have made something."

"Not today. Happy to help." Elle walked back to the oven and removed the lasagna. The salad had been prepared and sat waiting in the fridge. She moved to the edge of the kitchen and called out to Jessie.

"Dinner's ready!"

Jessie entered the kitchen in less than thirty seconds. He came up behind Ava and hugged her. "Feeling okay?"

"Yes, and thank-you for forcing me to take that nap." She smiled sweetly at him.

He sniffed the air. "Smells amazing, Mom. Can I help?"

"Nope. Have a seat." She set the salad on the table and then the dish of lasagna.

The three of them served themselves and dug in.

Elle asked Ava, "Will you be taking the rest of the week off?"

"The doctor suggested that I do."

"Then that's what will happen," Jessie added, around a mouthful of food. He set his fork down and spoke again. "Luke and I have come up with a plan for you and the girls, Mom." He went on to relay the conversation he and Luke had shared.

"Okay, that should work," Elle replied. "I only have one request."

"Sure. What is it?"

"If you're leaving earlier in the mornings, then Ava has to stay in bed until I get here. I should be here by seven o'clock."

"Okay. Better safe than sorry."

Ava cleared her throat. "Uh, I'm right here, guys."

Jessie lay his hand on her shoulder. "We know that. But we also know how stubborn you are."

"Yeah, that's true." She held up her hand and placed it on her heart. "I solemnly swear to say in bed until Elle gets here."

Jessie and Elle burst out laughing.

Once dinner had been devoured, Jessie stood to clear the table. Ava tried to rise at the same time to help. He gently pressed his hand on her shoulder to keep her from standing.

"First rule: no helping!"

"Jesus, I'm not a damn child, Jessie." She stayed seated.

"No. But, you are carrying our child, and you need to take it easy this week."

"Fine," she snapped.

Jessie looked at his mother and rolled his eyes. "See what you'll be dealing with?"

Elle smiled at the two of them. "Ava, honey, why don't you go have a nice hot bath while we tidy up?"

Ava looked up at Jessie. "May I stand now?" She smirked at him.

"You may." He lay a hand out to help her up.

"Idiot," she grumbled.

He laughed as she took his hand. He gave her a kiss and a swat on the ass. "Mom said to go have a bath, so go." He pointed at the stairs.

"You just wait until she leaves, Jessie." She raised her eyebrows at him.

Elle giggled to herself as she went about putting the food into storage containers. She loved the constant joking between the two of them.

Jessie cleared the dishes from the table and carried them to the dishwasher. Ava had already climbed the stairs for her bath.

"Hey Jessie, I never got the chance the ask you what it was you wanted to 'run by me' last night."

He chuckled. "We were planning on coming over to tell you about the baby!"

Elle smiled. "Well, you certainly accomplished that! I thought maybe you had wanted to come over to talk about Chase. You haven't said too much about it." She set the last container down and rested her hip against the counter to give him her full attention.

"There isn't really much to say, Mom. I haven't heard back from the police yet, so I don't know what's happening with him."

"Maybe I'll give Jillian a call tomorrow and find out what's going on. Better yet, I should go to the hospital and talk to the little bastard myself." She fiddled with the towel in her hand. She was getting agitated just thinking about it.

Jessie moved closer and placed his hand on hers. "This is probably one time you should let the police do their job." He smiled at her as he said it.

"We'll see. I guess I could call Jake."

She turned her attention back to the food. Once everything had been put away and cleaned up, they moved to the family room to sit and wait on Ava.

She came down the stairs a short while later.

"How did that feel?" Jessie asked as she entered the room.

"Either the water was too warm, or I stood up too fast. I felt kinda light-headed for a minute," she answered.

Jessie jumped up from the sofa to reach her side. He guided her to where he had been sitting. "Are you still light-headed? Should I call the doctor?"

"I'm okay now." She sat and curled her feet under herself.

Jessie sat beside her and put his arm around her. He stole a glance toward Elle.

"I'll get you a glass of water." Elle headed for the kitchen with worry on her mind.

She came back and handed the glass to Ava. "Just sip at this, and once you're done, I think you should go back up to bed for the night."

"Thanks Elle." She sipped at the water. Jessie still had his arm around her.

"Are you sure you're okay?" he asked.

Ava nodded.

Once she had finished, Elle and Jessie helped her back up the stairs. They settled her in bed with the television turned on.

"Do you guys want me to stay?" asked Elle.

"No, that's okay, Mom. I think I'll just go to bed with Ava for the night."

Elle kissed Ava's head and said she would head for home. Jessie walked her to the door.

"Call me if you need anything at all, Jessie."

"Thanks, Mom." They hugged before she left.

He locked up the house and turned off the lights before he went to join Ava.

CHAPTER 10

ELLE AND DANNY FINALLY HAD A CHANCE TO CATCH UP ON EACH OTHER'S DAY when they arrived home.

"How was your dinner with the boys?" she asked, as she poured herself a glass of wine. She grabbed a beer from the fridge and handed it to him.

He gave her a kiss and answered, "It was so nice to spend time with them. They said that the four of them are planning to head up to the cottages next weekend."

"Nice! I'm hoping we can get up there in the next couple of weeks."

They moved from the kitchen to the family room and sat on the sofa. Danny reached over and ran his thumb along her bottom lip.

"You look tired, babe." There was concern in his voice.

"A little. But sitting here with you sure is nice." She leaned in to kiss him.

"How was Ava today?"

She went on to tell him of her day with both Nora and Ava. She was still concerned about Ava feeling light-headed.

"You had a stressful day. I can see it in your eyes."

"Luke and Jessie are going to be spending more time with the girls over the next couple of weeks, so that will help. For now, I think I'll just go to bed early." She finished her wine and set her glass in the sink.

"Are you sure you're okay?" He followed her to the kitchen and set his empty beer bottle on the counter.

"Yeah, I'm okay. Would you do me a favor, though?" she asked.

"Of course. Name it." He took her by the hand and led her to their bedroom. As she undressed, he went to start a hot bath for her.

"I was wondering if you'd talk to Jake tomorrow and find out what's going on with Chase. It's been playing on my mind for the last couple of days. I just need to know what the outcome of his stupidity will be." She yawned on the last word.

"I'll call him in the morning. Come on, let's go have a bath. You'll sleep better." He held out his hand to her.

She smiled at his thoughtfulness and allowed herself to be led to the en suite bathroom.

Danny climbed in first, and then Elle climbed in to sit between his legs. She rested the back of her head on his chest.

He reached into one of her little dishes sitting on the edge of the tub and plucked out a hairband. He sifted through her hair until he had it all in one hand. He affixed the band and lay her hair over his shoulder. He could feel the tension leave her body. Within minutes, he could hear her breathing change to complete relaxation. He massaged her shoulders and rubbed her arms.

"You're too good to me." She sighed deeply.

"You're too good to everyone else. I wish you would slow down a bit."

"I will. I promise." She yawned again.

He rolled his eyes, knowing that she wouldn't slow down at all.

"I can feel you rolling your eyes at me." She smiled and turned her head slightly to get a glance at him.

He chuckled and kissed her forehead. "Come on, let's get outta here and get you into bed."

"Deal."

Elle threw on one of Danny's T-shirts and crawled under the blankets. She was asleep before the tub had time to drain.

It was early the next morning when the aroma of coffee drifted into the bedroom. Elle yawned, stretched, and sat up. She'd had a wonderful sleep.

Danny came into the room with two steaming mugs. He bent to kiss her and handed one to her.

"Good morning."

"Good morning. Thanks for the coffee."

His weight dipped the mattress as he sat beside her.

"What would you like to do today?" At the look of confusion on her face, he said, "It's Saturday."

"Really. Shit. I thought it was Friday. In that case, what the hell are we doing up so early?"

He laughed. "Want to take a drive down to Dune Lake?"

"Yes, please! It's been so long since we've been there."

"Perfect. Let's get dressed and make a picnic lunch."

They were on the road within the hour.

"What time do you have to be at Ava's on Monday?" he asked as he maneuvered the roads.

"I told them I would be there around seven o'clock. Why? Do you need something?"

"You are a liar."

Her eyes widened. "What do you mean I'm a liar?"

"Do you remember how you said last night that you would slow down?" She nodded.

"And here you are offering to help me now."

"Sorry. I can't help myself."

"I know you can't." He tapped the end of her nose with his finger and smiled. She grinned back at him.

They arrived at the beach and decided to take a nice long, relaxing walk. They kicked off their sandals and made their way to the sand.

They spent a wonderful weekend enjoying time alone. She had only checked in on the girls once. They had told her that everything was fine and that she was to enjoy her weekend. They would see her Monday.

Elle and Danny had shared amazing dinners and had worked in the yard. The weather had been beautiful.

Both were disappointed to see Monday morning arrive.

He rose from the bed. "What would you like for breakfast? I'm cooking."

"Hmm. I think eggs benedict would be nice."

"Eggs benedict? I was thinking more along the lines of toast or getting you a bowl of cereal."

She laughed out loud.

They enjoyed a very simple breakfast together, and then went their separate ways to start the day.

Elle arrived at Jessie's by seven o'clock, and was surprised to see him still there.

"I thought you'd be gone already."

"I should be, but I got a late start."

"How'd the night go? Is Ava feeling better?"

"She had a restful weekend and slept through the nights without another incident."

"Is she still in bed?"

"Yep. She was afraid to get up before you arrived!" He laughed.

Elle smiled. "Have a good day. I'll just go on up."

"Hey Mom, if Ava feels off again, can you give me a call? I'll try to get her back in to see Doctor Evans."

"Of course." She made her way to the staircase.

"Thanks. Have a good day."

Elle knocked lightly on the door frame and stuck her head into the bedroom. Ava was sitting up in bed with a book.

"Hi, Elle."

"Hi. Feeling better?" She crawled onto the bed to sit beside her.

"I am. I don't think I can lie here all week, though." She scowled.

"You sound just like me." Elle smiled. "Let's get you up slowly and see how you do."

Elle left the bed and came around to Ava's side. She offered her hand. Ava scooted to the edge and set her feet on the carpeted floor. She slowly stood and waited a few seconds. She smiled at Elle.

"So far, so good."

"Okay. Bathroom?"

"Yes."

Elle held her arm as they walked to the bathroom. She left Ava at the door and returned to the bed to pull up the sheets and blankets.

Ava returned a moment later. "Can I have some coffee now?"

"Of course." Ava dressed in leggings and a T-shirt. Elle was wearing the same. People would definitely mistake them for mother and daughter. Both women had their blond hair pulled back in a ponytail.

They slowly descended the stairs. Elle sat Ava down at the table, and grabbed two mugs from the cabinets. Jessie had left the pot of coffee warming for them.

"Is Danny getting annoyed with all of us yet?" Ava asked with concern in her voice.

"No! Not at all. He's been amazing," Elle replied.

Ava nodded. "Okay. I'm sorry that we've all been such a pain in the ass lately."

Elle reached across the table and took her hand.

"Danny and I are just fine. Plus, he knows how much I love all of you, and he would never step in the way of that. He has kids, too, and completely understands."

She released Ava's hand and rose from her chair to prepare breakfast for her.

"I feel completely useless sitting here while you cater to me." Ava pouted.

Elle laughed. "Just wait until you're about seven months pregnant. Jessie won't allow you to do anything for yourself!"

After breakfast, Elle settled Ava on the sofa with a blanket and pillow, turned on the television and said, "Let me know if you need anything else. I'm just going to tidy up the kitchen and start laundry."

UNITY

Ava dozed off while Elle made herself busy. Jessie called a few times. Elle reassured him that Ava was resting and that she was fine. He promised to be home by early afternoon.

Elle's phone rang as she was pulling a roast from the freezer for Jessie and Ava's dinner.

"Hi, Elle. How's Ava?"

"Hi, Nora. She's doing okay. Is everything okay with you and the boys?"

"We're good! I didn't want to disturb Ava in case she was sleeping." "Jessie will be home in a couple of hours, and then I'll be over to see you."

"You don't need to come over, Elle. You should go home when you leave Ava! I'm sure you have better things to do than to hang out here."

Elle smiled into her phone. "Well, there's lots I could be doing at home if you don't need me."

"Enjoy the time off while you can. You never know what will happen next in this crazy family of ours!" Nora laughed as she said the words.

"Okay, well, just call if you need something. Love you."

"Love you, too. Say hi to Ava and let her know that I'll call her later."

Elle continued with the preparation of dinner. She could hear Ava waking a few moments later. She went back to the family room to check on her. Ava sat up and rubbed at her eyes.

"Why am I so damn tired?" she asked.

"You're nurturing a baby in there. You may be tired for a few months. Every woman is different. You stressed yourself last week, honey. Just give it time." Elle moved to sit beside her. "Do you need anything?"

"Were you this tired when you were pregnant?"

"I don't think I was with Luke, but I sure was with Jessie. With the boys only being eleven months apart, it was pretty hectic for a while." Elle chuckled at the memory.

"Jesus! I don't know how you did it!" exclaimed Ava.

"Thinking back, I don't either!"

Jessie walked in the door as the two women were laughing.

"Well, that's a great sound to hear!"

Both women smiled at him. "Hi, babe."

He bent to kiss his wife. "Did you behave today?" She rolled her eyes at him.

Elle laughed. "No episodes today and lots of rest."

She sat and chatted with them for a few more minutes and then returned to the kitchen to set the roast in the oven. She gave Jessie the cooking instructions and hoped he wouldn't screw it up.

Ava thanked her for taking care of her.

"No worries. Call if you need something." Elle retrieved her purse and walked to the door.

"Are you off to Nora's now?" asked Jessie as he walked with her.

"No, she called and said everything was fine. I'll just go home and get caught up on my housework. I'd like to start on more drawings as well. Did I tell you that Kim wants me to do another show?"

"Hey, that's great! Thanks for being here today, Mom." Jessie gave her a hug and walked her to her truck. He re-entered the house and went to sit with Ava.

Elle called Danny on her way home.

"Hi, babe! How's it going?" asked Danny.

"Good. I was just calling to let you know that I'm on my way home."

"Whoa! You actually listened to me!"

"Not funny! Jessie got home early, and Nora didn't need me."

Danny chuckled. "And how many times did you ask Nora if she was sure you weren't needed?"

"Once or twice."

Danny laughed again. "I'll finish up here and be home in a couple of hours."

"I'm looking forward to a nice quiet dinner with you," she said softly.

"Hmm ... maybe I'll say 'fuck it' and leave now," he growled.

"Think you can slip past Lois?"

Danny groaned. "No."

Elle laughed out loud. "See you in a couple of hours then."

Elle arrived home and walked through the house to see what needed to be done. Nothing. The house was spotless and in perfect order. She dug through the freezer for two steaks. Next, she made sure she had everything she needed for the rest of their dinner. Once that was done, she wandered out to the deck with her sketch pad and pencil.

Her hand hovered over the page, not knowing what she felt like drawing. She set down her supplies and returned to the kitchen for a glass of red wine. Now, she was ready.

Danny arrived home in record time to find Elle still sitting out on the deck. He peeked over her shoulder to get a look at the new sketch. He was taken aback by the beauty of it.

Staring back at him was the most intricate drawing of lilies. They seemed to come to life in front of his eyes.

"Wow! That is breathtaking!" he exclaimed.

She tilted her head back and smiled. "Thanks. How was your day?"

He couldn't take his eyes off the page. "Good. How do you create something like that? I can't draw a stick man."

Elle laughed. "I honestly don't know. I got the talent from my dad, I guess." She stood to hug him. "What time is it?"

"Close to five o'clock."

"Would you like a drink before we have dinner? We could sit out here and watch our lazy river."

"Sure. That sounds good."

Elle scooped up her drawing and pencil. She walked past him to set them in the house and grab a beer from the fridge for Danny and more wine for herself.

She handed him his beer and clinked her glass against it. They each took a sip. He set his beer on the deck railing and pulled her in close.

He released her and said, "I'm glad you found some time for yourself today."

Elle smiled. "Me too." She rested her head on his shoulder and sighed.

They moved to the patio furniture to sit and enjoy the quiet.

"Did you talk to Jake today?"

"I did. It's not looking good for Chase."

She raised her eyebrows. "What did Jake say?"

"Chase is being charged with brandishing a weapon. It means that he could serve up to a year of prison time and also receive a fine of about five thousand dollars."

"Good." She didn't need to say anything else.

"His jaw will likely be healed in a couple of weeks, and then he'll have his day in court."

Elle nodded.

"I'm going to contact our lawyer tomorrow and have our contract with Chase dissolved."

Danny nodded. "Good idea."

"He doesn't deserve a damn thing from any of us. He was given the chance to better himself and threw it away. You know, I haven't been to confront him yet. That might just be a stop that I'll make as well."

Danny clinked his bottle with Elle's glass again. "Should we enjoy the rest of the evening without any more talk of that idiot?"

Elle smiled. "Absolutely."

He stretched his arm across the back of the sofa and rested his hand on her shoulder.

"It'll be nice to get back to the cottage on the weekends, won't it?"

"Can't wait," Elle replied. Danny gave her shoulder a squeeze.

CHAPTER 11

ELLE ARRIVED AT JESSIE AND AVA'S SHORTLY AFTER SEVEN O'CLOCK THE FOLlowing morning. He was coming out of his office with an armful of paperwork when she walked in.

"Hi."

"Hi. Is Ava sleeping?"

"She is. I can't believe how tired she is."

"Can I talk to you for a minute?"

"Sure. You okay?"

She waved off the question. "Yeah, I'm fine. I just wanted to ask you about this contract we have with Chase."

"Okay. What about it?" He raised his eyebrows.

"I'll talk to Luke too, but Danny and I were talking last night. I thought I should contact the lawyer and have the contract dissolved. What do you think?"

"Dissolved, as in he won't get any more money?" Elle nodded. "I have no problem with that. The guy's a fucking idiot."

"Agreed. Okay then, I'll talk to Luke later. I just didn't want to bring it up in front of Ava. She doesn't need to worry about anything but herself right now."

"Yeah." He looked up the staircase to where his wife lay sleeping. "I hope today goes as well as yesterday. I feel we'll be out of the woods then. I called the doctor, and we have an appointment this afternoon around three o'clock. I'll be home by two."

"Sounds good." She pointed at the coffee. "I'm gonna grab a cup of that."

"Help yourself. I guess I'll take off for work."

"Have a good day. I'll let you know what the lawyer says."

Elle sipped her coffee and then climbed the stairs to check on her daughter-in-law. She was just swinging her legs over the edge of the bed.

"How's the patient this morning?"

"Hi. Guess we'll find out as soon as I stand up." She smiled.

Elle moved to her side as a precaution. Ava stood and ran her hands through her hair.

"Okay?" asked Elle.

"Yep."

Elle made the bed while she waited for Ava to come out of the bathroom.

She came out dressed casually in jeans and a T-shirt. "You know, I think I could go back to work tomorrow."

"Sure! Just as soon as you convince Jessie." Elle stood with her hands on her hips and smirked.

"Guess I'll go back on Monday." She pouted.

"So, I hear you have a doctor's appointment today," Elle said as she poured a new coffee for herself and another for Ava.

"I hope it's good news." Ava worried.

"It'll be fine. I'm guessing she'll just suggest rest for the remainder of the week."

"Ugh. I'm so sick of lying around."

"Enjoy it while you can. In about six months, you'll be begging for sleep!" Elle said it cheerfully.

Ava laughed. "According to Nora, that's the truth."

As the women enjoyed their coffee, Elle looked around the kitchen. "It doesn't look like Jessie left much for me to do today."

"Nope. Maybe we could go for a walk?" she asked hopefully.

"Now, that sounds wonderful!"

They cleared their mugs and slipped on their sandals. They spent an hour wandering around the acreage. Ava pointed out where she'd like a play structure and sandbox placed. Elle was confident that the play area would be beautiful when Jessie finished it.

Once they were back in the house, Elle pointed to the couch. "And now, you need to sit for a while. I'll get water for us."

Ava gladly plunked herself on the sofa and waited for Elle to return. She found the air outside to be humid.

A storm could be heard brewing in the distance. Elle glanced out the window as she handed Ava her water. "Looks like we timed our walk perfectly."

"Yeah. You may not be stuck babysitting me tomorrow if we get all the rain they're calling for. Jessie won't be able to work."

Elle smiled sweetly at her. "It's hardly babysitting. I love being here and helping out."

"And we love you for everything that you do for us!"

Within minutes, big fat raindrops began hitting the windows.

Elle and Ava settled back further on the sofa and turned on the television. Ava was sound asleep twenty minutes later. Elle stood and covered her with one of the throws lying across the back of the sofa.

Jessie arrived home, soaked to the bone. He stood under the roof of the porch and ran his fingers through his hair to relieve it of some of the water. He left his work boots on the porch and walked in, carrying an armload of fresh-cut flowers. Elle closed the door behind him.

"Man, it's getting nasty out there!" exclaimed Jessie.

Elle held her index finger to her lips. "Shh, Ava's asleep."

"Oops, sorry," he whispered.

"Nice flowers!"

"I thought they would brighten Ava's mood." He smiled shyly.

"She'll love them. Let me get a vase for them." Elle searched the cupboards and finally came up with a tall glass vase. She cut the ends of the flowers, placed them in the vase, and set them on the table for Ava to see.

"How was she feeling today?" he asked.

"Good. No incidents. We went for a walk just before the storm hit. It may have tired her out a bit, but now she's sound asleep on the sofa."

"Thanks again for being here, Mom."

"No worries. You guys will be leaving shortly, so I guess I'll take off. I might go see Nora and the boys."

"Okay. I'll let you know what the doctor says, and I'll let you know if we're working tomorrow or not."

Elle retrieved her purse and opened the door. "Jesus, it really is getting nasty."

"Why don't you wait for it to pass?"

"Nah, I'm good. Talk to you later." She hugged him and ran for her truck.

Jessie closed the door behind her and climbed the stairs to have a shower before Ava woke and they had to leave for their appointment.

The rain was still pouring down when Elle arrived at Luke and Nora's. She parked as close as she could to the door and made a dash for it. She knocked and opened the door simultaneously.

Nora and the boys were lying on the floor. Jarrett lay on his belly while Nora practiced tummy time with him. He was not impressed. He fussed the entire time. Justin lay on his back, smiling and cooing. Nora looked up when she heard the front door open.

"Hi, Elle!"

"Hi. What's going on?"

"We're trying tummy time." She turned to Jarrett and said, "but someone doesn't like it."

Elle laughed. She lowered herself to her knees and rolled Justin onto his belly. "Well, let's see how you do?"

The same reaction came from him. The women stuck with it for a few minutes and then let them relax on their backs again.

"So, everything's going well?"

"Yep. We've got ourselves into a pretty good routine now. How's Ava doing?"

"Better. They'll know for sure after they see the doctor today."

"I bet she's anxious to get back to work!"

"She sure is. Jessie won't even allow her to do his or Luke's accounting right now." She played her hands along the boys' tummies as she spoke. Her reward was the sound of smacking lips. She smiled broadly.

"It's probably for the best." Nora scooped up Jarrett. "Want to help with the feeding, Grandma?"

Elle scooped up Justin. "I sure do!" She nuzzled his neck.

Luke arrived home just as they sat in the overstuffed chairs with the babies to feed them their bottles.

"Hi!" He was happy to be home to his wife and kids.

"Hi, yourself," replied Nora.

"Hey, Mom. How are you?"

"Good. I timed my visit perfectly!"

Luke chuckled. "And how are these two today?" He came forward and kissed the tops of their heads.

"You're home early," Nora said after Luke kissed her lips.

"Got rained out." He softly stroked the back of her hair and then moved to the sofa.

Nora laughed. "I didn't even realize it was raining! Guess I was having too much fun with these two munchkins." She nuzzled Jarrett.

Luke and Elle couldn't help but smile.

"What are you up to tonight, Mom?"

"I don't know yet. Just a quiet evening, I suppose."

"Us too."

"Do you and Danny want to go out for dinner Friday night?" he asked.

"That sounds nice." She tickled Justin's chin and said to him, "You're first big night out on the town."

"Let's hope it goes well!" exclaimed Nora.

They chatted for a bit longer before Elle decided to head for home. She was looking forward to drinking some wine with Danny and settling in for an evening of stormy weather. She loved a good storm!

"I'll call you tomorrow, Mom, and see what time works best for everyone."

"Sounds good!" She darted to her truck and headed for home.

Once she had left, Nora turned to Luke and asked, "What's going on Friday night?"

He smiled and told her what the plan was.

"I've already spoken to Jessie, Mike, Dave, and Danny. Dave and Mike were going to head to the cottages for the weekend but have postponed it until Saturday morning. They thought this would be more fun." He chuckled.

"I can't wait to see her face!" Nora was excited for Friday to arrive.

Elle arrived home a couple of hours before Danny. She prepared dinner and then sat with a glass of wine, waiting for him to get back.

She greeted him at the door with a cold beer.

He kicked off his work boots and climbed the three stairs, smiling. "That's a hell of a way to get greeted!" He took the beer from her hand and scooped her up by the waist with his free arm. He set her down, lowered his head, and took full advantage of her position.

She was grinning from ear to ear once he released her.

He pushed his sleeves up a little further and asked about her day.

"Luke asked if we wanted to go out for dinner Friday night. Did you have plans made already?"

"Nope. Dinner out sounds great. Where are we going?"

"Not sure. He said he'd call tomorrow." They moved to the family room and sat. Danny grabbed the converter and turned on the sound system.

They spent a relaxing evening of dinner, drinks, and sharing a hot bath.

Jessie called later in the evening to let Elle know that Ava's appointment had gone well and that she could return to work on the following Monday. He had added that he would be home the next day to work in his office due to the weather. Elle had the day off.

The following morning, while she was having her coffee with Danny, Luke called to say he would be home all day as well. He had made dinner reservations at Black Door Bistro for five o'clock Friday night.

Elle conveyed the message to Danny. She was excited to be going out with everyone. They usually met at one of their homes, so this would be a nice change.

The week seemed to fly by. Elle was relieved to see that Ava had improved so much. Her energy level had risen, and her happy attitude had returned. Nora and the twins had a great routine going. Elle was a little sad that she wouldn't be needed quite as much.

The girls had told her to enjoy Friday to herself and that they would see her at the restaurant.

Elle walked Danny to the door, reminding him of their dinner plans.

"I'll be home by three," Danny stated. He wiggled his eyebrows at her. "Or earlier, if you're interested in some of this." He splayed his hands to encompass his entire body.

Elle laughed out loud and shoved him toward the door. "Have a good day, babe."

"Spoilsport," he mumbled as he left the house.

Elle spent her day weeding the flower beds and taking photos of the budding flowers. She had always drawn flowers in their full bloom. Now, her thought process was to draw them as they were just beginning to bud. It would be a series for her art showing about "new beginnings." She was excited to get started.

It was nearing lunchtime when she finally sat down with her sketch pad and pencil. The weather had cleared, and it had turned into a beautiful day to sit on her back deck. She loved the sound of the Relic River running just beyond her.

Danny arrived home at the promised time of three o'clock to find her drawing again. He studied the two she had completed after he had given her a kiss.

"These are beautiful, Elle."

"Thanks, babe. Just trying something different." She set her supplies aside and stood.

"Shall we go have a shower before dinner?"

"You bet!"

They stripped as soon as they entered their bedroom. Elle tried to sashay past him to start the shower. Before she took two steps, he picked her up and tossed her on the bed. She laughed as she hit the mattress.

"You first. Shower second." He crawled on top of her.

She spread her legs, and he settled between them.

"You drive me crazy," he growled in her ear.

"Ditto."

They finally left the bed an hour later and took the intended shower.

"We have about thirty minutes before we have to leave for dinner," announced Elle.

"If you would stop distracting me, we could have already been drinking cocktails."

Elle gave him a swat and then started to wash his muscular body. He returned the favor with enthusiasm.

CHAPTER 12

ELLE AND DANNY ARRIVED AT BLACK DOOR BISTRO WITH TWO MINUTES TO spare. The rest of the crew had only arrived a few moments earlier. Luke and Nora were unbuckling the twins. Dave, Mike, Emma, and Maggie were just exiting their vehicle.

"Hi, you guys! This is a nice surprise," Elle exclaimed as she made her way over to the foursome.

"Hi, Elle," they said in unison.

"I thought you were heading to the cottages," she said as she hugged each of them.

"Tomorrow is another day," remarked Maggie.

Danny greeted each of them as well and then walked toward Luke and Nora. Luke smiled and jerked his head towards the highway. Jessie was just turning into the parking lot.

Elle reached their truck as the babies' car seats were being released. She kissed each of them and then moved to the side so the doors could be closed. She hugged both Luke and Nora.

Jessie pulled into the parking lot, honking his horn. He and Ava slipped out of the truck as soon as it came to a stop.

"Did you buy a new truck?" asked Elle as she wandered towards it.

"What do you think of it?"

"It's beautiful." She stuck her head inside the driver's door and looked around the interior. The seats were a burgundy leather and smelled wonderful. Elle took a big sniff.

Luke walked up and said, "Get in, Mom."

She slid into the driver's seat and ran her hands over the steering wheel.

"It's so nice! Just like mine, but newer." She smiled at Jessie. She stepped from the truck.

"We're glad you like it! Here you go." He took her by the hand and dropped the keys in her palm.

She looked down at the keys and then up to him with a questioning look.

"Brand new, top of the line, fully loaded, 2019 Lincoln Navigator," Luke announced.

Jessie smiled broadly as Luke slapped a stick-on red ribbon to the side window.

"It's all yours!"

"Wait. What?"

"Just our way of saying thank-you for all that you do for us. It's been a crazy month!"

"Well yeah, but a new truck?"

Her sons took turns hugging her tightly.

Nora and Ava moved in to hug her as well.

Ava's eyes filled with tears. "Thank-you, and we love you."

Nora moved in next. "I don't think we could survive without you."

Elle's eyes filled with tears. She looked to Danny, who stood by, grinning from ear to ear.

"You were in on this?"

UNITY

He nodded and rocked back on his heels. She shook her head at him in disbelief.

Mike, Dave, Maggie, and Emma came forward to hug her.

"Congratulations on your new truck!" exclaimed Mike.

"Sweet ride!" chirped Dave.

"Will you pick us up some time for a road trip?" asked Emma.

"It's beautiful, Elle," said Maggie.

Once she had been released, she turned. "I don't know what to say! Thank-you! I love it!"

Danny stepped forward and bent his arm so Elle could slip hers through it. "Shall we go eat?"

She slipped her arm through his, briefly rested her head on his shoulder and smiled. She turned to her family. "You guys are too much!"

The gang entered the Italian restaurant full of loud talk and laughter. Jarrett and Justin were set on empty chairs in their portable car seats. They weren't left belted in for long before Maggie and Emma scooped them up. The two women sat next to each other, cooing and cuddling the twins.

"So, where will your first drive take you?" Dave asked once they were seated.

Elle laughed out loud. "Probably to Ava's or Nora's!"

The group nodded knowingly. Ava and Nora smiled shyly.

The server arrived with menus and glasses of water. Next, she asked to take their drink orders. Ava stuck to her glass of water while everyone else ordered alcohol. Nora was anxious to have a glass of red wine. She hadn't had a drink in quite some time, and couldn't wait to wrap her hands around the stem of a wine glass.

There was talk of being cottage bound over the next couple of weeks. Dave, Mike, and the girls would be leaving in the morning. They had planned on doing some yard work and checking all of the cottages for any damage that may have occurred over the winter.

The entire group was happy to be out and spending time together. Emma and Maggie didn't contribute much to the conversation. They were far too busy giving their attention to the twins. Nora had glanced at the girls a few times and then relaxed enough to settle in to enjoy the evening. She had a canvas bag full of bottles, diapers, and toys in case the boys became fussy. Any one of her family would be happy to relieve Emma and Maggie if needed.

Jessie laughed when Nora's wine arrived. He turned to Luke and said, "I guess you don't have a designated driver anymore!"

Luke groaned and then smiled. "But now we have Ava!"

Ava rolled her eyes at her husband and his brother. They were having a great time at her expense.

Danny took in the scene before his eyes. He watched his sons and instantly filled with pride. They had been without a mother in their lives for many years, yet here they were with their girlfriends, spending time with their new family. Of course, they would never call Elle "Mom," but they treated her with kindness and respect. They received no less in return. Elle loved his sons and made sure that they were aware of it. She took the time to call them and speak with them whenever she had the chance. They spent time together when they were at the cottages, and here around home as well. Dave and Mike, along with Maggie and Emma, were always included in any family get-togethers and dinners. Danny loved that about this family. They were really turning into a unit. The laughter around the table made his heart swell.

His thoughts were interrupted by a ringing cell phone. Everyone around the table reached into their pockets or purses to see if it was theirs. Elle retrieved hers from her purse and held it up "It's mine." She looked at the name on the screen and scowled.

"Who is it?" asked Danny when he saw the look on her face.

"Chase."

"Put it on speaker, Mom," suggested Jessie.

The table fell silent as Elle tapped the speaker button and said, "Hello?"

"Enjoying your little family dinner and fancy new truck?" He snapped the question at her.

Jessie, Luke, Mike, and Dave scraped their chairs back from the table and marched to the entrance of the restaurant. They pushed through the door and searched the parking lot for Chase. Luke walked straight to Elle's truck and looked around it. Jessie, Mike, and Dave walked among the rest of the family vehicles. There wasn't any sign of him. They entered the restaurant after a few minutes.

Jessie shook his head from side to side when the family looked his way. He pulled out his wallet to retrieve Officer Riley's business card. Luke pulled his phone from the front pocket of his jeans and took the card from Jessie. He stepped to the end of the table to speak with him. As he waited, Elle continued her conversation with Chase.

"Following us around now? What do you want, Chase?"

"I want you to stop spending my money!"

"We're not spending your money. You gave that up when you decided to get high and hold my son at gunpoint." She spoke calmly. "How did you get out of the hospital?"

"I walked out. They can't fucking hold me against my will!"

"Actually, they can. You're going to be charged."

"Fuck you!"

"You'd better hope to hell that the police find you before I do, you piece of shit! You and I aren't even close to being done with this."

"Tough talk coming from someone like you."

"Ha! Someone like me, huh? You have no idea who you're dealing with."

"I know exactly who I'm dealing with!"

Elle looked at Luke to see if he had Jake on the line. He gave the thumbs up. Jake was tracking Chase's phone.

"Really? Why not come face me then? There's nothing I would like better than to knock that fucking smugness right out of you!"

Every face at the table had their eyes on Elle. Their mouths hung open. Danny concentrated on the phone in her hand. He wanted to crawl right through it and grab the bastard by the throat. His body vibrated with anger. Jessie stood next to her with his fists clenched.

"We'll see each other soon enough, bitch!" He snapped the words at her and disconnected.

Elle calmly set her phone on the table.

Danny put his arm across her shoulders. "You okay?"

"I could strangle him!"

Dave spoke up. "Wow!" He raised his beer mug to her.

"Holy Christ! You had me scared, and all I did was listen!" said Mike.

The babies started to fuss just as Luke ended his conversation with Jake. Nora rose from her seat and went to them. She told the girls to hold them closer together. They did as they were told, and were shocked at how they stopping fussing as soon as their hands touched. Nora smiled and returned to her seat.

Luke returned his phone to his pocket.

"So, it turns out that Chase is about five miles from here. Jake and a few other officers are on their way to find him."

Elle simply nodded. "How the hell did he get past the men posted outside his hospital room?"

"Jake figures it happened during a shift change. Chase would know their routine by now." He sat. "You gave him quite a tongue lashing." He tipped his beer bottle toward her.

Elle shrugged her shoulders.

"So now what?" asked Ava.

"Now we wait for the police to pick him up," said Danny.

"And if they don't find him?"

"We should all be very careful and watch each other's backs."

"Okay." Ava worried her napkin in her hands.

Jessie moved to sit beside her again. He ran his hand down her back to calm her down. She gave him a shaky smile.

The server came back to the table to take food orders. She made her way around the table, taking notes on her pad of paper.

Once the food orders were taken, the conversation picked up again.

Jessie had anger in his voice when he spoke. "This was supposed to be a happy occasion. I'm sorry that Chase ruined the evening, Mom."

"He didn't ruin anything, Jessie. I'm surrounded by my family, enjoying a nice evening of dinner and drinks." She raised her wine glass and said, "Cheers to all of you. And thank-you for my new truck!" Danny leaned in and kissed her cheek.

Everyone raised their glasses and said "cheers." The mood around the table had changed from excited chatter to anger and then to less enthusiasm.

Elle set her glass down and asked if she could hold one of the boys. Maggie rose from her seat to hand over Justin. Emma handed Jarrett to Ava.

"Guess we were being baby hogs!" Emma said.

"It's easy to do with these two!" Elle said, as she held Justin and played with his pudgy fingers.

Ava was the mirror image with Jarrett.

The twins were returned to their seats once the meals were served.

Chatter picked up again as everyone tried to enjoy their dinner. Thoughts of Chase were moved to the back of their minds.

"So, you have a few days to clean out the old truck, Mom. We traded it in, and the dealership will be picking it up at your place."

"Okay. I'll clean it out tomorrow. Thanks."

All talking ceased when Luke's phone rang. All eyes turned to him.

"Jake?"

"Luke. Just wanted to let you know that we found Chase's phone, but, unfortunately, he's not with it. We've tracked it right to where he tossed it.

"Okay. What happens now?"

"We're going to keep searching for him. We just got a call about a stolen car. We have the description and license plate number. I have a feeling Chase has it."

"He's been busy since he left the hospital."

"I want you all to be very careful until we track him down. We'll be sending cruisers by each of your homes until then. Also, we'll need Elle to come down to the station tomorrow for her statement. Should I call her directly?"

"She's here with me now. I'll pass along the message. I'm sure she'll be in to see you first thing in the morning. Thanks for the help, Jake."

"No worries. Talk to you later."

Luke pocketed his phone and relayed the message to everyone at the table.

Ava began feeling agitated immediately.

Elle agreed to meet with Jake the following morning. Danny would be joining her.

The server returned to clear the dishes and hand out dessert menus. Dessert was declined as everyone rubbed their full bellies. The server smiled and left them to finish their drinks and conversations.

Danny pulled out his wallet to pay for dinner, but didn't get very far before Mike shut him down.

"Not a chance, old man. This meal is on us." He pulled out his own wallet and waited for their server to return with the bill.

"Well, that's really nice. Thank-you."

"You're welcome. Tonight is, well was, for you guys," replied Mike.

Mike was thanked by everyone. Dave slapped him on the back and told him to invite him for dinner anytime he wanted.

Jarrett and Justin were buckled back into their car seats as the family slid back from the table.

They all said their good nights in the parking lot. Elle was excited to drive her new truck home. Danny would be driving the older one. He followed her home and kept a keen eye on his surroundings.

Elle began to shake once she was alone. She had been angry during the phone call from Chase. She had acted calm and brave, but now the reality of Chase actually harming a family member became clear. He was obviously desperate for money and figured that she was his meal ticket.

She dialed Jillian's number.

"Hello? Elle?"

"Jillian, is Chase with you?"

"No. Why?"

"Are you aware that he has checked himself out of the hospital?"

"What?"

Elle went on to relay to her what had taken place while she had been out for dinner with her family.

"He threatened you?"

"Jillian, if you have any idea of where he might be, you should contact the police."

"But I don't know where he could be."

"Think hard! If he comes after another member of my family, he'll have more than a damn broken wrist and jaw!"

"I'm so sorry, Elle."

"Call Officer Jake Riley." With that said, she disconnected.

Elle cranked up the truck's stereo system. The country music blaring from the speakers occupied her mind. She made a mental note to get back to her music writing soon.

She wouldn't be needed quite as much by the girls soon. Ava would be going back to work on Monday morning. Nora seemed to be settling into a routine with the boys. Luke and Jessie were busy with their companies. Everything was good with Mike and Dave. Maggie and Emma were both enjoying their jobs. Elle was looking forward to spending weekends at the cottage. The lazy easy days by Giggling Creek and lazier nights by the campfire was just what everyone needed.

Danny parked beside her in their laneway and stepped out.

"How does she handle?" asked Danny when he saw the smile on her face.

"It's great! I still can't believe the kids bought me a truck." She shook her head.

He walked toward her and trapped her between the truck and himself. He ran his thumb along her bottom lip. "Do you recall the conversation you had about the inheritance?"

She furrowed her brow and then nodded.

"Specifically, the part where you said 'it would put my heart to ease if you guys would accept this gift of money.'" He raised his eyebrows at her.

Her eye widened at the memory.

"This would be their way of 'putting your heart to ease.'" He patted the truck.

Elle laughed out loud. "Those buggers!"

He took her by the hand and led her to the house. "They love you, Elle, and appreciate everything you do for them."

He unlocked the door and then bent to kiss her.

"That was so nice of Mike to pay for dinner, too," Elle remarked.

"Yeah, well, they each got a pretty big raise from their very generous boss." He smirked as he pointed to himself.

"Nice boss!" She teased.

Danny closed and locked the door behind them. He pulled off his cowboy boots and took the couple of stairs up to the living area. Elle kicked off her sandals and followed him.

"Wine?" he asked.

"Yes, please."

He grabbed himself a beer and poured his wife a large glass of wine. Once they were seated on the sofa, Elle curled her feet under herself.

Danny reached over and tucked her hair behind her ear.

"So, now that you've probably worked the mad off in your truck, would you like to talk about Chase?"

She smiled at him. "You know me too well."

"You were so calm in the restaurant; it was scary."

She told him about her conversation with Jillian.

"What's she going to do?"

"I hope she'll call Jake and give him some kind of clue as to where they can find her idiot son."

He tapped the neck of his beer bottle against her wine glass. "Let's hope so."

CHAPTER 13

LUKE AND NORA ARRIVED HOME WITH BOTH BOYS SOUND ASLEEP IN THEIR CAR seats. They carefully unbuckled them and easily slid them free. Nora carried Jarrett to his crib. Luke followed with Justin and placed him beside his brother. Their little hands reached for each other. Luke and Nora smiled at the bond between them.

They left the nursery and went straight to their bedroom. Both were tired and ready for sleep.

Unfortunately, the stress of the evening played on their minds. Nora tossed and turned, trying to find comfort. Luke lay still with his hands stacked behind his head.

"The boys will likely be up in a couple of hours," Luke said into the darkness.

"Yeah. I'm just restless." She left the bed and walked to the bathroom for a drink of water. She crawled back into bed a few moments later and curled into Luke. He unstacked his arms and pulled her close. They eventually fell into a light sleep.

Nora woke with a start an hour later when she heard a voice coming through the baby monitor. She sat up straight and gave Luke a shove. He woke instantly.

"What's wrong?"

She put her index finger to her lips and then pointed to the monitor on her nightstand. Luke concentrated and then heard the whisper of a voice.

"Your grandmother thinks she's so fucking smart. Now, you two will be my ticket to a whole bunch of money."

Luke darted from the bed. He quietly opened his closet and reached for his baseball bat. He motioned for Nora to stay put and to call the police.

He crept down the hall to the nursery. He slowly opened the nursery room door without a sound. There, leaning over the crib, stood Chase. The anger in Luke's entire body raged. He carefully walked closer. He could see that Chase had not picked up either of the boys yet. He simply stood over them, talking nonsense.

Luke cocked the bat and moved closer. Chase reached down into the crib to pick up one of the children.

Before he even had the chance to straighten, the bat hit him with full force behind his knees. His grasp on Jarrett loosened, and he was dropped back into his crib. Chase hit the floor with a loud thud. He hollered out in pain. The second blow landed on Chase's lower back. Luke quickly looked down into the crib to see that his sons were fine. Jarrett and Justin cried out at the disturbance. Nora came running into the room a second later. She saw Chase on the floor, and Luke standing over him with the bat cocked once again.

"Luke. No!" She screamed the command as she raced to her children. She scooped them up and ran from the room. She set them on their king-size bed. She closed the door behind her as she ran back to the nursery. The fear of what Luke would do to Chase raced through her mind. Although he deserved everything he would receive, she didn't need Luke in prison for murder.

Luke stood over Chase's crumpled body with one foot pressed down hard on the back of his neck. The bat was ready to inflict more pain if Chase even twitched.

"Go ahead and move, you son of a bitch!" He ground the words out through his teeth. He was barely in control of his anger.

Chase groaned but didn't move a muscle.

"Luke. Don't!" Nora yelled. "The police are on their way."

Nora's voice pulled Luke back from his trance. He desperately wanted to kill this bastard.

He turned his attention to his wife. "The kids?"

"They're fine."

Sirens could be heard coming up the laneway. Nora rushed from the room to unlock the front door. The cruiser came to a halt. Jake Riley and his partner Pete Roberts exited the vehicle with their weapons drawn.

Nora pointed to the direction of the nursery once they had reached her.

"Is he armed?" asked Jake.

"I don't know. Luke has him pinned down."

Jake nodded. He and Pete rushed to the nursery.

They found Luke standing with his foot pressed down on Chase's neck.

"Luke?"

He turned at the male voice. Jake moved closer. Pete holstered his weapon and reached around for his handcuffs. He bent and yanked Chase's arms behind his back and snapped the cuffs onto his wrists. He stood and tapped Luke on the back.

"We've got him now. You can step back."

Luke stood where he was for another few seconds.

"Step back, Luke. We've got him cuffed," said Jake.

Luke pressed a little harder and then removed his foot from Chase's neck and stepped back.

Pete and Jake grabbed Chase by his cuffed arms and hauled him to his feet. He yelped out in pain.

"I hit him behind the knees and then his back." He still held the bat in his hands. Jake looked at the bat and then back to Chase.

"Can you walk?"

"No!"

"Then we'll drag you."

Pete looked at Jake with questioning eyes.

"Now!" The officers dragged him from the room. Nora stood outside the entranceway. She stepped forward and slapped Chase so hard across the face that the sound echoed off the walls in the hallway.

"You've gone too fucking far this time! You're lucky you're still breathing."

Jake smiled and gave Pete the nod to keep moving. "Let's get him to the cruiser."

The officers secured Chase in the car. Pete stayed with him while Jake returned to the house to speak with Luke and Nora. Nora came out of their bedroom with the boys in her arms. Luke was standing in the kitchen doorway. The bat was still in his hands. He was ready to pounce.

When Jake reached him, he placed his hand on the bat. "Easy, Luke."

He set the bat against the wall.

"Any idea of how he got in here?"

"I haven't had the time to look around." He explained how they had heard his voice over the baby monitor and then went on to tell what had happened after that.

Jake nodded. "Let's take a look around."

They wandered the house together. Nora moved to the sofa and sat with her sons. They had settled down again.

Jake and Luke returned to the kitchen. Luke turned to Nora and said, "He broke the window in my office to get in."

Nora shook her head in disbelief. She held her sons just a little tighter.

Luke turned his attention back to Jake. "Need me to come down to the station?"

"No. It's pretty clear cut what's happened here. Looks like he was still angry after the phone call with Elle earlier. We'll lock him up for the weekend. Monday morning, we'll contact the judge and get his case moving. The guy is an animal. Jesus! Who the fuck tries to steal someone's kids?"

The rage ran through Luke once more. If Nora hadn't stopped him, he knew he would have been capable of killing Chase.

He shook Jake's hand and thanked him for arriving so quickly.

"We were doing our rounds of all your homes when we got the call. He won't be causing any more trouble for you or your family."

Nora stayed seated with Jarrett and Justin while Luke walked Jake to the door.

Luke went to his bedroom to pull on a pair of jeans, and then went to his truck for a piece of plywood to cover the broken window for the night. He would have it replaced in the morning.

He returned to sit beside Nora. He slipped Justin from her arm. "Are you sure they're okay?"

"Not a mark on them."

He nodded. "Should we put them back to bed now?"

"I'd like to sit with them for a bit longer." She rested her head on his shoulder. He leaned his head into hers.

"I can't even imagine what his plan would have been if he'd gotten out of the house with the babies." Her voice was a little shaky.

"Thank God you heard his voice over the monitor!"

"I hear everything now that these two are here." She bent to kiss Jarrett on the top of his heard.

"Just like a lioness with her cubs."

They sat for a few more minutes and then took the boys back to the nursery. They were placed in the crib that hadn't been used earlier. Nora would strip the other crib and scrub it down in the morning. There would be no sign of Chase when she was done.

Luke returned to the kitchen and re-locked the door. He picked up his phone and dialed Jessie's number.

"Luke? What's wrong?" he said in a sleepy voice.

"The police have Chase now."

"They found him? Where the fuck was he?"

"In my house."

"What?" Jessie sat up straight in his bed.

He unfolded the details to his brother.

"The boys are okay?"

"Yeah. I was ready to kill him," said Luke angrily.

"I'm not so sure I could have stopped myself." Jessie's angry voice mimicked his brother's.

"I'll talk to you tomorrow. I want to call Mom and tell her that the police have Chase." They disconnected.

Elle answered on the second ring.

Luke conveyed the same story to her.

"We'll be over tomorrow unless you want us there tonight."

"Tomorrow is good. We've just put the boys back to bed."

Danny reached for his phone once Elle had disconnected with Luke. He called Dave and Mike to relay the situation.

Everyone would sleep a little better knowing that Chase was behind bars.

The following morning, Elle and Danny arrived at Luke and Nora's by seven o'clock. Luke stood in the kitchen, drinking coffee. Elle wrapped him in a hug and kissed his cheek.

"Are you okay?"

Luke nodded. Danny stepped forward. "I'm glad they have the bastard now. The boys and Nora are okay?" he asked.

Nora walked in with Jarrett and Justin in her arms as the question was asked.

"We're all okay."

Elle rushed to her. She kissed each of her grandchildren and then hugged Nora. She slipped Jarrett from her arms and cuddled him. The two women moved to the family room to sit and feed the twins.

"I'll show you where he broke in, Danny," said Luke.

They walked down the hall to Luke's office.

"Have you ordered a new window yet?"

"I was just about to." He pulled his phone from his pocket and punched in the number of one of his suppliers.

Danny wandered around the room to inspect for any further damage. The frame of the window had not been damaged. He left the room to ask Nora where the vacuum could be found. He wanted to clean up the broken glass before anyone cut themselves. He went to work as soon as he had retrieved it.

Within an hour, the new window had been delivered and installed.

Once the twins had been fed and entertained, Elle and Nora set them back in the crib. Nora stripped the sheets from the other crib. Elle went looking for disinfectant to scrub it down.

The four adults sat and drank coffee while the boys slept. Everything that needed to be cleaned had been dealt with.

"So, what happens now?" asked Elle.

Luke spoke up. "Jake said that they would be holding Chase for the weekend. He won't be going too far for the next while. He also said he would be contacting the judge to move his hearing along."

"Good." Elle took a sip of her coffee. She placed her hand on Nora's back. "Are you sure you're okay, honey?"

"The boys are fine, and that's the most important thing." She set her mug on the table. "He knew damn well we weren't home when he broke in here. He knew we were all at the restaurant. He could have broken into any one of our homes." She shook her head.

"I feel like this is all my fault," said Elle. And then she added, "If I hadn't pissed him off even more than he already was, none of this would have happened."

UNITY

"He would have come after one of us at some point. He's a drug addict, and he's desperate. He wants the money we promised him, and that's all he's focused on," said Luke.

"Yeah, I guess so." It didn't make Elle feel any better, but she knew it was the truth.

Jessie and Ava arrived as the group sat chatting.

"Jesus Christ! Is everyone okay?" Ava needed to know. She rushed to Nora and hugged her.

"We're fine. And the boys are fine, too. Thank God!" Nora answered.

Ava chose a chair and slumped into it.

"I wish to hell that this guy had never entered our lives," growled Jessie.

"Just one more thing to thank Max for." Elle ground her teeth as she spoke the words.

Danny reached over and rubbed her back. "They're both out of our lives now."

Dave, Mike, Emma, and Maggie arrived within minutes of Jessie and Ava.

"We have got to stop spending so much time together!" exclaimed Mike. The entire group erupted in laughter. It was exactly what they needed to hear.

"I thought you guys were going to the lake," remarked Danny.

"We can go any time. Next weekend will be soon enough. We just wanted to check in and make sure everyone was okay," said Dave.

Nora rose from her seat to make another pot of coffee. "Have a seat. Thanks for coming over."

Maggie said shyly, "I know Chase has never directly come at me, but I'm damn glad he's locked up right now. To come after your sweet innocent children is despicable."

"As far as we can see, Jarrett and Justin are fine, but I wouldn't mind if you took a look at them when they wake up, Maggie."

"Of course, I will."

"If none of you have plans for dinner, we'd like you all to join us at our place," said Danny. "We'll just have an easy barbecue."

Everyone agreed that they would be there. The girls would prepare salads and appetizers.

The boys made their presence known through the monitor.

"Our life saver," stated Luke as he pointed at the monitor sitting on the kitchen counter. He and Nora went to get the twins. Maggie followed so she could fulfill Nora's request of checking them over.

Nora stripped the boys down so that Maggie could inspect them. Neither of them made a fuss when she gently moved their arms and legs. She found no sign of bruising on either of them. Luke let out a sigh of relief and went back to the kitchen to report the good news.

Maggie and Nora followed once the boys had been changed and re-dressed. Maggie handed Justin to Emma, and Nora gave Jarrett to Ava. Both little guys were snuggled closely.

"Okay, so we're gonna head for home and start getting things organized for dinner," Elle announced. She made her way around the table, hugging each family member. Danny followed suit. Even though they were out of danger, he wanted them all close for the evening.

CHAPTER 14

MONDAY MORNING ARRIVED WITH A FULL HOT TEXAS SUN SHINING DOWN. ELLE stepped outside to the deck with her coffee. She wore shorts and a tank top. Her first stop on her travels today would be to Ava's. She would pick her up and bring her to Nora's for the day. After Friday night's fiasco, Jessie wanted Ava to take Monday off and return to work on Tuesday.

Elle knew Ava would sit at home and worry herself sick, thinking about what could have happened to her nephews.

Elle arrived just as Jessie was preparing to leave for work.

"Mornin', Mom."

"Hi, Jessie. Is Ava up?"

"I could hear her moving around a minute ago. What are you two up to today?" He rummaged through the fridge for bottled water as he spoke.

"I thought I'd get Ava out of here and take her to visit with Nora and the boys."

"That's a great idea!"

"That's what I figured. We'll be back home later this afternoon."

"Sounds good. Have a great day." He left the house with a wave.

Elle helped herself to a cup of coffee while she waited for Ava to come downstairs.

"Hi, Elle."

"Hi. How are you feeling?"

"I feel great!"

"Perfect! I thought we'd go visit Nora and the boys for the day."

"Really? Oh, that would be wonderful!"

"We'll leave as soon as you've had some breakfast." Elle rose from her seat to put bread in the toaster. Ava rested her hand on her shoulder.

"I can make my own toast, Elle." She tilted her head to one side. "Sit. I'll get you another coffee."

"Thanks."

Twenty minutes later, the two women arrived at Nora's door. A vehicle, which Elle did not recognize, sat in the driveway. She opened the door and called out to Nora.

"Nora? It's me, Elle."

"Come on in. We're in the family room."

When Elle and Ava walked in, they were surprised to see Jillian sitting on the sofa.

"Good morning," Jillian said.

Elle looked at her oddly. "What are you doing here?"

"I came to apologize to Nora for Chase's behavior last night."

"Behavior? Is that what you call it? He intentionally broke into their home and tried to kidnap their children!" Elle said angrily.

Jillian lowered her head. "I know. What I don't know is how to deal with Chase anymore."

UNITY

"The courts will deal with him now," snapped Elle. "I don't think you should come around us anymore, Jillian. We've had about all we can take from Chase." She crossed her arms.

Ava moved from Elle's side to sit on the floor next to Nora and the boys.

"You're probably right. I'll leave." Jillian stood and turned to Nora. "I'm so sorry about all that has happened." She looked at Ava, and then Elle. "I won't bother you again." She picked up her purse from beside the sofa and walked out the door.

"She's got some fucking nerve coming here," Elle stated.

"She feels really bad," said Nora sadly.

"And so she should. Her son is an idiot. Good parenting goes a long way." Elle knelt on the floor and began to play with her grandsons. "And how are you two little munchkins?" she asked in baby talk as she touched their toes.

She was rewarded with small gurgling noises. Elle smiled at the cuteness of it.

She looked up at Nora. "I'm sorry if I stepped out of line with Jillian. This is your home. Not mine."

"It's okay, Elle. I really didn't want her here. I just didn't know how to ask her to leave."

Ava laughed. "Leave it to Elle. She'll take care of everything!"

The women smiled at each other.

"Well, we did all promise to watch each other's backs," said Elle with a shrug.

The women thoroughly enjoyed their day together. There was a lot of talk about Nora's upcoming wedding. They would check with Maggie and Emma to see which weekday evening would work to try on dresses. Of course, Nora already had an idea of what she wanted.

"What do you think of black bridesmaid dresses?" she asked.

"That's a pretty bleak color, don't you think?" questioned Ava.

"I've thought about it, and I think with all the colors of summer and full foliage at the cottages, it will be a nice contrast." Nora was feeling excited about her decision.

"Hmm. That's true. I think it would be lovely," Elle stated.

"I was thinking about short and airy dresses. Like chiffon," Nora said.

"Oh, nice! That should help cover up this growing belly! And the guys will be in black, too?" asked Ava as she ran her hands over her growing stomach.

Nora smiled and nodded. "I don't think we need to be colorful. I think it will look quite elegant."

"I think you're right," added Elle.

"How does next Thursday night sound for dress shopping?"

"Good with me," Ava said happily.

"Me too," Elle said.

"Okay, I'll text the girls now and hope that it works for them."

The reply from both girls came back immediately. It worked for them both.

Now that they had picked a night, Nora turned to Ava and asked, "Are you sure you're up for this?"

"Of course, I am! I feel fine. The doctor and Jessie are just taking precautions."

"Okay. But, if something changes, you let me know, and we'll reschedule."

"Got it." Ava nodded to both women.

UNITY

Elle had promised Jessie that she would have Ava home by the afternoon, so they said their goodbyes and headed out the door.

Ava yawned the entire drive.

"When we get back to your place, you should go have a nap." Elle was a little concerned at how tired Ava was.

Ava covered up another yawn with her hand and nodded. "Sounds like a great idea."

Once they arrived home, Elle sent her up the stairs. "I'm going to take off for home. So, get some rest, and I'll lock the doors behind me."

Ava gave her a hug and thanked her for the nice day. She trudged up the stairs and crawled under the sheets.

Elle dialed Jake's number as soon as she sat in her vehicle. She threw it in drive and headed for home.

Jake was working at his desk when his phone rang. "Riley," he said when he answered.

"Jake, it's Elle Jackson."

"Oh, hi, Elle. How are you?"

"Doin' okay."

"How are the rest of the family?"

"Everyone's fine. Is there any word on what will happen with Chase?"

"I've called the judge and explained the circumstances. He agrees that Chase will not be leaving his cell until this case gets to court. He's lawyered up, but it won't do him any damn good."

"What exactly does he think a lawyer can do for him?"

"I would imagine it will all come down to that damn inheritance."

"That's kind of what I thought too. I've gotta say, I'm happy he won't be able to reach any of us."

"You and your family are safe now, Elle."

"Thank-you. By the way, I've told his mother, Jillian, to stay away from us, too."

"Good idea. I'll keep you updated on what's happening with Chase."

"Okay. Thanks again."

Elle continued on her way home as she disconnected the call. She was so relieved that Chase was behind bars. The entire family could relax for now.

When she arrived home, she noticed her old truck had been picked up. She smiled at the generosity of her children. Jessie and Luke were certainly keeping up their end of the bargain about buying her anything that she needed. She certainly didn't need a new truck, but apparently her sons felt that she did.

Elle unlocked the house and pulled her phone from her purse to call Danny.

"Hey, babe," he said when he answered.

"Hey, you. Working hard or hardly working?"

Danny chuckled. "Funny lady. What are you up to?"

"I just got home from seeing the girls."

"And how are they?"

"Good. I sent Ava up to bed once I got her home. I can't believe how tired she is."

"I wonder how she'll survive going back to work," he remarked.

"I was wondering the same thing. Maybe she'll have to work half days and nap in the afternoons," Elle replied.

"I would love a job like that!" He laughed out loud.

Elle chuckled. "What time will you be home?"

"Want to have a nap with me?" he asked with a smile in his voice.

"Hmm ... maybe."

"I'll leave now. See you soon." He disconnected and walked out of his office.

Lois looked up from her computer. "Heading out?"

"Yep. See you tomorrow. Have a good night." He smiled broadly.

Lois looked at him curiously. "You too."

Danny arrived home in record time to find Elle preparing dinner.

She laughed when he walked through the door. "I thought you were kidding!"

He kicked off his boots and scooped her up. "Lady, I never joke around when it comes to having sex with my beautiful wife!"

Elle giggled as he carried her to the bedroom.

He tossed her onto the bed and dove on top of her.

It didn't take long for the passion to take over. Zippers were tugged at, and shirts were flung to the floor. Danny barely had his jeans pulled off before Elle tackled him.

His cell phone could be heard ringing in the kitchen. Neither one of them paid any attention to it. Whoever it was could damn well wait.

A little time for themselves was exactly what they both needed.

They lay sated and completely relaxed with smiles on their faces.

"I could get used to you working half days," Elle said.

"I'm thinking about retirement." He pulled her close for another kiss.

"We would spend all day in this bed."

"I'm not seeing the problem."

Elle laughed at him as she pushed away and climbed out of bed. "Well, some of us need to eat. I'll get the rest of dinner ready while you start the grill."

"Spoilsport." He groaned, but rose from the bed to do as she asked. She smiled and sashayed from the room.

"Keep walking like that, and you'll find yourself right back in this bed!"

She turned her head and winked at him.

He loved her sassiness.

"What's for dinner?" he asked, as he came up behind her and wrapped his arms around her waist.

"Chicken."

He dropped a kiss on her neck and released her. "I'm gonna have a beer. Would you like a glass of wine?"

"Sure. Thanks."

He poured the wine and set the glass on the table before going out to start the grill. His cell went off again. He picked it up and answered it as he went through the patio door.

"Hello?"

"Darling, how are you?"

He scowled and pulled the phone from his ear to check the name of the caller. He frowned deeper when he saw his ex-wife's name.

"Grace?"

"Yes! How are you?" she asked again in an excited tone.

"Fine. Why are you calling?"

"I'm back in town!"

"And?" he asked warily.

"I thought we could get together for dinner." After a few seconds of silence, she continued. "You don't sound too happy to be hearing from me."

"Why the hell would I be happy to hear from you?"

Elle walked through the door with the plate of chicken as he said the words. She raised her brows.

He shook his head angrily. Elle set the food beside the grill and frowned.

"Don't you want to see me?" Grace asked.

"No, I don't."

"Wouldn't it be nice for the four of us to have dinner together?" she asked.

"The four of us?"

"Yes. Me, you, and our sons."

"Have you spoken to Dave and Mike?" He paced the deck as he spoke.

"Well, no, not yet. I thought I'd call you first."

"I can tell you it was a waste of your time calling me. I have no intention of having dinner with you. As for the boys, they can do as they please. Goodbye, Grace."

"Danny! Wait!"

"What?" He snapped the word.

"Couldn't we at least meet somewhere for a drink?"

"No."

There was complete silence on the phone.

"Goodbye, Grace. Lose my number." He disconnected and jammed his phone in his pocket.

Elle moved closer to him and placed a hand on his arm. "Are you okay?"

He nodded. "I can't believe she had the nerve to call me. What an idiot. Sorry, babe. I'd better call Dave and Mike and warn them that she's back in town."

He pulled his phone out once more and dialed Mike's number.

"Hey, Dad."

"Hi, Mike. Is Dave with you?"

"He's on his way over, actually. Why? What's going on?"

"You won't believe who just called me." He sounded sad.

"I have no idea. Who?" asked Mike.

"Your mother."

"What? Why now?"

"I'm not sure. I just got off the phone with her." He went on to tell him about their conversation.

"I'll let Dave know."

"Do you want me to come over?"

"No, that's okay, Dad."

"Don't be surprised if she calls you, okay?"

"Okay. Thanks for the heads up."

He disconnected and turned to Elle. "I'm sorry about that." He moved in to hug her.

She rubbed his back. "Our exes sure are a pain in the ass."

He laughed lightly. "Do you think I should go over to Mike's?"

She pulled back. "That's up to you, babe. We can hold off dinner if you want to go."

"How did I ever luck into finding you?" He pulled her in again and hugged her tightly.

Elle smiled. "We both got extremely lucky."

"Would you come with me to see the boys?"

"If that's where you want me, then that's where I'll be." She picked up the food and returned it to the kitchen. She stacked everything in the fridge and then went to get dressed.

She came back out wearing a black skort and a white tank top. Danny pulled on a pair of shorts and a blue T-shirt. Elle went to the hall closet and pulled out a cooler. She filled it with beer and a bottle of wine. She covered the drinks with ice and then added two blocks of cheese along with a length of salami before closing the lid. Next, she went to one of the kitchen cabinets and pulled out boxes of crackers. She set them atop the cooler, snatched up her purse and walked to the door. Danny stood back, watching her move around smoothly and methodically.

"What's with the cooler?"

"Your kids need to eat and drink." She looked at him as if he had asked the stupidest question in the world.

"You never stop worrying about others, do you?"

She shrugged her shoulders. "Ready to go?"

They walked out, locked the door, and climbed into his truck.

They arrived at Mike's within half an hour. He met them at the door.

"You didn't have to come over, Dad."

He hefted the cooler. "Elle packed beer and food."

Mike smiled and opened the door wider. "Well then, come on in!"

He hugged Elle and thanked her for her kindness.

"Your welcome, honey. Are Dave and the girls here?"

"Yep. They just arrived. They're out on the deck. Go on out."

Elle greeted each of the kids with a hug.

Mike came out with a bottle of red wine and a glass for Elle.

"I just need the glass, Mike. I brought wine."

"And you can take it home with you. I always have wine here for you."

She smiled up at him and accepted the glass of wine.

Danny handed out beers to the gang. "Has she called yet?"

Dave spoke up. "Nope. I really don't care if she calls or not." He took a sip of his beer.

"Me neither," said Mike.

Elle sat quietly with Emma and Maggie.

The two girls had never met Grace, and they weren't anxious to meet her anytime soon. Dave and Mike had lost all respect for her when she had walked out the door years before. They rarely mentioned their mother.

When the doorbell rang, all eyes landed on Danny.

"You don't think that's her, do you?" There was a hint of panic in Dave's voice when he posed the question.

Mike stood and walked back into the house. Dave and Danny stood to follow. The three women looked at each other and rose. If it was Grace at the door, they wanted to get a glimpse of her. Especially Elle.

"Hey, how's it going?" asked the male voice. Elle's shoulders relaxed a bit with relief.

"Hi, Jessie. Hi, Ava. Come on in."

"Oh, hi, Mom. Hi Danny." He set down his cooler to hug his mother and shake Danny's hand. Ava stepped forward and hugged everyone.

"We're just hanging out on the deck. Come on back."

Jessie hefted his cooler again and followed Mike.

UNITY

Dave pointed at Elle's cooler. "You're just like your mom."

"She taught me right!" He opened his cooler and offered beer to everyone before he twisted the cap off one for himself.

He turned his attention to Mike. "You sounded a little pissed when you called about your mother. We thought we'd come over and see what we could do to help."

"That's so sweet," said Emma.

"Everyone needs support. You guys were all there when we needed you, and now, we're here to help you," added Ava.

The doorbell rang again. Once again, all eyes landed on Danny.

Jessie stood. "I'll get it." He marched through the house and opened the door.

Luke handed the baby seat cradling Jarrett to his brother. "Be back in a second." He went back to his truck to help Nora with Justin and to grab the cooler he had packed.

Dave entered the house as they all came in.

"The whole family is here!" he called out to the others.

Luke and Nora followed Dave out to the deck. The girls snatched up the babies instantly.

"Hey, everyone!" He set his cooler down and made the rounds of hugs for the women and handshakes for the men. Nora hugged everyone but gave an extra squeeze to Dave, Mike, and Danny.

"It amazes me how this family pulls together after one quick phone call," announced Mike.

Beer bottles were lifted and clinked. "To family!"

"So, what's happening with your mother?" asked Jessie.

"Nothing yet. She's only contacted Dad so far," answered Dave.

Jessie nodded. "Okay, so let's sit, drink, and wait for her next move."

"And eat," added Elle. "Where would I find a platter?"

Emma handed Jarrett to Ava and rose to find a platter. Elle removed the food from the cooler and followed. The two women worked side by side to pile it high.

"You doing okay, Emma?"

"I'm fine. I'm more worried about Dave and Mike," she said sadly.

"I know; me too. But that's why we're all here. We'll get through this together." She placed her hand on Emma's back.

"Thank-you, Elle. Have you ever met her?"

"Not yet."

"Aren't you nervous about meeting her?"

"Not in the least."

Emma nodded and opened the doors for Elle. The overflowing platter was big and heavy, so Luke jumped up to relieve her of it.

"Thanks, Luke."

"No problem, Mom." He walked around the circle of his family and offered the food Elle had prepared.

"This is so nice! Thanks, Elle," said Maggie.

Elle smiled at the group surrounding her. She loved how they all blended together so well.

The doorbell rang for the third time. Panic enveloped Mike and Dave. It had to be their mother. Everyone else was already sitting here with them.

Jessie rose again. "I got this." He strolled through the house once more. He swung the door open. There stood a tall, slender woman with black, short-cropped hair. She wore a slinky, low cut, red dress that barely reached her knees.

"Can I help you?" he asked innocently.

She looked up at him and then at the house number. "Does Dan Jackson live here?"

"No."

"Oh, I'm sorry. He must have moved." She took a step back. "Are you Grace?"

She stopped in her tracks. "Yes, I am. Do I know you?"

"Not yet."

She warily took another step back, and then Danny came into view. Grace looked at Jessie with questioning eyes and a scowl on her face.

Jessie turned to see Danny and then back to Grace. "What? He doesn't live here anymore. Mike does."

Danny rested his hand on Jessie's shoulder and said, "I'll take it from here." He moved into the doorway. "Hello, Grace. What are you doing here?" Jessie made his way back to the group.

"Since you didn't want to go out for drinks, I thought I'd stop by and bring a bottle of wine for us to share." She looked down at the bottle in her hand and back up at Danny. "Who was that guy?"

Elle came up behind Danny and looped her arm through his. "My son. What's going on, honey?" she asked Danny, way too sweetly.

"Elle, this is my ex-wife, Grace," he said quietly.

"It's nice of you to finally come to visit your sons." She glanced at the bottle of wine in her hand. "Unfortunately, Dave and Mike don't like wine. They only drink beer. I suppose you wouldn't know that though, would you?" Elle tilted her head slightly.

"I just came to ..." Grace paused. She lowered the bottle.

"Oh, Grace, I know exactly why you came here." Elle shook her head slightly. "Now, let me go see if Mike would like to welcome you into his home. Danny and I are just here visiting." She stood on her tiptoes and kissed her husband's cheek. He chuckled softly and smiled.

All eight of the kids stood quietly in the family room. Jessie and Luke smiled broadly at their mother as they flanked Mike and Dave.

Elle stopped in front of Dave and Mike and took them by the hand. "If you don't want to see her, all you have to do is say so, and she's gone. If you want to talk with her, we can all step outside, or we can leave. The choice is completely up to you two."

The boys looked at each other. "We might as well get this over with," said Dave. He hugged Elle and whispered, "Please stay."

She hugged him back and then hugged Mike. "Your dad will be right by your side, and we'll all be out on the deck. Come have another beer when you're done." She winked and shooed the rest of the crew out the door.

"Nicely done, Mom," said Jessie.

She simply smiled and moved her chair closer to the open patio door, where she would sit until Grace left. Luke grinned and took his seat next to Nora. Maggie and Emma sat with Jarrett and Justin, unsure of what to do. The uncertainty in their eyes made Elle sad. Ava sat, wringing her hands. Jessie moved to sit beside her.

"It's okay, honey. Just relax," he said as he put an arm around her. He squeezed her shoulder as he added, "We're all just here for support."

Dave and Mike made their way to the front door. Their father filled the doorway with his frame. Neither could see their mother's face.

"Dad?"

Danny turned to face his sons. The anger in his eyes changed to concern. He moved to the side to allow his sons through. They stepped closer to the door.

"Boys! Oh, my goodness!" Grace rushed forward to envelop them in a group hug. Neither of them returned the hug. She took a step back.

"You're both so grown-up and handsome." She reached out for Danny's hand and smiled. "Just like your daddy." He swiftly removed his hand from hers.

Dave and Mike stood stiffly, staring at her. Little emotion showed on their faces.

Grace clapped her hands together. "It's so nice to be all together again."

"We're hardly 'all together again,'" Mike replied.

She looked at him oddly. "Well, of course we are!"

"Why are you here?" asked Dave.

"Well, I just thought it would be nice for the four of us to spend some time together. Maybe dinner or something?"

Danny laughed. "I'm not so sure my wife would appreciate that."

"That woman is your wife?"

"Yes."

"Hmm. I guess I just thought she was the flavor of the month or something." She dusted a non-existent piece of lint from her shoulder.

Dave raised his eyebrows. "You should be thankful that Elle didn't hear that comment."

"She's a wonderful woman, and has come to mean a lot to us. We love her." Mike said it simply and honestly.

Now it was Grace's turn to raise her eyebrows. "You love her?"

Both boys nodded. Danny stood, smiling from ear to ear.

"Grace, I think it's probably best for you to leave now."

"Why? I'm not able to come and visit my family now?"

"You didn't think we were your family when you walked out the door six years ago," snapped Mike.

"I needed my own space." She said it sadly as she hung her head in shame.

"And now we need ours," Dave replied.

The three men took a step back inside the house. Grace stood with her mouth hanging open. "Well, I never …"

"Never what—gave a damn about anyone but yourself?" asked Mike.

"That's not fair!"

"What exactly is fair, Mom? What is it that you want from us? Dad divorces Elle? I sell this house back to him, and then Dave and I and our girlfriends all find somewhere else to live? All of this because you're tired of traveling, and you want us all to be one big happy family again?"

She glared at Danny. "What kind of bullshit stories have you been feeding my sons?"

UNITY

Dave interrupted her. "We all stood right here over six years ago while you walked out this door. We remember it well." He crossed his arms over his chest. "Dad didn't have to feed us any bullshit lies. I think our little reunion is over. Have a nice evening." She stepped away from the door to avoid it being closed on her.

"Goodbye, Grace," Danny said as he slowly closed the door. Once it was shut, he placed a hand on each of his son's shoulders.

"I'm sorry if she upset you."

"I'm not upset," said Mike.

"Me neither," replied Dave. "I could use a beer, though."

Danny chuckled as he walked through the house with them to rejoin their family.

After a few hours of discussion, Elle and Danny left the kids out on the deck with the coolers of beer and headed for home.

He reached over and took her by the hand. "Are you upset?"

"I'm upset for Dave and Mike. I can handle a woman like Grace."

"So, you're not angry with me?" he asked warily.

She smiled sweetly. "Why would I be angry with you?"

"When you get quiet, it kinda scares me," he said sheepishly.

"Danny, I'm not a jealous person. But when someone comes after the people I love, I have a problem with that."

He nodded in agreement. He had felt the same way about Max when he'd had his car accident and tried to win Elle back.

"I would like to add that if you decide to leave me for Grace, you will never be seen or heard from again." She smiled sweetly once more.

"See what I mean? You scare me!"

Elle laughed out loud. "I love you and your sons. Grace can spend all the time she wants with them." She put up her index finger and added, "as long as she's kind to them." Before she put her finger down, she also added, "she will not have the privilege of spending time with you."

"Point taken. Let's get the hell home. I want to show you just how much I love you." He squeezed her hand a little tighter and hit the gas pedal.

CHAPTER 15

LOIS SAT AT HER DESK TYPING CONTRACTS FOR DANNY TO DELIVER TO HIS clients, when he walked in. The scowl on his face had her alarmed.

"Good morning, Danny. Is everything alright?"

"Yeah, just great." He moved past her to his office. It had been many years since she had seen him in such a sour mood. She rose from her chair and went directly to his office door. She knocked and opened it at the same time. She took the chair across the desk from him.

Danny looked up and raised his eyebrows as he rested his elbows on the desk.

"Is there something you need, Lois?"

"Just wondering what's wrong with you. Did you have a fight with the boys? They walked in here earlier with the same look on their faces."

"No, we didn't have a fight," he said, as he ran his hands through his hair.

"So, what then?" She crossed her arms in stubbornness. She had no intention of leaving until he told her the problem.

"Their mother is back in town."

"What? Grace is back? What the hell for?" She was practically yelling. Lois remembered the day that Grace had left. Danny had come to work later than usual and had crossed the reception area with the same scowl on his face. He had slammed his office door and hadn't opened it for hours. When he had finally resurfaced, he was drunk and weaving his way toward the entrance. Lois had called two of his employees to help get him home. She had followed in her vehicle and had stayed the night on his couch.

Lois had waited for the boys to arrive home. They were just as drunk as their father had been when they finally arrived at midnight.

"What the hell is going on around here? Why are all the men in this house fucking drunk?" she'd shouted.

Dave had stumbled toward her and answered with, "Mom walked out on us this morning."

"When will she be back?"

"Not coming back," he slurred.

Lois shook her head and told both boys to go sleep off the booze. She was pretty sure they'd be in bed for the majority of the day.

Although they were grown men at the ages of eighteen and nineteen, they had been hit hard by the news.

When Danny had woken the following morning, she had breakfast and coffee waiting for him. She sat patiently while he worked his way through it. He had finally told her about Grace leaving.

She had moved around the table, hugged him tightly, and said, "You have two sons sleeping their hangovers off in their rooms right now. Their hearts are aching, too. You need to be there for them. You can drown your sorrows once they've dealt with theirs."

He had nodded and thanked her.

Lois gave her head a shake as she came back to the present. "And what do the boys think about all of this?"

He went on to tell her how Elle's family had surrounded his with love, support, beer, and food.

Lois pictured the scene and laughed.

He then relayed the conversation his sons had shared with their mother.

"So, it doesn't sound like they want to spend time with her. Can't say that I blame them."

"Me neither. But the choice is theirs. I certainly won't get in the way," he said. "Grace will have to give them time and space if she plans on sticking around."

Lois stood to leave. She leaned across his desk and said, "You're not going to lock yourself in here and get drunk again, are you?"

Danny smiled for the first time that morning. "No, Lois. I'm not going to get drunk."

"Alright, then. Let's get to work. I have a stack of contracts on my desk for you."

Danny rounded his desk and stooped to wrap her in a hug. "Thank-you for everything you do for me."

Lois patted his back and returned the hug. She returned to her desk with a smile on her face.

Danny came out a few minutes later. "Just going to the warehouse," he told her.

"Okay."

He strolled out to the building to talk with his sons. They were trying hard to look busy, but Danny knew they were hungover. Jessie had stayed and drank with them until the early morning hours. Ava, of course, waited to drive him home.

They looked up when the door opened.

"If you have a hammer in your hand, drop it," growled Mike.

Danny chuckled and held up both empty hands. "Not today."

"Thank Christ," mumbled Dave.

"You guys doin' okay?" he asked as he moved closer.

Both nodded.

"It smells like a brewery in here."

Mike smiled weakly. "We drank enough last night to drain a damn brewery."

Danny chuckled once again.

The boys set their tools on the workbench and leaned against it.

"So, do you think Mom will come around again?" Dave asked.

Danny tilted his head. "I'm not too sure. I don't think she was overly happy with the outcome of last night's visit."

"Too bad for her," commented Mike.

Danny felt bad for his sons. For Grace to waltz back into their lives and expect them to fall all over her was disgraceful. The chances of them reuniting were pretty slim. Right now, he knew they were angry with her, and forgiveness would not come easily.

"I guess the decision is up to you two. There isn't any hurry to decide. But I want you both to know that whatever you decide is fine with me. Whether you spend time with her or not makes no difference to me. For myself, I have zero intention of seeing her again."

"Okay. How was Elle last night on the way home?"

"Her main concern is you two. She's worried about you both. I actually came out here to invite you and the girls for dinner tonight. And just so you know, Elle will be keeping a very close eye on all of you, but don't tell her I told you that."

The boys smiled broadly at their dad. "We meant it when we told Mom that we love Elle. She's the kindest and most generous person we know," said Dave.

"Glad to hear it. She loves you guys, too." Danny hugged both his boys. "I love you too. See you for dinner?"

"You bet. Wouldn't miss it. Will the rest of the family be there?" Mike asked, hopefully.

"I don't think so. Elle just wants to concentrate on you guys for now."

"Okay. Thanks Dad. See you later." The boys picked up their tools and continued working on the task at hand.

Danny walked out to his truck and sat heavily in the driver's seat. He pulled his cell phone from his pocket and dialed Elle.

"Hey, babe."

"Hi. I was just calling to let you know that Dave, Mike, and the girls will be over for dinner."

"Perfect! What time do you think you'll be home?"

"Probably around five o'clock. Did you need me to come home earlier?" he asked hopefully.

Elle rolled her eyes and laughed. "You are insatiable. Five o'clock is good. See you then. I love you."

"Stop rolling your eyes, and I love you, too." He disconnected with a smile on his face. He threw the truck in gear and headed out to one of the homes where they were currently installing cabinets.

He pulled in the lane and saw Luke's truck parked there. He hopped out and went looking for him.

"Hey, Danny!" Luke yelled from the roof.

Danny shielded his eyes from the sun and looked up. Luke and his crew were setting the last sheet of tin in place. "Hot day to be up there."

"Yeah. Almost done. What are you up to?"

"Checking on the cabinet installation. You guys want some water?"

"Nah, we'll be down in five minutes."

"Okay. See you in a few." He opened the door to the house and did his walk around the kitchen. He was delighted to be setting cabinetry in the homes Luke was building. A real family affair!

Luke walked through the door a few minutes later and shook Danny's hand. "It's lookin' good in here," he commented as he looked around the house.

"Shouldn't be long before they're able to move in."

"Yep. Hey, how're Dave and Mike doin' today?"

"Besides being hungover?" Danny chuckled. "They're doin' okay. They're coming to the house for dinner tonight."

"Jessie feels like shit today, too." Luke chuckled as well. "Dave and Mike will be fine. They just need some time." He slapped Danny on the back and said, "A good homemade meal by Mom will sure help!"

UNITY

"I think you're right. Anyway, I have to get back to the office. See ya later, Luke." They shook hands and went on about their day.

Luke pulled out his cell phone from his front jean pocket.

"Hey, Luke."

"Hey, Jessie. Feeling any better?"

"Ugh. No! Fuck, I hate hangovers!"

"There's an easy cure for it ... don't drink so damn much!"

"Haha ... funny guy. What are you up to?"

"Just finishing up one of the jobs. Hoping to get home early to see Nora and the boys and then crack a beer."

"Say hi to them for me."

"You bet."

Luke and his crew worked for a few more hours before they called it a day. They packed up their gear and cleaned up any mess they had left behind. They would move on to the next house the following day. Luke was thankful for the work they were receiving. He had proven himself on many occasions, and the word had spread. He smiled when he thought of how Danny, Mike, and Dave were doing the cabinetwork and how Jessie was doing the landscaping. He thought for a second that they could all become one company and then instantly disregarded it. Not a chance would that work—too many bosses!

He arrived home to find Nora and the twins on the big blanket in the middle of the family room floor. He had sure lucked out with this woman. He smiled as he kicked off his boots and walked toward them. He kissed Nora on the top of her head and then scooped up Jarrett. He cooed and chatted with him and then set him down to do the same with Justin. These two little boys made his heart swell.

"How was your day?" Nora asked.

"Good. We finished up one of the jobs and are ready to move on to the next. How was your day, babe?" He reached over and gently stroked her back.

"We had a great day!" She tweaked the boy's toes. "Didn't we, my loves?" She was instantly rewarded with gurgling noises and a huge grin from Luke.

"If you want to start the grill, I'll get the table set."

He kissed the top of her head again and stood. "You bet."

Nora picked up each of her sons and nuzzled their necks before she set them in the playpen. She would let them entertain themselves while she and Luke prepared dinner.

It was always a nice surprise to have him home early. He was a fair and tough boss on the job, but when it came to his sons, he was just a big teddy bear. She wondered how he would be with Jarrett and Justin when they reached the teenage years. Getting themselves into trouble was a certainty. She knew they would have to deal with it when the time came, so for now, she would enjoy the complete innocence of her twins.

As they sat to have dinner, Nora reminded Luke that she and the girls would be dress shopping Thursday evening.

"Okay." He glanced at his sons. "I think I'll call in Jessie for reinforcement."

"Just remember you'll be parenting, not drinking."

Luke smirked at the comment. "I know. I know."

Elle had just finished setting the table when Danny arrived home. He removed his work boots and came up behind her to wrap one strong arm around her tiny waist. He kissed her neck and produced a beautiful bouquet of flowers with a flourish.

She laughed when he stuffed them in her face. "Smell good?" he asked.

"You idiot!" She pushed them from her face and turned with a huge smile on her face. He smiled back.

He released her waist to rub his thumb across her lower lip. "I love you, babe."

"I love you, too. Thank-you for the flowers." She kissed him deeply.

He pulled back and scowled with raised eyebrows. "You are not allowed to kiss me like that when you know damn well we have company arriving shortly."

She shrugged her shoulders and gave the sweetest smile he had ever seen.

The knock on the door interrupted them.

Danny tapped her nose and whispered, "You will pay for that later."

Elle laughed again and called out, "Come on in!"

Dave, Mike, Emma, and Maggie all entered with smiles on their faces. They loved coming to Danny and Elle's for dinner.

Elle gave each of the kids a big hug and an extra squeeze. She made sure to ask each of them how they were doing. Danny did the same before they all moved out to the deck for drinks.

Danny served cocktails while Elle served appetizers. It was going to be a relaxing evening along the shore of the Relic River. The soft gurgling noises of the water were soothing.

Each of them took turns recalling the events of their day at work.

"So, you're all feeling better after last night's drinking festivities?" asked Elle with a smile on her face.

Emma and Maggie groaned about their hangovers, but they were feeling more alive now.

Mike said, "I don't know how the hell Jessie can drink so much beer!"

Dave added, "Seriously, it's like he has a hollow leg!"

Elle laughed out loud. "He, unfortunately, gets his drinking habits from his mother." She pointed to herself good-heartedly. "Don't let him fool you, though. He felt like shit all morning, too!"

"He's so damn funny when he drinks. He could be a professional entertainer!" remarked Maggie.

Elle nodded in agreement. "He's definitely the clown of the family! Luke, on the other hand, likes to join in on the laughter but kind of stays on the sidelines."

"These two are no different." Danny pointed at his sons. Maggie and Emma completely agreed.

The group moved into the house to have the dinner Elle had prepared. They thoroughly enjoyed the roasted pork tenderloin.

Once everyone had finished the main course and had started on their dessert of pie and ice cream, Elle asked, "So, no further word from your Mom?"

"Not yet," answered Mike.

"How do you feel about that?"

"I don't care either way. I have to wonder why she even came back at all." He ran his fingers through his shaggy brown hair. "I guess she thought we could all start over as one big happy family, but after last night's discussion, she knows that's never going to happen."

"Maybe she'll just head back to wherever the hell she came from," stated Dave.

The two girls sat quietly listening while they enjoyed their dessert.

"Well, you're all adults, and you can certainly decide for yourselves which way you want the relationship to go. I just want you to know that your father and I support you one hundred percent. Okay?"

The boys nodded and thanked her for her kindness.

They moved on to other conversations and topics while they enjoyed the remainder of the evening together.

Once the kids had left, Danny and Elle walked back into the house and locked the door.

Elle turned toward the kitchen to finish tidying up, but Danny stopped her in her tracks. He wrapped his arms around her and said, "I told you that you'd pay for that little kiss stunt earlier. Time to pay up," he growled in her ear.

"But I have work to do!"

"Don't care. Don't want to hear excuses." He took her by the hand and led her to their bedroom. She fought weakly, very weakly, to not be pulled to the room. He simply shook his head at her and tossed her onto the bed.

CHAPTER 16

THE FOLLOWING MORNING, DANNY STROLLED THROUGH THE FRONT DOORS OF his office building and greeted Lois with a smile.

"Well, you're in much better humor today."

"I am. We had a wonderful dinner and evening with the kids."

"Nice." She handed him a stack of paperwork before he could walk away.

"Jeez Lois, can't I even get a coffee first?"

"I'm sure your lovely wife has already made you a coffee this morning."

"I actually made the coffee," he retorted.

"Then, you're ready to get to work." She smiled up at him and set her fingers on her keyboard again. "Go on!"

Danny scowled at her and then laughed. "Dammit, you're bossy."

She completely ignored him and went on with her work, smiling.

Dave and Mike entered the building and greeted Lois.

"Good morning, boys. I hear you had a nice evening!"

"We sure did. Is Dad in his office?"

"Yep. Go ahead in."

They entered his office and said, "Mornin', Dad."

"Good morning! Everything okay?"

"Yeah, we just wanted to come in, and thank you again for last night. We all really enjoyed ourselves."

"We had a great time, too. I'll let Elle know you enjoyed it."

"I've already called her," replied Mike. "She's a great person, Dad."

"She sure is."

"Anyway, I just wanted to say that, and now we'll get back to work."

"Okay. Thanks guys. Talk to ya later."

He started back at his paperwork once his sons had left. He had only been at it for a couple of hours when he heard Lois speaking harshly to someone in the reception area.

"What are you doing here?" Lois asked.

"Nice to see you too, Lois. I came to see Danny."

"He's busy."

"I'm sure he'll make time to see me."

Lois came around from behind her desk. Her hands were firmly settled on her wide girth. "I'm sure he won't."

Grace walked around her and strolled into Danny's office. Lois was directly behind her. "I told her you were busy." She scowled at Grace.

Danny smiled weakly at Lois and said, "It's okay, Lois. I'll take care of it. Thank-you."

She knew she had been dismissed and didn't like it one bit. She marched back to her desk and sat down heavily. She watched Grace close the office door for privacy, and she liked that even less.

UNITY

Grace hiked up the edge of her low-cut, short, silky summer dress to settle herself on the corner of his desk. She crossed her legs and leaned in toward him, her strappy high heels dangling from her feet.

Danny narrowed his eyes. "There's a comfortable chair right there that you can use." He pointed to the empty seat across from his desk.

"I think I like it up here better."

"Suit yourself. I'm busy, so what do you want?"

"I want us to go out to lunch together."

"You've already wasted your breath with that question the other day. Same answer. No." He bent his head to go over the papers in front of him.

Grace snaked her hand out and rested it on his.

He looked at her hand and then up at her face.

Elle walked into the reception area with a smile for Lois. "Good morning! Is Danny in his office?"

"Uh, yes."

"Great! I came to surprise him by taking him out for lunch."

"Elle, he already has a surprise visitor in there."

"Oh, he does? Okay." She sounded disappointed.

Lois scowled. "Grace is here."

"Really? Well, I think I'll just go say hi." The disappointment left her voice immediately. It had been replaced with anger.

Lois shook her head from side to side. Here we go, she thought to herself.

Elle confidently strolled toward Danny's office door. She turned the handle and walked in to see them holding hands.

"Oh, hello Grace." She walked around the desk, took a glance at Grace's hand covering Danny's. His lay flat and motionless. She smoothly removed it from her husband's and then bent to kiss him soundly on the lips.

"Hi! I came to take you out for lunch." She placed her arm around his shoulders as she straightened to stand beside him.

"Funny. Grace just asked me to join her for lunch as well."

"Really? I would have thought that she'd want to spend her time and energy repairing the damage she's done to your sons." Elle directed the comment directly at Grace with raised eyebrows.

Grace slid from the desk and stood awkwardly.

"Don't you think that would be a better plan, Grace? I mean, I don't see why my husband would want to have lunch with his ex-wife." She smiled sweetly. Danny bit his inner cheek to keep from smiling.

"Mike and Dave are our sons, and I want the four of us to dine together." Grace stated.

Elle nodded. "I see. A nice little family meal together. Have you asked the boys yet? They're out in the warehouse if you'd like to speak to them. I just brought them each a coffee. Oddly enough, they didn't mention that you had asked them out." Elle tilted her head to one side, waiting for an answer.

"I wanted to ask Danny first." Grace stuttered slightly.

"And what was Danny's answer?"

"It really isn't any of your business."

Elle chuckled and took a step toward her. Grace took two steps back. "Actually, it is my business. You see, Danny and I have a very open and honest relationship. When he told me that he never wanted to see you again, I believed him.

Walking in here and seeing you dressed like that, sprawled across his desk, won't change our marriage in the least. By the way, is that really how people in Europe dress for lunch?"

Grace looked down at her attire and answered with, "We're a little more refined than the people around here." She took in the clothing Elle had chosen to wear that day. She thought the black skort and baby blue tank top looked trashy.

"Well then, I suggest you take your refined ass out the door and go ask your sons if they would like to join you for lunch." Elle moved forward, taking her by the arm to escort her from the room.

Grace pulled her arm free. "Don't touch me!"

"Don't touch my husband." She growled the words.

Grace marched from the office. As she passed Lois's desk, she scowled deeply at her.

Lois smiled happily and said, "Have a nice day!"

Grace stormed out the door to her rented vehicle. She left without a second's thought of asking her sons to join her for lunch.

Elle turned to face Danny as soon as Grace had left.

He sat with his arms crossed.

"Sorry," Elle said.

"For what? That's the best fucking thing I've ever seen. No one talks to Grace like that!" He stood and crossed the room to her. He ran his thumb across her lower lip. "I didn't think I could love you any more than I already do, but my God, you're incredible." He lowered his thumb and kissed her deeply.

Lois cleared her throat as she entered Danny's office. The two broke apart and smiled. Lois gave Danny a small shove out of her way so she could wrap Elle in a hug.

"Sorry for eavesdropping. But I think I love you even more now, too! That woman disgusts me, and it's about damn time someone stood up to her." Elle returned the hug.

"I had just told Danny last night that I'm not a jealous person, but when I saw her hand on his, I kinda lost it." She was a little ashamed of herself for the reaction.

"Jealous? Jesus, do you not own a mirror?" Lois laughed at her own remark. She was rewarded with a warm smile from Elle and a big laugh from Danny.

He had settled on the edge of his desk after Lois had pushed him out of the way. Now, he uncrossed his ankles and stood again to round his desk. He glanced at the paperwork and stacked it.

"Cancel any appointments I have today, please, Lois. My wife is taking me out for lunch."

"Sure thing, boss. Enjoy!" She left the room feeling extremely happy for Danny and Elle. "Screw you, Grace!"

Elle smiled at her handsome husband. "So, you're not mad at me?"

"Not in the least."

"Do you think Mike and Dave will be?"

"Nope."

"You sure?"

"Would you like to go speak with them yourself?"

"Maybe I should."

"Okay. Let's go."

They crossed the yard, hand in hand, to the warehouse.

Elle greeted them with, "Hi, guys."

"I thought you two were going out for lunch?" commented Mike.

"We had a bit of an interruption."

"Oh?" He noticed the look on Elle's face and then asked. "What's wrong?"

Danny was about to speak when Elle lay her hand on his wrist. "I'll tell them."

"Okay. Now you're scaring me," said Dave.

"Your mother was here, and we had a few words for each other." She went on to relay the events of the conversation. "I hope you're not upset with me."

"Not in the least. I doubt she's ever been spoken to that way." Mike chuckled.

"Phew. Okay." Elle was quite relieved.

"Thank-you for standing up for us, Elle."

"At first, I was just blowing off steam, and then I unfortunately involved you two."

"Go and have a nice lunch. We're good with it all," said Dave.

"Do you want to join us?" asked their father.

"No, thanks. We'd better finish up here and get these cabinets delivered."

"Alright. See you later."

"See ya."

"See? Told you they'd be fine with it."

"Yeah. Still, it wasn't my place to say anything to Grace."

"Well, it's over now, so let's go have some lunch. Where are you taking me, anyway?"

"Is Ruby's okay?"

"You bet."

They had only been at the restaurant a few minutes when Elle's phone rang. She smiled when she saw Jessie's name pop up on the screen.

"Hi, Jessie."

"Hi, Mom. How are you?"

"Good. How's Ava feeling?"

"Really good. I stopped by to have lunch with you, but you weren't home."

She smiled at Danny. "Yeah, I decided to surprise Danny and take him out for lunch." The thought of Grace offering the same hit her like a hammer.

"Nice. Well, enjoy it. I'm working just up the road from you, so I'll try again tomorrow."

"Come for drinks later tonight."

"Yeah? You gonna have time to make lasagna?" He chuckled into his phone.

"Not tonight."

"You okay, Mom?" He didn't like the tone in her voice.

"Sure. I'll text Luke and see if they're available."

"Okay," he said warily.

"I love you."

"Love you too, Mom."

She texted Luke immediately. Drinks at our place tonight?

He received the text message as his phone rang.

"Hey, Jessie."

"Hey. Have you talked to Mom today?"

"I just got a text as you called. Drinks tonight."

"So, you don't know why she's upset?"

"Mom's upset? Why?"

"I don't know. I'm asking you."

"No idea. Guess we'll find out later?"

"See you there."

Luke answered Elle's text. Sure. Everything okay?

She typed one word. Grace.

Got it. See you tonight. Mike and Dave too?

No.

Luke left it at that and called Nora to let her know the plan.

Elle placed her phone back in her purse and grinned at Danny.

During her phone and text conversation, she had missed the server coming to take their drink order. Danny, of course, had ordered wine for her a beer for himself.

"Maybe I should have accepted Grace's invitation. She would have paid more attention to me."

"Are you trying to be funny?" She tilted her head as she asked the question.

"I'm kidding. What's wrong?"

She settled back in her chair. "Nothing."

He reached across the table to take her hand in his. "Elle, there is nothing to worry about when it comes to Grace."

"I know."

"Okay. So, what's the problem?"

"Nothing."

He settled back in his chair. "So, Luke and Jessie are coming for drinks tonight?"

"Yes."

"Why?"

"So, now you have a problem with me spending time with my sons?"

"Wow! You need to relax."

"Danny. Don't ever tell me to relax." She said it so calmly that it startled him.

"Maybe we should leave."

"Maybe we should."

"What the hell is going on with you?"

"Nothing."

"Stop feeding me bullshit."

She leaned forward. "Fine. I need to know that if Grace keeps coming after you if you'll eventually want to get back together with her."

He sat forward and took her by the hands once more. "Elle, she was my practice marriage. You are the real deal. I have zero interest in her. I don't know how many sunsets I have left in my life, but I know I want to spend every one of them with you."

"Okay."

"I can't believe you're so sensitive over this situation."

"How would you feel if you were in my position?"

He squeezed her hand. "I've been in your position."

Her mouth dropped open at the memory of Max. "Jesus. Yes, you have. I'm sorry."

He grinned and said, "You can make up for it as soon as we're done lunch."

"I love you, Danny. And I know I'm being an idiot. It just pisses me off that she came back to try to win you and the boys over. She doesn't deserve any of you."

He waggled his eyebrows at her. "How hungry are you?"

"Not much."

He took her by the hand as he stood. "Let's go."

UNITY

The servers showed up with their cocktails as they began to stand. "Do you still want your drinks?"

"Yes, and the bill," he replied, as he smiled at his wife.

She grinned back and took a huge gulp of her wine.

"Hurry up."

He guzzled his beer like he had lived in the desert for a month.

The six ounces of wine went down like a shooter. "Let's go." Elle placed her glass on the table and stood. They had been in the restaurant for a total of twenty minutes.

Danny grinned and downed his beer. "Now."

They didn't even make it home. Danny found a side road that had apparently been unoccupied for years.

Elle's tank top was tossed in the back seat of his truck. The skort followed.

"Jesus, woman!" He threw the truck in park and tugged at his jeans. Elle had already pressed the button to lay her seat flat. She unsnapped her bra and flung her panties on the floorboard. He couldn't get out of his clothes quickly enough.

They were like two teenagers trying to get at it before curfew. Once they had ravished each other and were both sated, he lay on her heavily.

"We need to leave," Elle said.

"In a minute."

"We'll look like fools if we get caught here."

"Don't care." He breathed heavily into her ear.

"Danny. Seriously, I know the owners of this property. We gotta go."

"Does he have a shotgun or something?"

"I really don't want to find out." She laughed as she pushed him off.

"Spoilsport. Can we pick up on this later?"

"Yes."

"Deal. Where is my underwear?"

She laughed out loud. "When you find yours, hand me mine!"

They arrived home in time to have showers before Danny needed to be back at work for the afternoon. They drove back to his office hand in hand. Elle had to pick up her truck from his parking lot.

She arrived home shortly after, to tidy up the house and prepare snacks for when the family arrived. She was feeling kind of bad about not making dinner for them.

Luke and Nora arrived first with the twins. Elle greeted them with a hug. Nora leaned in. "You don't look nearly as upset as I was led to believe. You look like ..."

The smile on Elle's face answered her comment.

Luke questioned his wife's look. "Like what?"

"Nothing." She chuckled and moved toward the kitchen to set the boys' diaper bag down. Luke scowled, but went to the fridge for a beer.

Jessie and Ava showed up shortly after. "Hey, everyone!"

"Hi! Busy with the boys," Elle called out.

"Of course, you are!" Ava sat next to Elle. "You okay?"

"Mm-hmm."

"I thought something was wrong ... oh, never mind!" As soon as she saw the look on her mother-in-law's face, she knew to shut up. Ava grinned and moved toward Danny to take Justin from him.

"Hi, Mom." Jessie bent over to give her a kiss on the cheek.

"Hi, honey."

"You okay?"

"I'm fine now."

"What was wrong earlier?"

"I had a bit of an altercation with Grace and then Danny."

"And?" Luke had moved closer by this point.

"She left. I told Dave and Mike what had been said, and then Danny and I went for lunch. The boys were fine with it all. Apparently, they've never heard of anyone speaking to their mother that way." She smiled a little sheepishly.

"Do you think there'll be any backlash?"

"I doubt it. I put Grace in her place, and hopefully she stays there."

"How about Danny?" asked Luke.

"We're good."

Both boys nodded.

"Who needs drinks?" Danny called out.

The group moved out to the deck with the twins and enjoyed the beautiful evening.

"You're feeling okay, Ava?" asked Elle.

"Yeah, I feel great. Still tired, but I guess that's normal."

"No more headaches or light-headedness?" Nora inquired.

"Not really."

"What does that mean?" demanded Jessie.

"Well, I still have a bit of a headache now and then."

"We're going back to the doctor tomorrow," he stated. He was angry that she hadn't told him earlier. She was his everything, and he wanted her to be happy and healthy.

"Yes, Mom."

He rolled his eyes and glanced at his own mother. "She gets that smartass attitude from listening to you, ya know."

Elle laughed out loud. "You're probably right."

The twins had started to fuss a bit, so Elle handed Jarrett to Ava so they could be closer. As soon as they sensed the closeness of each other, the fussing stopped. Nora rose from her seat to warm up their bottles.

Once the boys were fed, they were rocked to sleep and then placed in one of Elle's cribs. They slept soundly for two hours.

The discussion of Grace was not brought to light again. Luke and Jessie knew that their mother and Danny would figure it out. Grace would not pull the wool over Elle's eyes. The poor woman just didn't know it yet!

CHAPTER 17

ELLE PICKED UP EACH OF THE GIRLS IN HER NEW VEHICLE FOR WEDDING DRESS shopping. Ava had met her at Nora's. Jessie would be the extra set of hands for Luke if he needed them. Luke was a little overwhelmed about staying alone with the kids.

The women chatted excitedly about the evening ahead of them.

When they entered the salon, they were greeted warmly and handed glasses of champagne. Ava asked for water as she gave her glass to Nora.

A room had been prepared for Nora with the dresses she had asked about after seeing them on the internet. She came out of the dressing room after trying on four dresses. The first ones hadn't been what she had anticipated and the reaction of the women proved it to her. Of course, she was beautiful in each gown, but Nora just hadn't loved any of them.

As the assistant, Helen, tied and adjusted the fifth dress, Nora looked at herself in the mirror and sighed.

"Oh my God, this is it! This is the one!"

Helen smiled hugely and took a step back. "Should we show you off?"

"Yes!"

"Okay! Let's go." Helen held the small train of the dress as Nora made her entrance.

All eyes grew wide.

"Oh my God! I love it!" Ava's eyes teared up as she gasped the words.

"Really?"

"Honey, that dress is perfect for you!" Elle exclaimed.

"It suits you to a tee!" Maggie gushed.

Emma spoke next, "You are gorgeous in that dress!"

"Thank-you! I think this is the one!"

The scooped neckline and small capped sleeves were sheer and the slim, body-forming bodice boasted antique lace. The rest of the dress fell perfectly. Nora stood, looking like a Greek goddess. The short train was the perfect length for walking down the aisle and then to be bustled up for later in the evening. Nora scooped up the front of her dress to reveal her flip flops.

"And the perfect footwear, too!"

The women laughed, knowing that Nora was serious. They would all be wearing flip flops, including the men.

Elle moved toward her to inspect the handiwork of the dress and then to wrap her in a hug.

"You will be such a beautiful bride. I love you, Nora."

"Thank-you, Elle. I love you, too. Thank-you for being here tonight."

"I wouldn't be anywhere else."

The women stepped forward to hug and admire Nora.

UNITY

She was led back to the dressing room to return to her street clothes. The assistant had placed dresses in the other change rooms for Elle, Ava, Maggie, and Emma to try on.

Nora sat, patiently sipping her champagne while she waited for them to change.

The four women came out side by side with their arms linked. They were smiling from ear to ear.

The dresses were exactly how Nora had imagined them. The length reached mid-calf. The crystal embedded band around their necks allowed the sleeveless dresses to flow like a waterfall. The lightly pleated black chiffon material swayed around the women's legs as they walked toward Nora. The clicking of their crystal clad sandals made her smile. Elle's dress reached her ankles. It was meant to make her look just a little bit different.

She clapped her hands together. "Do you like them?"

"It's as comfortable as a pair of pajamas. I love it!" Ava responded. She ran her hand down the front of her dress. "And it hides this belly of mine."

Nora winked at her. Ava's pregnancy had made her choice of dress easy.

"I adore it, Nora. It's just beautiful!" Maggie could hardly contain her happiness.

"What a wonderful choice!" This from Emma, as she ran her finger across the jewelled neck.

"I love everything about it." Elle swished her dress and wiggled her foot to show off her sandals.

"Oh, I'm so glad! You all look lovely." Nora's eyes filled with tears.

The seamstress stepped forward to inspect the fitting of each of the dresses. "You girls made my job easy. I still had all your measurements from Ava's wedding. So, we'll box them up, and you can take them home with you tonight." She turned her attention to Nora. "I should have your dress ready by next week."

"Thank-you. This has been a successful evening!"

The women went back to change into their street clothes. When they re-emerged, Nora was scowling.

"What's wrong?" asked Ava.

Nora walked toward Elle and frowned.

Elle grabbed Maggie's arm and placed her in front of herself. "Uh oh."

"You pre-paid the bill." Her hands were on her hips.

Elle peeked around from behind Maggie. "Yeah, well ... you guys bought me a truck!"

Nora gently pushed Maggie to the side and took another step closer. She wrapped Elle in a hug and kissed her cheek. "Thank-you, and I love you for everything that you are to me."

Elle expelled a sigh of relief and returned the hug. "I love you, too."

The tension had eased, and everyone in the room smiled at the exchange between Nora and Elle.

With the bill paid and Elle's truck waiting outside, they climbed in and headed out to a fancy restaurant in town.

Drinks and dinner were served as the group of women talked about the June wedding that was to happen at the cottage property.

UNITY

When the bill arrived at the table, Elle reached out to the server to retrieved it. Nora smiled sweetly as she took the bill and said, "Two can play this game."

Elle shook her head and laughed.

She drove Maggie and Emma home and then drove to Nora's to drop her and Ava off.

"How'd the dress shopping go?" asked Luke.

"Great! I found the one I want! It'll be ready next week. How were the boys?"

"Good for you. The boys were fine. They're in bed for the night. Jessie was a big help."

Jessie grinned. "Gotta practice before mine comes along." He stood and walked toward his wife. "Did you girls find the dresses you wanted?"

"We did. They're beautiful! We were able to bring them home, so mine's in the truck already."

Jessie waggled his eyebrows at her as he placed his hands on her slim hips. "Maybe you can try it on for me later."

"You've already gotten me pregnant."

"Well yeah, but I could still use the practice."

She gave him a light slap as Luke laughed at his comment.

Nora giggled as she went to check on her children. They were sound asleep in one crib, holding hands. She smiled at the wonder of them, and then returned to the family room.

She sat beside Luke and rested her hand on his knee. "Your mom paid for all the dresses tonight."

Luke smiled and nodded. "I didn't think you'd get the chance to pay."

Jessie laughed. "She did the same for Ava."

"Well, at least I was able to grab the dinner bill before she did."

Ava spoke up. "I wanted to ask you how you managed to do that."

I pretended I was going to the washroom and found our server. I told her to give me the bill no matter how hard Elle tried to pay it." She smiled at the memory of the confused look on the server's face.

"I'll have to remember that!"

After a few more minutes of chatting, Ava and Jessie headed for the door.

"Thanks for the help tonight, Jessie."

"No worries. It was fun." He shook Luke's hand and hugged Nora.

"Okay, let's get home and take a look at this new dress." He lowered his hand to squeeze Ava's ass. That got him another swat.

Luke and Nora laughed at the two of them as they left the house.

Once the doors were locked and the lights turned off, Luke took Nora by the hand and led her to their room.

She smiled at him and said, "You don't get to see my new dress."

"I don't want to see you in anything right now."

"Has it been that long since we've had sex?"

"Forty-five days." He growled the words as he walked quickly to the bedroom with her.

"Who's counting though, right?"

CHAPTER 18

AS THE WEEKS PASSED BY, THE TWINS WERE GROWING AND BEGINNING TO become more active. They were almost two months old and starting to show their characters. Their smiles came easily when they were surrounded by the love of their family.

Luke and Nora had slipped into a routine that worked well for them. Elle would often visit just to get her baby fix. Nora didn't require her help as much, but certainly enjoyed her visits. Luke and his crew of men were busy Monday through Friday. He tried hard to avoid having his employees work on weekends. He figured that if he enjoyed spending weekends with his family and friends, they would, too.

Ava was feeling like herself again. She rested as much as she could. Jessie made sure of it. He would call her at least twice a day at work to check on her. He also avoided working weekends like the plague. He wanted to spend time with his family and friends at the cottage. He and Ava were hoping to drive up there this coming weekend.

Dave and Maggie were hoping to get up to the cottages for the weekend as well. With Maggie's new position at the hospital, weekends were never an issue for her. Unless there was a rush job for cabinets to be installed, Dave and Mike only worked weekdays as well.

Mike and Emma had planned on joining the family. Emma had always refused to work weekends; it had been written in her contract. She was kicking herself in the ass now for suggesting hair and makeup for weddings. She knew that would involve Saturdays. Mike wasn't impressed with it, but knew it was her passion and supported her completely. She wasn't booked for any weddings this weekend, and she was extremely happy about it.

Danny and Elle were packed and ready to go by Thursday afternoon. Kim and her husband were planning on joining them. She and Elle hadn't had the opportunity to have that lunch to discuss the showing of her artwork, so Elle extended the invitation. Danny was looking forward to getting the chance to meet Kim's husband, Tony.

After his divorce from Grace, he had lost contact with many of his friends. Married couples didn't know how to deal with divorced people. Whose side should they take? Even though Grace had moved away, his friends had spent more time with couples rather than a single man. He had been lost for quite some time and had focused on the well-being of his sons. Once he had reunited with Elle, she and their blended family had become his priority.

Elle had been in the same predicament when she and Max had divorced. She was lucky to be so close to Luke and Jessie. Kim had been a huge support, as well. Elle hadn't wanted to work on friendships with past friends. She couldn't be bothered with all the questions. "What happened?" "Did he have an affair?" "Did you have an affair?" "How are the boys handling it?" "Are you okay?" Ugh!

Danny arrived home at noon from work. Elle met him at the door with a kiss and a duffle bag to be loaded into his truck.

He smiled and chuckled. "Ready to go, are you?"

"Yes! Let's get the hell out of here!"

They loaded the truck with the pile of stuff Elle had sitting by the door. Two hours later, they arrived at their beloved cottage. Elle sighed and set her head on the headrest.

"God, I love this place."

Danny smiled at her peacefulness and placed his hand over hers. "I love to see you so relaxed."

She smiled back and squeezed his hand. "I guess we'd better tidy up the cottage before we start unloading."

"Yep. C'mon old girl. Let's clean, unload, and then take a walk down by the water."

"Deal!"

Within an hour, the cottage had been cleaned, and the truck unloaded. Elle was just finishing putting new linens on their bed when Danny came up the stairs with a glass of wine for her and a beer for himself.

"Almost ready for that walk?" He held out the glass of wine to her.

"You bet!" She spread her hand across the comforter to smooth it out. She took the wine and kissed him.

"Are Tony and Kim taking our bed for the weekend?"

"Nope. They said they wanted the whole camping experience, so they bought a tent."

Danny chuckled. "Well, it'll certainly feel like a campground with all the noise of our kids and grandkids!"

Elle joined in on the laughter. "They may never want to come back!"

They took their walk down to the water to sit on the shoreline with their drinks. The water was calm, and the sun hot. Elle stripped out of her shorts and tank top and walked into the water to cool off. Danny followed suit. They lay on their backs and floated around for a bit before they decided it was time to head back up and get ready for their guests.

"I wonder if we should have the kids build a small cottage for guests." Elle mused.

"Hey, that's a good idea. We'll talk to them when they get here tomorrow night."

"Maybe we should make up a bed in Jessie and Ava's cottage for Kim and Tony for the night."

"Another good idea. Two nights sleeping on the ground might be a little much for them. I know I wouldn't do it!" Danny chuckled again.

Elle texted Jessie. Is it okay if Kim uses your spare room for the night?

Sure. We won't be up until later Friday.

She turned to Danny. "I'll get the spare sheets and go ahead down to Jessie's to make the bed."

"Okay. I'll get the grill out and get the porch furniture out of the shed."

With their chores done and dinner prepared, they sat on the porch with drinks, enjoying the quiet and the beautiful weather.

UNITY

Tires coming up the laneway could be heard crunching the gravel. Elle smiled. She was excited to be spending time with her girlfriend. Kim jumped from their truck in a cute little summer dress, with her phone in her hand. She stopped and snapped a photo of Elle and Danny.

"Now, that is complete relaxation!" She smiled broadly. "Hi!"

Danny and Elle went to greet them. Elle wrapped Kim in a huge hug. "I'm so glad you guys could make it up here for the weekend!"

"Us too!" She returned the hug with as much enthusiasm.

Elle moved to Tony. "Hi! How was the drive?"

Tony bent his six-foot-four frame and hugged her. "It was great! Very scenic."

Elle stepped back to introduce him to Danny.

"Tony, this is my husband, Danny. Danny, this is Tony."

The two men shook hands. "It's nice to finally meet you, Tony."

Tony's black eyes searched Danny's blue ones. "So, you're the man that my wife is infatuated with."

Danny's mouth dropped. "What? I've never—"

Tony clapped his hands and rolled his head of pitch-black hair back, laughing out loud. "You should see your face!"

Danny stood, looking confused. He turned to face Kim.

"Guilty." She pressed her right hand to her heart.

He then turned to Elle. She stood back, laughing.

"You'll get used to these two fools! But honestly, Kim does think you're pretty hot." She smirked

Tony slapped Danny on the back. "Beer?"

"Uh, yeah."

The foursome made their way to the cottage. Kim and Tony were given the tour before drinks were handed out.

"I've made up a bed for you in Jessie's cottage for the night."

"Oh, thank God! It was never my idea to sleep in a damn tent." She sent a dirty look at her husband.

"C'mon Kim, it'll be fun." He grinned from ear to ear.

"Not for me! You're the country boy, remember. I'm a city girl."

Tony turned to Danny. "She has zero sense of adventure."

Danny chuckled as he handed him a beer. "Have a beer, and then I'll help you guys unload the truck."

Tony clinked the neck of his bottle against Danny's. "Cheers."

The two women were served wine as they settled into the deck chairs.

"My God, you guys must love it up here!"

Danny and Elle smiled. "We sure do. The kids will be up tomorrow night. Jessie and Ava won't mind if you use their spare room for the weekend."

Tony spoke up. "We wouldn't want to intrude."

"Yes, we would!" Kim said loudly and clearly.

"Okay, so the tent stays in the truck then." Danny laughed at Kim.

After unloading the truck, the foursome packed a cooler and headed down to the water for a boat ride. The peacefulness and scenery were so enjoyable that Kim wanted to skip dinner and stay out on the water. Tony was okay with sleeping in the cottage, but he was not willing to give up dinner. They headed back for grilled steaks.

Kim set her fork down and picked up her glass of red wine. "So, any word on what's going to happen with Chase?"

Danny set his fork down as well. "We should know what's happening by Monday morning."

"Good. I hope they put the bastard away for a long time."

"Us too. We're just thankful that Luke, Nora, and the boys weren't harmed."

Tony spoke up. "I'd like to meet him in a dark alley sometime."

"You and me both!" Danny was getting worked up about the conversation.

Elle placed her hand on his wrist. "He'll get what he deserves."

Kim spoke up. "Sorry. I didn't mean to upset anyone. I just wanted to ask before any of the kids showed up."

"It's okay, Kim. The waiting game is pretty frustrating."

She smiled. "Okay, so new subject. When are we going to have your next art show?"

Elle smiled back. "Maybe in the fall? I think I'd like to enjoy the summer after all we've been through."

"Perfect! We'll discuss it more later in the summer." She raised her glass. "Cheers to a wonderful weekend with friends!"

Tony and Danny went back outside to start a bonfire, while the women began clearing the table and washing dishes.

They spent a great night settled around the fire, drinking and catching up.

The following morning was a little fuzzy as they sat and had breakfast together.

"Probably shouldn't have pulled out the bottle of tequila last night." Tony groaned as he placed his hand on his forehead.

Danny smiled. "The weekend has just begun. Wait until the lads get up here tonight. You may not survive it!"

Tony groaned again.

Kim laughed. "It's been a while since we've seen them."

"I imagine they'll be here by dinner time tonight," Elle stated.

"The twins must be getting big."

"They sure are. They smile and gurgle constantly," Elle said proudly.

Tony smiled broadly at her response as he continued to hold his head. Danny rose from the table to pour more coffee. He set the bottle of Tylenol in the center of it.

"Thank-you." Tony reached for it.

Once the table had been cleared and dishes done, they walked the property.

"I could get used to this place." Kim sighed.

"Good! We were thinking of having the guys build another cottage or at least a bunkhouse for guests," Elle said.

"We'll burn the tent tonight." Kim gave Tony a sideways glance as she said the words.

Tony laughed as he took her by the hand to continue their walk.

The afternoon was spent down by the water. Elle and Kim sunbathed while the guys tried their hand at fishing. By the time late afternoon arrived, the fish were still safe and sound in the water.

"Good thing we brought burgers for supper!" Elle laughed at their hunched backs as they packed up the tackle box.

Car doors could be heard slamming in the laneway.

"Sounds like some of the kids are here!" Elle stood to go and greet them.

"Hey, you guys!" she yelled as Dave, Maggie, Mike, and Emma stepped from the truck.

"Hi!" They each gave Elle a hug as the others made their way toward them.

Introductions were made, and then everyone grabbed a bag to help make the process of unpacking go a little quicker.

Drinks were about to be served when Jessie and Ava showed up. Luke and Nora and the kids were next. Kim and Elle swooped in on the twins while the rest lent a hand to unload the vehicles.

Jessie came back to the main fire pit to place a cooler full of beer next to the picnic table. He twisted the cap off one and started handing them out to Danny and Tony.

Tony took one and looked long and hard at it.

"I have other brands in the cooler if you don't like that one, Tony."

"Oh no, it's not the brand." He chuckled. "It's the way I felt this morning after drinking way too many of these last night."

Jessie laughed out loud. "Hair of the dog ... bottoms up!" He clinked his bottle against Tony's and drank deeply.

Tony sighed and did the same.

Luke joined them with his cooler and opened a beer for himself. Dave and Mike were right behind him. The six men continued to drink as the women made dinner and handed Jarrett and Justin back and forth amongst themselves.

By the time dinner was ready to be served, the only sober ones were the women. The boisterous laughter around the picnic table had the women rolling their eyes but enjoying the fun. The men were guided back to the fire so the girls could clean up and get the twins ready for a bath and bed. Emma and Maggie sat snuggling the twins until Nora announced it was time for them to be laid down for the night. She settled them, and brought the baby monitor back out to the fire.

Luke picked at his guitar by the fireside. The others began singing to the requested songs. It was decided that they all sounded better when alone in the shower. Mike, however, surprised them all with his deep baritone voice.

"You should come sing with the band at our next practice, Mike," said Luke.

"I'm not good enough to join all of you." He said it seriously.

"Yeah, you are. I'll let you know when the next session is."

The evening ended, not surprisingly, early for the men.

Saturday morning was a repeat of Friday morning for Tony and Danny.

"I honestly don't think I could survive too many more weekends up here," Tony said, holding his head once more.

Danny laughed. "Welcome to drinking with the lads."

Kim interrupted. "Speaking of the lads. Didn't all of you make plans to go out on the ATVs for the day?"

"Sweet Jesus!" Tony groaned.

They stepped outside to see the ATVs lined up and being fueled by the four younger men.

"Good morning! How are ya today?" said Luke.

Danny scowled. "Apparently in a lot worse shape than you four."

Mike came up around behind them. He clapped two huge stainless-steel pot lids together. Danny and Tony just about had heart attacks on the spot.

UNITY

"What the fuck is happening?!" Tony yelped as he grabbed at his head again.

Dave was bent over in half, laughing. "It's not a hammer on a tin wall, but it gives the same effect!" Everyone except for Tony and Danny was laughing.

Danny told him how he had a habit of hitting the tin walls of his warehouse with a hammer when he knew his sons were hungover.

"Payback is brutal."

The four younger men couldn't contain their laughter.

They finally disbanded to grab coolers full of food and beer.

Tony held up his hand as Kim walked toward him with a cooler for himself and Danny. "If there's beer in there, please take it out."

"Ya big baby." She laughed as she went to add more bottled water.

The cottage area immediately quieted as soon as the ATVs left. The six women spent an enjoyable day down by the water and fussing over Jarrett and Justin.

Emma and Maggie offered to make a seafood dinner for the crew. As the tables were being set and the twins being fed, the ATVs could be heard returning.

Elle and Kim rolled their eyes as they watched Danny and Tony try to climb off the bikes. They were filthy and stiff. Standing straight was proving to be a problem. The women stood back and crossed their arms, with smiles on their faces, as they continued to watch the show.

Tony turned to Danny. "I think I'm getting too damn old for this shit."

"Same."

Kim winked at Elle as she walked into the cottage to grab two bottles of beer. They walked toward their husbands and handed them over.

"Don't need it, but will gladly drink it. Thank-you." Tony took a swig. Danny followed suit.

Emma and Maggie had cooked a delicious meal of cod. The men told the events of the day as they all enjoyed the food and each other's company.

The bonfire had been lit again. Within a couple of hours, the men were nodding off and starting to make their way to their beds. The women stayed up, drinking wine and chatting.

Sunday was a lazy day for all. Tidying up the area began late in the afternoon. The boats were secured, ATVs locked up, and grills put away. Kim and Tony were the first to leave. They thanked everyone for such an amazing weekend and promised to be back before the summer's end.

"I'm going to need the summer to repair my liver." Tony rubbed his stomach as he spoke.

Elle hugged him while she laughed at his humor. He and Danny shook hands. They knew they would be the best of friends in the years to come.

Kim wrapped Elle and then Danny in a huge hug and thanked them once more.

"Talk to you soon." Elle kissed her cheek.

The kids said their goodbyes and thanked them for the fun.

Their first weekend at Giggling Creek had been a success.

CHAPTER 19

CHASE WAS NOT HAVING A TYPICAL MONDAY MORNING. HE HAD BEEN HAND-cuffed and led into the county courtroom for his day of judgment.

Jillian sat quietly in the row of seats behind him, wringing her hands as she listened to the judge berate her son and then sentence him. She knew he deserved everything he had been handed for what he had done. He had gone off the rails because of drug and alcohol abuse, and this was the price he would pay. His greed for the inheritance money had pushed him over the edge.

Chase turned to face his mother after his sentencing. There was anger in his eyes. She smiled weakly in a show of support. The bailiff grasped him by the arm and roughly led him from the room.

The court stenographer continued to tap the keys on her keyboard.

Jake stood from his seat in the back row of the room and left. He pulled his phone from his pocket and called Jessie. It was mid-morning.

"Hello."

"Jessie? It's Jake."

"Hey Jake, how's it goin'?"

"Better now."

"Oh yeah?"

"The judge has just sentenced and fined Chase."

"Okay. So, what did he get?"

"He'll spend one year in jail for brandishing a firearm."

"And what about trying to kidnap my nephews? Did he get anything for that?" Jessie was not impressed. It could be heard in his voice.

"I should probably talk to Luke about that."

"When does his sentencing begin?"

"He was hauled off to the state prison this morning. You won't need to worry about him for quite a while."

"Sounds like he got some time for his other crime." Jessie smiled, knowing that Jake had slipped up.

"Uh, yeah. Listen, I have to call Luke. If you have any further questions, give me a call anytime."

"Okay. Thanks, Jake." He wanted to call Luke, but figured Jake would be on the phone with him momentarily. He'd call in ten minutes. He needed to know how long the bastard would be locked up.

He called his mother instead.

"Hey, Jessie. That was a fun weekend!"

"It sure was! Tony's a blast!"

Elle chuckled. "What are you working on today?"

"Landscaping a new job. I was calling to let you know that Chase was taken to prison this morning."

"Good. For how long?"

"For pointing the gun at me, he got a year. Jake wanted to tell Luke about the attempted kidnapping charges himself, so I don't know how much more or what he got for that."

"A year! What a fucking joke!"

"I don't care about that part. I just hope he's put away for a lot longer for his stunt with Jarrett and Justin."

"I know, honey. It just doesn't make sense to me is all. Christ, he could have pulled that trigger at any second. It still makes me sick to think of it."

"Me too. I'm gonna let you go and call Luke now. I'll talk to you later, Mom." He disconnected and called his brother.

"Hey."

"Hey. Did you get a call from Jake?"

"Just got off the phone with him."

"And?"

"For escaping custody, making verbal threats to Mom, breaking into my home, and the attempted kidnap of the twins, he got three years added to the one he got for you and a five thousand dollar fine."

"Pfft. Hardly seems like enough for that dirtbag."

"At least he got something. It's more than I thought he'd get."

"Yeah. You'd better give Mom a call. She's waiting to hear from you."

"Got it. Coming over for a beer tonight?"

"Sure. See you later."

Luke called Elle and relayed the message about Chase once more.

They batted back and forth what Chase should have received for punishment, but in the end, no one was injured and the twins were fine. Just maybe, Chase would clean up his act while at the crowbar hotel.

He was not likely to have an easy prison term. When it came to harming children, it was not well accepted behind prison walls. His tough-guy attitude would more than likely be beaten out of him. Chase had every right to be scared and nervous.

When Luke arrived home to his wife and children, he told Nora the news about Chase.

She sighed in relief. "I guess we won't have to worry about him for the time being." She stood from her seat on the sofa and wrapped Luke in a hug. Jarrett and Justin continued to coo from their haven in the playpen.

Luke released Nora and walked over to pick up his sons. He cuddled both of them. He knew just how lucky he was to be able to come home to them. He'd had terrible nightmares after the incident. They always included him searching for his sons and never finding them.

Nora made her way to the kitchen to set the table for dinner. She knew Luke needed time with the twins.

Jessie and Ava arrived shortly after dinner. Ava helped Nora bathe the boys and then sat with them in the rocking chairs. Ava inhaled Justin's "baby smell," and the softness of his blue pajamas had her smiling. Jarrett wore the identical set. She loved being here with them. She could hardly wait for her child to be welcomed into the world.

Jessie and Luke grabbed a couple of beers from the fridge and joined the women and children in the family room. Their large frames filled the majority of the sofa, while their long, jean-clad legs stretched out in front of them.

UNITY

They discussed the situation of Chase, and then moved on from the subject. It would probably not be brought up again until the day of his release in four years' time. They were all glad to be done with him.

Jessie changed the subject. "So, Ava and I were talking last night about baby names."

"Ohh!" Chirped Nora. "What have you come up with?"

"Nothing," replied Jessie.

Nora scowled. "Well, you've got to have some kind of an idea."

"Nope. Not a thing."

Luke laughed out loud. "You seriously don't have any inclination of a name?"

Ava spoke up. "We thought we'd leave that up to you guys."

"Us?" Luke sounded shocked.

"Yep. We'd like you to pick the name for our child. It'll be your first job as legal guardians." Jessie smiled.

"Not fair. That's too big of a responsibility." This from Nora.

Jessie smiled. "You have a few months to figure it out."

"What if you don't like the name we choose? I hope you have a backup name."

"We only have two conditions on the name."

Luke turned his attention to Nora. "And here we go." He rolled his eyes.

"Okay, what are these conditions?" he asked Jessie.

"One, it has to start with the letter J, whether it's a boy or a girl. And secondly, it can't be a stupid name."

Luke laughed again. Nora rolled her eyes.

"Why the letter J?" Luke asked.

"Wouldn't it be cool for the three cousins to all have the same initials, J.C.? Plus, it would be fun for Mom to say 'I'm babysitting the three J's tonight!'"

The foursome laughed at the image of Elle saying that.

Luke clinked the neck of his beer bottle against Jessie's.

"Okay, we'll do it."

Nora shook her head at the wonderment of the two brothers. Seriously, who would ask someone to name their child for them?

The two women rose from their chairs. It was bedtime for the twins. Luke and Jessie took turns snuggling and kissing them goodnight before they were swept off to their room.

The men sat again. "So, do we give you a few choices, or what's the deal here?"

Jessie smiled. "Just put a few names for a girl in one hat and a few for a boy in another. When the baby's born, we'll pick one from the hat."

Luke shook his head. "You're crazy."

"Bat shit crazy." He clinked his beer again.

The girls returned to the family room with the wedding book. Jessie caught a glimpse of it. "Oh shit."

Nora laughed. "I just want to go over a few things. Relax."

"Is there a list of jobs in that book for me?" he asked.

"A few."

"Okay, hit me with it." Jessie leaned forward.

"I want to be married by the water. All I need you to do is clear the beach area a bit and bring in fresh sand."

Jessie nodded. "That's easy enough. If we all go back up to the cottages this coming weekend, you can show me exactly what you want."

Nora smiled. "Thank-you."

"That smile was a little too fast." Warily he asked, "What else?"

"I'm a little worried about what the weather will be. I'll pray for sunshine, but we could get rain. I'll need something to cover both scenarios."

"Easy. Tarps."

Nora raised her eyebrows. "Tarps? I'm not really going for a redneck theme."

"Well, not construction tarps! I meant silky, flimsy things that look like sails on a boat."

"Now you have us all confused," Luke added.

Jessie went to the kitchen for paper and a pencil. He returned to the sofa to draw out his idea. The other three crowded around him.

Once he was done, he held it up to show them. "See? The sails will be strung from the trees. They'll overlap and blow gently in the breeze. We can hang lights on them, and in the trees too if you want."

Nora smiled from ear to ear and kissed his cheek. "I love it! How did you come up with this?"

"I just finished a patio, and this is what they're using for shade instead of a solid roof."

"It's perfect! Thank-you, Jessie."

"Anything else?"

"Nope. Only the suit fitting."

"Ugh. That was a bad experience for me last time."

Luke laughed. "I won't be giving whiskey-filled flasks as a groomsman gift."

"Thank God for that!" Ava added.

They left shortly after the planning session and said they would see each other at the cottages the following weekend.

Danny was pleased with the news Elle had given him about Chase. Elle had added that the lawyer was in the process of dissolving the contract between themselves and Chase. He would not have access to the money when he was released.

"I hope that bit of news doesn't set him off when he gets out." The concern in Danny's voice was clear.

"What do you mean?"

"He was obviously trying to kidnap the twins to collect a ransom." He looked Elle in the eyes. "Probably for the sum of his inheritance."

"Yeah. I think I'll give Jillian a call tomorrow. I'll explain the situation and also see how she's coping."

Danny wrapped her in a hug. "Even with all the anger you have toward Chase, you still have concern for his mother." He held her back and raised his thumb to her lips. "You never cease to amaze me."

"Well, I was pretty rude to her that day at Nora's. It was said in anger, and I haven't been feeling very good about it. It's not Jillian's fault that Chase makes the choices he does."

"You're right about that. I'd say a lot of it comes from his father." He smirked a little and then took her by the hand to lead her to the couch. "Let's have a drink and head for bed."

"Sounds good."

Elle was tired by the time they reached the bedroom, but when Danny started to make advances toward her, well, she simply couldn't resist the urge to make love to him. She gave in willingly.

CHAPTER 20

LUKE MADE THE PHONE CALLS TO HIS GROOMSMEN ABOUT THE FITTING appointment for their suits. It was to be Thursday evening at the same location where Jessie had had his fittings.

"Are we going for beer and pizza after?" Mike wanted to know.

"Sure."

"Okay, then I'll be there."

Luke laughed out loud. He remembered just how much fun they'd had after Jessie's night out.

Mike promised to pass on the message to Dave.

Luke called Jessie next. "You still good for suit fittings on Thursday night?"

Jessie groaned. "I'll be there. We're going out to eat and drink later, right?"

Luke laughed again. "Yes. We'll go to The Bar for pizza and beer."

"Perfect. See you Thursday."

Next, he called Nora.

"Hi, babe. How are the boys behaving today?"

"They're little angels … when they're sleeping." She smiled into the phone.

Luke chuckled. "So, the guys are all set for Thursday night."

"Great! No grumblings?"

"As long as I take them for food and beer."

Nora laughed. "Of course."

"Can you call and make sure that Thursday night still works for the salon?"

"The word 'salon' sounds funny coming from you." She smiled to herself. "I'll call them right now. See you tonight."

"Thanks. Yep, see you tonight. Give those munchkins a kiss from their daddy."

"Will do. Luke, did you call Danny?"

"Shit. No. I'll call now. Thanks for the reminder, babe."

He dialed Danny as soon as he disconnected from Nora.

"Hey, Luke."

"Hey, Danny. How are you?"

"Good. You?"

"Good. I just got off the phone with the guys, and it looks like Thursday night is the night for trying on our suits. Are you able to make it?"

"Yeah. That should be fine. Food and beer after?"

Luke laughed. "I've had the same question with every phone call. Yeah, we'll go out after the fitting."

"Perfect. See you then."

Elle had finished framing a few of her drawings, and felt like going to see her grandchildren. She climbed in her truck and arrived at Nora's twenty minutes later. She knocked on the door and walked in.

UNITY

Nora stood in the kitchen, preparing the bottles of formula for the twins.

"Hi, Elle!"

"Hi. How are you?"

"Good. What are you up to today?"

"Did some work at home and decided it was time to come see these two." She made her way to the playpen where Jarrett and Justin were batting their arms around, trying to reach the toys that hung over their heads.

"Well hello, boys." She reached in to pick up Justin.

Nora handed her a bottle. "Have a seat, Elle. I'll get Jarrett, and we'll sit and feed them."

Elle made herself and Justin comfortable on the sofa.

"You have a great routine going with the boys, Nora."

"I think so, too. Their schedule is pretty good, and they don't wake during the night anymore." She played with Jarrett's cheek as she spoke. "Mommy and Daddy are sure happy about that, right buddy?"

Elle bent to kiss Justin's cheek. "They're such happy little guys."

"They sure don't cry much."

"You're doing a wonderful job of raising them, Nora. I hope you know that."

"Thanks for saying that, Elle. It means a lot to me. My mother has never said those words." She turned a little sad.

"Well, your mother doesn't spend much time with you, so don't take it too hard, honey."

"Yeah, I know."

"Are your parents going to make it to the wedding?"

"I've sent them an invitation and called a few times, but there hasn't been any answer."

"Well, I hope they make it. It's going to be such a quaint and elegant evening. Let me know if you need any further help with anything, okay?"

"Thanks. The guys are going Thursday night for their fittings."

"Oh, boy! Are you going with them?" Elle laughed.

Nora groaned. "I probably should."

"Well, if you decide to go, just let me know, and I'll come over to watch the boys."

"Okay. Are you and Danny going to the cottages this weekend?"

"We're planning to."

"Oh, good. Will you help me decide on the exact location down on the beach to say our vows?"

"Of course! I look forward to it." Elle ran her finger along Justin's chest and then placed her hand over his heart. Her own heart melted.

After an hour of visiting, Elle went home to prepare dinner for herself and Danny. The evenings were lovely, and they enjoyed eating out on their deck.

They spent a wonderful night soaking up the beautiful sunset and view.

Elle turned to Danny. "I forgot to call Jillian today."

"Oh well, tomorrow's another day, babe."

"Would you mind if I called her right now?"

"Not at all."

She reached for her phone that was sitting on the table.

"Hello?" Jillian's voice sounded wary.

"Hi, Jillian. It's Elle. How are you?"

"Fine. I thought you didn't want to speak to me anymore."

Elle sighed. "I'm sorry about what I said to you that day at Nora's. It was said in frustration and anger."

"I don't blame you. I'm sure I would be feeling the same way if our roles were reversed."

"Thank-you for understanding. How are you doing?"

"I'm okay."

"And Chase?" Danny lay his hand on her knee.

"As well as can be expected, I guess. I've been to see him a couple of times, but he doesn't have much to say."

"I'm sure he doesn't. He'll have time to contemplate his actions while he's in jail." She waited for a second and then added, "Jillian, I was calling to let you know that the contract with Chase has been dissolved."

"Okay."

"I wish all of this could have turned out differently. We all had high hopes."

"We sure did. Thank-you for the opportunity. I know Chase doesn't feel the same way, but I want you to know that I appreciate the kindness of your family."

"I hope there won't be any repercussions once he learns about the cancellation."

"What do you mean?"

"We think his attempted kidnapping of Jarrett and Justin was for a ransom for the money he was to receive."

"Sweet Jesus! That never even crossed my mind!"

"It all kind of makes sense when you think about it. First, he held Jessie at gunpoint, then threatened me when he saw my new truck, and then the twins."

"Yeah, I guess it does." Jillian ran her hands through her hair. "How is Danny?"

Elle covered his hand with her own and smiled. "He's good."

"I've been seeing someone." She blurted out the words.

"Hey, that's wonderful news!"

"We met online a couple of weeks ago."

Elle smiled into the phone. "Well, good for you. I hope it goes well."

Jillian deserved some happiness in her life. Chase had put her through hell.

"Thanks. Anyway, thank-you for the call, and maybe we'll talk again soon, Elle."

"Talk soon." Elle disconnected and stared off into the distance.

Danny sat silently beside her. His hand still resting on her knee.

By the time the weekend arrived, everyone was ready to spend some quality time together.

Danny and Elle had arrived Thursday evening with a truckload of food and drinks. They spent a quiet evening settled around a small campfire, listening to country music. When one of Elle's songs came across the airwaves, Danny reached over to crank it up. He smiled broadly as they sang along to it. He still couldn't believe the songs he was listening to had lyrics written by his wife.

When morning arrived, they took their coffee mugs and walked down to the beach. It was going to be a beautiful day.

"So, Luke and Nora want to have their wedding down here by the water." Elle looked around and thought it would be lovely.

"I think Jessie is having sand delivered up here tomorrow."

"We'll never get a truck down this path!"

"And that's why he's bringing wheelbarrows. I hope you're feeling strong." He smiled as she rolled her eyes.

"I think I'll be busy babysitting the twins."

Danny laughed. "I wish I could use the same excuse, but I don't think the lads will let me off the hook."

Elle laughed as she took him by the hand and led him back up the path. She refilled their coffee mugs and brought them out to the porch. Danny sat rocking in his chair. He looked content and happy.

"Enjoying the peace and quiet?"

"I'm so damn happy we bought this place." He kissed her lips as she bent to hand him his mug.

"Me too." She let out a sigh and sat.

They turned their attention at the sound of a vehicle coming up the lane. "Are you expecting someone?"

"Nope." Danny craned his neck a little more as he answered.

A shiny new black pickup truck slowly approached the cabin. Danny squinted his eyes as the driver waved out the window.

He turned to Elle and smiled. "Well, shit. It's Hank!" Elle smiled and rose.

"Hi, Hank!"

"Hello! How are you two?" He ran his hand down the front of his plaid shirt and made sure it was tucked into his jeans.

"Great. Nice truck!" Danny approached it to run his hands along it. Elle stepped forward and gave Hank a hug.

"It's so nice to see you again."

Hank hugged her warmly. As he pulled away, he glanced around. "You guys have done a great job up here." He continued to look around. "I love how all of it blends in with the surroundings."

"Come and have a seat. I'll get you a coffee," Elle offered.

"Thanks."

"So, when did you get the new truck?" Danny asked.

"Not long after I sold this place to you. It's quite a step up from what I used to drive." He chuckled. "The place really does look super."

"Thanks. The kids worked pretty hard to get their cabins done. Now we can relax and enjoy our weekends up here. What's new with you, Hank?"

"Oh, not much. I do some volunteer work a couple of days a week, but other than that, I just kinda hang out around home." He shrugged.

"Well, I'm glad you stopped by. You're more than welcome to come up and visit us anytime."

Hank nodded. "Thanks. I kinda miss the place." He winked and added, "I don't miss the work of it, though."

Danny chuckled. "We have lots of hands up here to help. Luke and Nora are having their wedding here in June. Jessie has a load of sand being delivered tomorrow to freshen up the beach area."

"Nice. It'll be a beautiful spot to exchange their vows."

Elle handed the men a coffee and set a plate of the cookies she had baked the day before on the table between them. She sat on the top step of the deck and smiled when Hank reached for one.

"It's been a long time since I've had home-baked cookies." He took a bite of the soft oatmeal cookie and closed his eyes. "These are amazing."

Danny rubbed his belly. "And that's why I've gained ten pounds since we got married."

Hank laughed. "It'll happen to a man every time."

The three sat and visited for a couple of hours before Hank decided it was time for him to leave. Danny admired his truck again before he pulled away with a wave out the window.

"That was nice of him to stop by," Elle stated as they watched him leave.

"We should ask Luke and Nora if they'd invite Hank to the wedding. I'm sure he'd love to be back here on the property for the day."

"Good idea. We'll ask them tonight."

The kids started arriving around dinner time. Elle and Danny had prepared a feast of burgers and salads. The food was devoured in no time.

"What time is the sand coming tomorrow Jessie?" asked Luke.

"It should be here by nine o'clock. Oh, and Nora, I brought up some of those tarps for you to try out."

"Great, thanks!"

Elle turned to address the family. "We forgot to tell you guys that Hank stopped by today."

"How is he?" asked Jessie.

"He looks great!"

"He bought a new truck! It's really nice," Danny added with admiration in his voice.

Elle smiled at her husband and turned to Luke and Nora. "We were wondering if it would be okay with you if we invited him to the wedding."

"Of course! It would be wonderful to see him again."

"Great. I'll get an invitation from you and send it to him."

"Should we take a walk down to the water and figure out what needs to be done?" asked Ava.

"Yeah, let's go."

Maggie and Emma scooped up the twins and started to make their way down the path.

Nora smiled at how comfortable they were with her children. They were both going to be amazing mothers. She and Elle grabbed a bottle of wine, four glasses, and then followed. The men reached into the coolers for beer.

Nora started pointing at some of the small limbs that she wanted trimmed for a clear pathway.

"We'll start trimming tomorrow before the sand comes. I brought my chainsaw just in case," said Danny.

"How are we getting the sand down here?" asked Luke.

"With the wheelbarrows I loaded in the back of my truck," answered Jessie.

Luke groaned.

"It's your wedding, man. Not mine." Jessie shrugged and moved on.

"Yeah, yeah."

"We'll all pitch in," said Maggie.

"Not me. I'm babysitting," said Elle.

Jessie spoke up. "Ava isn't helping either." He looked at his wife and smiled sheepishly. "We're not taking any chances, babe."

UNITY

"I won't argue this time. I'm good with helping Elle take care of Jarrett and Justin." The two women smiled at each other.

Nora splayed her hands out and said, "Okay, I think right around this area will be nice for the ceremony." It was the one area of the beach that had lots of space and needed the least amount of work. They would add the sand, level it out, and be done.

"If you get married along the water's edge, we could set up chairs or benches back here by the tree line." Elle stood where she suggested the guests sit.

"Benches would be nice," Luke said. "My guys and I will start making them on Monday and have them here next weekend."

Nora walked to him and kissed his cheek. "Thanks, honey."

Maggie and Emma stood swaying with the kids in their arms. Ava rubbed her baby bump, dreaming of when she would be swaying the same way with her little one.

The discussion continued for another twenty minutes before the gang made their way back up to the cottages.

Dave started the campfire while Mike carried more wood over from the small shed. Danny brought his cooler closer for everyone to be able to reach into and then went to retrieve more wine for the women.

Nora and Luke brought Jarrett and Justin around to everyone in the group so they could be kissed good night. Once they were settled for the night, the family enjoyed a nice evening around the fire.

Danny and Elle went off to bed first. "Lots of work to be done tomorrow, guys. See you in the morning."

"I don't think it will be a late night for any of us," added Jessie.

The load of sand was delivered on time, as promised. Jessie had the driver dump the load as close to the pathway as he could. Luke paid the man in cash before he left. The men wheeled load after load to the beach area. The women smoothed it all out with the rakes that Jessie had brought with him. Ava and Elle took turns delivering cold drinks and entertaining the twins.

It was late afternoon by the time the job was finished. They all took a swim to cool off before heading up to the cottages for the lunch Elle and Ava had prepared. Luke opened beers and handed them out. Jessie reached into the back seat of his truck and pulled out a couple of the tarps. He sipped his beer while he contemplated how he would hang them. Luke brought the ladder over, and they began stringing them between the trees to create a canopy. They started where the small reception area would be.

Nora came back out from her cottage and covered her mouth with her hands. "Oh, Jessie! That looks wonderful! I love the mixture of black and white."

"So, you think this will be okay? I ordered plenty so we can extend the canopy to whatever size you want."

"Thank-you!" She moved closer to him and kissed his cheek.

The reaction from the rest of the family was just as positive.

Luke and Jessie took them down again and stored them in Luke's cottage. They would bring the rest of the canopies with them the following weekend.

Nora planned on bringing the rest of her supplies with her as well.

UNITY

The wedding was only a couple of weeks away. It was going to be simple and elegant, with only thirty guests. Luke and Nora didn't want a big wedding with all the headaches that would surely come along with it.

CHAPTER 21

THE FOLLOWING WEEK PASSED QUICKLY. NORA KEPT HERSELF BUSY ORGANIZ-ing all of the supplies she would bring with her to the cottage on the weekend. Elle helped her as much as possible. The twins were awake a little more during the day, but the women were still able to accomplish quite a bit each day. Ava, Emma, and Maggie were a huge help as well. They came over a couple of nights during the week to lend a helping hand.

The evening of the suit fittings for the guys arrived. Each of them had taken off work a bit earlier than usual. They wanted the fittings over with so they could get to the beer and pizza that Luke had promised them.

When they walked into the salon, the woman who would be helping them rolled her eyes. She remembered very clearly how much fun this crew had had the year before when they'd had their fittings for Jessie's wedding.

Danny had been the last to arrive. He smiled broadly at the laughing and joking around. They were pulling pink ties from the shelving and wrapping them around their foreheads like bandanas.

Danny had piqued the assistant's interest. She didn't recall him being part of the crew from the year before. She would have remembered that body. Oh, how those jeans and plaid shirt fit him perfectly. His laugh was wonderful!

She walked up to him and introduced herself. She held out her hand to shake his and said, "Hello, I'm Connie, and I'll be assisting all of you tonight."

Danny shook her hand politely. "Hi, I'm Danny. The stepfather of the groom."

"Is there something I can get for you?" She eyed him up and down.

Luke nudged Jessie to get his attention turned to Danny. Jessie smiled and nudged Mike, who did the same to Dave.

"Looks like the old man still has it." Dave chuckled.

As Danny continued his conversation with Connie, the boys stood in a row and crossed their arms across their chests. Danny caught a glimpse of them and turned red in the face. He cleared his throat and excused himself from Connie.

He walked toward the men and said, "What?"

"Nothing. Not a thing," Jessie replied and laughed.

"Then wipe those damn smiles off your faces."

Connie interrupted them. "Okay, so I have the suits you chose. You can go ahead and try them on. I went with the sizes from last year, but we may need to make some adjustments." She turned her attention to Danny. "I'll need to take your measurements though, Danny. If you would come with me, please."

Mike laughed out loud as he walked into the changing area. Danny turned a deeper shade of red.

UNITY

The guys got dressed in their black suits and straightened their ties before they entered the salon again. Connie sure was taking her sweet time with Danny.

Dave cleared his throat. "Just about done, Connie?"

"Uh, um, yes." She stood and smoothed her black dress. "I'll just go and grab a suit for you to try on, Danny." She left the room in a hurry.

"Hey, you guys look great!" Danny exclaimed.

"Not too bad for a bunch of hooligans, eh?" Jessie looked down at himself.

Connie walked back in with a suit on a hanger. She handed it to Danny with a sweet smile. "Here you go. Go ahead and try it on. Let me know if you need any help."

He took the suit from her and said, "Thanks. I'm good." He walked away, feeling the smiles of the guys on his back. He shook his head and kept walking.

She checked each of the suits the guys were wearing. Each of them could have used a bit of adjusting, but Connie felt that they looked just fine. The guys were comfortable and could move easily. They would only be wearing the jackets for the ceremony, and then they would likely be tossed to the side for the rest of the evening.

Danny came out in his suit, and was a little wary of the way Connie was looking at him.

"Oh, it looks great." She walked to him and ran her hands along the arms of the jacket. She moved her hands a little lower to touch the pant legs.

"Yep. It fits just fine. I'll go change now." He couldn't get out of there quickly enough.

Everyone changed back to their street clothes. Luke paid the bill, and they left.

Connie called after them. "Thanks for coming in guys. I'll have the suits ready for pickup early next week."

Danny pretended he didn't hear her, and kept walking. Mike slapped him on the back and laughed.

He drove them all to The Bar for the promised beer and pizza. Jessie found a corner table for them. The server arrived to take their orders.

"What'll you have, guys?"

Luke answered with, "We'll have a couple of large pizzas with all the fixings and a round of beers, please."

"Sure thing."

"Keep the beer coming, too! Luke's paying." Jessie chuckled.

Luke shook his head at his younger brother. He could knock back the pints pretty good himself, but Jessie was another story. Jesus, he could drink!

The beer arrived in record time. The server knew the Chase boys and how her good service would be rewarded. She smiled as she set the drinks down. "Cheers," she said.

The men raised their pints and repeated, "Cheers."

Luke's band members entered the bar a few minutes later. They easily found the groom's table by the level of noise.

"Hey, Luke."

"Hey, guys. Pull up a chair."

Four more chairs were pulled from vacant tables and added to the already full table. The server had seen the group enter, and quickly went to take their orders.

UNITY

Rob ordered a round of shooters for the group. Once they arrived, the small glasses were raised for another cheer of congratulations to Luke.

The pizza was devoured, and the beer flowed freely. The laughter grew louder as the evening progressed. The server made her way around the bar to announce last call. It was nearing two o'clock in the morning.

Luke asked the men if they wanted anything else. When the answer came as a no, he asked for the bill.

When she returned with the bill, Danny asked Luke to hand him a napkin. As Luke did as he was asked, Danny took the bill from the server. Luke shook his head in anger.

"No way, Danny. This is on me." He tried to grab it from him.

Danny smiled and held it out of his reach. "It kills me how you young lads think you can wrestle the bill from me. Jessie couldn't do it last time, and you won't this time." He stood and made his way to the cash register.

He was thanked profusely for his kindness and generosity when he returned to the table.

The group made their way outside with loud laughter. The cabs had been called and were lined up waiting for them.

Danny hadn't had very much to drink, so he had planned on driving himself home. He made sure the guys were safely in the cabs before he walked to his own truck. There, leaning against his vehicle, was Grace. She wore a tight tank top, short skirt, and thigh-high black boots.

"That was a long evening. I've been waiting for you for at least an hour," she said.

He shook his head. "What do you want, Grace?" he asked angrily.

"You."

"Already spoken for." He tried to reach by her to open his door.

She leaned into him. "I've missed you."

"I haven't missed you. Please step aside so I can go home to my wife."

She pouted. "Can you give me a ride home? My car broke down."

"No, but I'll call you a cab." He slid his hand into the front pocket of his jeans to retrieve his phone.

She slid her hand in next to his. "I'd rather you drove me home."

"I don't even know where you live." He removed her hand and pulled out his phone.

"It's not far. Come on. It's only a few minutes out of your way."

He frowned and gave in. "Get in." He unlocked the doors as she ran around the front of the truck to the passenger side.

He threw the truck into gear. "Where to?"

"Just up on Hilltop Street." She slid her hand across the console to lay it on his arm.

"Cut it out, Grace." He pulled his arm away.

"What is your wife giving you that I can't?"

He scowled at her. "Love, honesty, trust … shall I go on?"

"I can give you that."

"You've proven that you can't. And I'm not having this conversation with you."

She settled in the seat with a pout on her face.

Danny pulled into her parking lot a few minutes later.

"Will you walk me up to my apartment?"

"No."

"So, I'm to walk in, in the middle of the night, alone?"

"Jesus." He climbed out of his truck and slammed the door behind him.

She joined him at the front of the truck and slipped her arm through his. "Thank-you, Danny."

"Yeah."

She unlocked the main entrance and stood to the side of the door.

"I'm not going up with you."

"Why? Afraid some of those old feelings will come back?" She said it a little to sexily.

"Not in the least. What I'm afraid of is my wife's reaction to this stupidity." He turned to leave.

She placed both hands on either side of his face and kissed him soundly on the lips.

He pushed her back and stomped to his truck.

She stood with one hand on her hip and the other on her lips.

He climbed back into his truck and once again threw it into gear.

He contemplated telling Elle of what had just taken place. It was a long drive home with the thought swirling around in his head. He had zero interest in his ex-wife. He loved Elle.

He arrived home to the lights off in the house. He unlocked the door and quietly entered. He went directly to the shower to wash any trace of Grace off of himself.

Elle woke when he finally made it to bed.

"Hi, babe. How was your evening?"

"Fine."

"Okay. Did something happen?" Now she was wide awake with concern.

"Everything is fine."

"Okay." She leaned over to kiss him. "Good night, then. See you in the morning."

Danny had a restless sleep, and it showed when he walked into the kitchen to have breakfast with Elle.

"Wow. You look like shit."

"Good morning to you, too." He smiled as he walked towards her to kiss her and wrap her in a hug. He hung on for a few seconds longer. "I love you, Elle."

"Love you too. Are you okay?"

"I have something to tell you."

"What is it?" She set the tea towel on the counter.

"First of all, Connie at the salon was hitting on me."

Elle laughed. "Of course she did. Have you looked in a mirror lately? You are a very handsome man."

He smiled weakly. "And then Grace was waiting for me at my truck when I left The Bar."

Elle's smile faded abruptly. "And?"

He went on to tell her about the broken-down car and how he had driven her back to her apartment. He lowered his head.

"And?" She repeated the one-word question.

"She kissed me." He raised his head and looked his wife in the eyes.

"I see. And did you kiss her back?"

"No! I shoved her away and raced back home to you. I made it very clear that I was not interested."

"Okay, then."

"That's it? You're not mad?"

"Not at you." She turned to pour them each a coffee.

He approached her from behind and kissed her on the back of her neck as he wrapped his arms around her tiny waist. "So, you're not mad at me?"

She turned in his arms to face him. "It sounds like you actually want me to be upset."

"Well, I thought we'd argue, I'd apologize a hundred times, and then we'd have makeup sex."

Elle smiled. "I'm not mad."

He leaned in for a kiss.

She placed her index finger on his lips. "What I am is surprised at how easily she reeled you in. You are a very naïve man, my dear."

He looked shocked. "What do you mean?"

Elle shook her head. "Babe, she played you like a guitar."

"No, she didn't."

Elle smiled again. "So, let's go over this again. Her car broke down at what, one o'clock in the morning and she didn't call for assistance? She literally stood in the parking lot of The Bar waiting for you to come out."

Danny ran his hand through his hair and looked at the ceiling. "Damn, she's good."

"Mm-hmm. And, where was it that you dropped her off?"

"The apartments on Hilltop Street."

"Good to know." She turned to return to the task of pouring coffee.

"Elle, don't you dare go over there!"

"Why not?"

"Well, because I've dealt with the situation."

She turned to face him and handed him his coffee, tilted her head to one side, and said, "Did you?"

"Yeah."

"I feel like maybe I need to deal with it, too."

Danny took a sip of his coffee while eyeing her. "What are you going to do?"

She tapped his nose lightly with her index finger. "Don't you worry about that." She moved to the sofa to sit. Oh, how she was looking forward to this conversation with Grace.

They dropped the subject and discussed their plans for the day.

Danny had a few job sites to check on, and Elle had planned on going to Nora and Luke's to help with the last of the wedding plans.

They kissed at the door and went their separate ways.

Elle drove directly to Hilltop Street. She found Grace's name on the plaque and pressed the button. No answer. She waited outside the door. As luck would have it, a resident of the apartment building came out and politely held the door open for her so she could enter.

She found Grace's apartment number on the brass plate and climbed the flight of stairs. She knocked on the apartment door. After a few minutes, her patience began to run thin. She pounded on the door with her fist.

Finally, a groggy Grace jerked the door open. "What?" She was shocked to see Elle standing there.

UNITY

Elle eyed her attire of an oversized T-shirt. Her hair was a mess, and her makeup had smudged under her eyes.

"I assume you would have worn something a little sexier if you'd been able to talk my husband into sleeping with you last night." Elle pushed passed her.

Grace was affronted. "Who the hell do you think you are barging into my home?"

Elle smiled. Perfect. She turned to face Grace. "Who the hell do you think you are barging in on my marriage?"

Grace crossed her arms under her breasts. "I have no idea what you're talking about."

"Oh, really? Let's see. You don't consider trying to tempt my husband up to your apartment at two o'clock in the morning barging in on our marriage?"

"He deserves better than you."

"And that would be you?"

"Yes."

Elle tilted head back and laughed out loud. "You are such an idiot! When you walked out on your marriage, it ended. Forever"

"Get out of my home!" Grace pointed to the open door.

"Sure. As soon as I'm done speaking with you."

"I'm not talking to the likes of you."

Elle took a step closer and spoke very precisely. "You have no idea who you're dealing with."

Grace looked her up and down. "You don't scare me."

Elle took another step closer. Grace took a step back. "If you come near my husband again, I promise you'll be sorry."

"Whatever."

"Hmm. I used to know a person who would say that to me. He's no longer walking among the living."

Grace's eyes grew wide. "What?"

"Yep, that's right. I'm not threatening you. I promise you that you will pay dearly for your actions." With that said, Elle walked toward the door. "Have a nice day."

"You're fucking crazy!"

Elle smiled. "Yes, I am." She left the building and returned to her vehicle. She was not surprised to see Grace's car parked in the lot.

She made her way to Nora's with a grin on her face. She knocked and opened the door. "Hi, Nora! It's just me."

"Hi, Elle. Come on in. I'm in the nursery."

She walked in to see Nora changing the twins' diapers. She stepped closer to the change table. "Hi, guys!" She was rewarded with gurgles.

Once Jarrett had been changed, Elle scooped him up and chatted away in baby talk. The women moved to the living room as soon as Nora finished changing Justin.

"Coffee?" asked Nora.

"Sure. Thanks." She placed the boys in the middle of the big comforter on the floor and knelt to play with them. "Are we going to make plans for Mommy and Daddy's wedding?" She asked the twins, knowing she wouldn't get anything but a smile from them. She tickled their bellies.

"I think I've got just about everything ready for the big day!" Nora called out from the kitchen.

"Great! Have you heard back from your parents yet?"

"No," Nora said with disappointment in her voice.

"Oh, I'm sorry, honey."

"Welcome to my life. It's just Mom being Mom."

"Well, you just let me know if there's something I can do to help."

Nora came into the room with two mugs full of coffee. "Thanks, Elle."

They spent time playing with the kids and making final arrangements for the wedding. The gang would head up to the cottages on the weekend with supplies, and do a quick rehearsal.

Elle left a few hours later and went directly to Danny's office.

Lois sat at her desk, tapping at the keys on her keyboard. She lifted her head when she heard the door open, and smiled when she saw Elle.

"Hi, Elle! How are you, honey?"

"Good! How are you, Lois?"

"Good. Danny's just going over contracts, but I'm sure he'd love to be distracted by you!" She laughed as Elle made her way to his office. She knocked and walked in. He was on the phone. Danny smiled and motioned for her to sit. "Okay, Bob. Thanks. I'll get back to you by the end of the day with a price." He ended his call, hung up the phone, and rounded his desk. He took Elle's face in his hands. "This is a nice surprise."

"Want to have lunch with me?"

"Of course!"

"Great! I was thinking I'd tell you how my morning went, and then we'd have makeup sex."

He raised his eyebrows. "Jesus. What did you do now?"

She went on to tell him about the conversation she'd had with Grace.

Danny laughed. "She must be shaking in her thigh-high boots."

"Thigh-high boots?"

Danny smirked. "That's what she was wearing last night."

"Hmm. Funny, you didn't mention that."

"So anyway, about the makeup sex?"

Elle laughed. "Come on. I'm kidnapping you for the rest of the day. We'll stop and buy some food and head to the beach."

"Is Lois at her desk?" he asked warily, as he peeked over her shoulder.

Elle smiled. "I'll handle Lois."

"Okay. She's a lot tougher than she looks, though," he said skeptically.

She took him by the hand and walked through the reception area. She stopped at Lois's desk and winked. "Danny will be back in the morning."

"Gotcha."

They walked out the door hand in hand.

"That was easy," said Danny.

"I know how to deal with women."

"Apparently."

They enjoyed lunch on the beach of The Dunes and each other's bodies for the afternoon.

CHAPTER 22

THE WEEKEND ARRIVED WITH A HEAT WAVE, AND THE SUN WAS SHINING BRIGHTLY.

Elle and Danny left their home on Thursday evening to get a head start on the weekend. They planned on spending plenty of time floating around in the lake.

They were surprised when Elle's kids showed up shortly after them.

"Taking tomorrow off?" asked Elle, as she helped with the twins.

"Yep. Way too fucking hot to work!" Luke answered. "Ava and Jessie are only five minutes behind us. Dave, Mike, and the girls will be up tomorrow." He shot a glance at Danny. "They said their boss would never give them a Friday off." He laughed as he said it.

"If they bought the business from me, they could do whatever the hell they want."

"Is that an option?" Luke asked, as he carried groceries to his cottage.

"It's always been an option." Danny grabbed some of the wedding supplies and followed Luke.

"How much are you looking for?"

"Couple million. Why? Are you interested?" Danny asked with raised brows.

"I'd like to talk to Mike and Dave first, but I think that Jessie and I could be investors for them to buy it." He kept walking.

"Sounds interesting."

"Owning your own business is much more profitable than being an employee."

"That's for sure."

Elle helped Nora settle the boys and asked, "Do you want to store the wedding supplies in our cottage? We have plenty of room."

"Oh, that would be awesome. Thank-you!"

Elle nodded and stopped Danny before he could put down the box he was carrying. She pointed to their own cottage and asked him to set it in the corner of the family room.

"Got it." He turned and walked in that direction.

Jessie and Ava showed up and pitched in immediately. The trucks were unloaded in record time.

Nora dressed the twins in their little swim trunks and handed Justin to Luke. "Let's go for a swim and cool off." She scooped up her long hair to cool her neck.

"Good idea." They changed quickly and made their way to the water. The rest of the family followed in their swimsuits.

The twins weren't overly happy about the temperature of the water, but were soon happy to be cooled off.

Luke and Jessie each held a child in their arms while they stood in the water. The girls floated close by.

"Hey Jessie, I was talking to Danny just before you got here."

"Yeah, about what?"

"He's thinking of retiring and selling the company to Dave and Mike."

"Nice. It'd be a great opportunity for them."

"Exactly. We'll talk to them tomorrow about it but, I was wondering if you'd be interested in investing in it."

"Absolutely! Danny's built up one hell of a business."

"He has. Okay, so we'll talk to the guys tomorrow?"

"Yep." Jessie dunked Justin in the water a little further. Justin gasped a little, but thoroughly enjoyed it.

Luke did the same with Jarrett and got the same reaction. The girls smiled at the scene.

Once everyone had had enough of the water, they made their way back to the cottages to change clothes and light the fire.

Nora came to the fire with the twins dressed in pajamas and light blankets around their shoulders. Danny and Elle held out their arms to take them from her. Nora smiled and handed them over.

It was an early night to bed for everyone. It had been a hot and tiring day.

The next morning was just as hot as the day before. A few chores were done for the wedding, and the rest of the day was spent by the lake.

Mike, Dave, Maggie, and Emma arrived by late afternoon. They could hear the laughter down by the water. They quickly unloaded the truck and changed into swimsuits. They came running down the path and dove straight in. All four of them came up gasping from the coolness of the water, but had huge grins on their faces. Smiling faces welcomed them.

"Hey, everyone!"

"That was quite an entrance." Luke laughed.

"Christ, it's hot!" Mike said.

"Glad you made it up early to enjoy this," Danny remarked with a smile.

"Don't worry, Dad. All the jobs are done."

"I never doubted it for a second." He strolled to the edge of the water with cold beer for the four of them. He was thanked before they all guzzled it down.

"Can I hold one of the boys?" Emma asked Nora.

"Of course. Here you go." She handed Justin over. Ava handed Jarrett to Maggie.

The women all seemed to congregate together, as did the men.

Luke and Jessie looked at each other and nodded.

"Hey guys, have you given any thought to buying the business from Danny?"

Dave shrugged. "We've been batting it back and forth for a while now. He says he'd like to retire in the next year or so. Why?"

"Well, if you're serious about buying it, Jessie and I would like to be investors if you're interested. We would just be the money guys. We wouldn't have or want any say in the day-to-day operations. That would be all up to you two."

Dave and Mike looked at each other and nodded.

"Sounds good. You realize Dad wants a couple of million for it, right?"

"Yep."

"Okay. So maybe we should sit down one day soon and work it out. We'll make Dad an offer and go from there."

"Perfect." Jessie shook their hands, and Luke did the same.

Elle left the group to make up a picnic lunch to be enjoyed by the water's edge. Maggie and Emma brought the boys out of the water to dry them off and wrap them in towels. Nora and Ava sat with them and chatted.

Luke and Jessie headed up to refill their coolers with beer.

Dave and Mike plunked themselves down beside Danny.

"What a great place to come up to." Mike lay on his back and stacked his hands beneath his head.

"It would be nice if you could spend more time up here, Dad," Dave said.

Danny smiled. He knew what was going on. He had overheard their conversation with Jessie and Luke.

"Oh, I don't know. I think I'd get pretty sick of it if I spent too much time up here."

Mike sat up. "Really?"

"No! I'm just kidding. I would love to be up here a lot more than we already are. Look, if you guys want the company, it's yours. Don't stress over it. We'll sit down Monday morning at the office and make a plan, okay?"

"Really?" Mike repeated.

"Really."

"Okay! Thanks, Dad," Dave remarked.

"Don't thank me yet. It's not free, and it's a lot of work."

"Yeah, we know."

Danny handed them each a beer. "Monday."

"Monday." His sons said in unison.

Dinner had been prepared while the twins napped, and the huge picnic table was set for the ten adults.

The chatter was lively as usual; there never seemed to be any shortage of conversation.

Luke pulled out his guitar once the fire was lit. Most joined in with the singing. Some just hummed along. It had been a wonderful day and evening.

Danny and Elle eventually excused themselves from the group and went ahead to bed.

He pulled her close once they had slid under the sheets. "So, how do you feel about spending a whole lot more time with this old guy?"

"I'd love it! Are you finally ready to slow down a bit at the company?"

He tucked her head onto his shoulder. "More than slow down. I think I'd like to retire. I was talking to the boys earlier, and they feel they're ready to buy it and take over."

Elle raised her head. "Oh, good for them! And, good for you!" She kissed him. "Let me show you how we'd be spending those retired days."

Danny laughed as she attacked his body.

The following morning, Danny and Elle took a walk along the pathways, with mugs of coffee in their hands.

"It'll be nice to spend more time up here next summer."

"You bet. I look forward to the nights." Danny smirked as he said the words.

Elle gave him a swat and giggled.

The gang was sitting at the picnic table, sipping their coffee, when Danny and Elle returned.

"Want some breakfast?" Jessie asked.

"Are you cooking?" Danny asked warily.

Jessie laughed. "No. Ava's making breakfast for everyone."

"Then sure." Danny smirked.

Luke went to get the paper plates while Jessie went for the condiments.

Ava came out a few minutes later with a platter loaded down with French toast. Maggie came out with the home fries and bacon that she and Emma had prepared.

"Wow! This looks amazing." Elle sat and admired the feast.

"Dig in," Mike said.

"So, I hear this big lug will be spending more time with me," she said to Dave and Mike as she ran a hand down Danny's back.

"We sure hope so."

"Good! And good for you guys."

Mike looked over at Jessie and Luke. "We already have investors lined up."

"Oh yeah? Who?" Elle had missed the look as she ate her breakfast.

"Luke and Jessie."

Elle's eyes grew wide. "Really? Hey, that's awesome!"

The conversation continued as they enjoyed their breakfast.

"We'll work it all out with Dad on Monday," Dave remarked.

Everyone nodded. It was a big step for Dave and Mike, but everyone was confident in their decision.

"So, what do we need to do today for the wedding?" Jessie asked around a mouthful of food.

Nora listed what she'd like to have done before the big day coming up the next weekend.

The table was cleared and jobs were given out for wedding preparations.

CHAPTER 23

ON MONDAY MORNING, DAVE AND MIKE SAT ACROSS THE DESK FROM THEIR father. He had already asked Lois to hold all of his calls.

"Ready to discuss the purchase of Dan's Designs?" He smiled encouragingly at his sons.

"Yes." They both felt nervous and a little overwhelmed.

"Okay. First off, I've changed my mind on the purchase price."

"Dad, I'm not sure we can make any more than two million work," Mike said a little sadly.

"I know, son. That's why I've lowered the price to one million."

Both boys' eyes widened. "What? Why would you do that?" Dave asked.

"Because I can. You guys have proven yourselves over and over again." He spread his arms wide. "I don't want to spend the rest of my days coming to work. I want to sit back, relax, and watch you guys spread your wings and fly."

Dave's eyes filled with tears. "That's quite a gift for us, Dad."

Danny smiled and put his hand forward. "Do we have a deal on one million?"

The boys looked at each other and smiled. Both of their hands shot out to shake with their father.

"I've already contacted the lawyer and had him draw up the paperwork. Take a look at it and sign it if you're comfortable with it."

Dave and Mike quickly glanced at it and signed with a flourish.

"Congratulations! You are now business owners."

Mike ran his fingers through his hair. "You're gonna hang around for a few months to show us the ropes up here in the office, right?"

"Sure."

Dave stood and went to hug his father. "Thank-you for everything you do for us."

"I wouldn't have it any other way." He hugged his son tightly.

Mike hugged him next. "We'll make you proud, Dad."

"You always do."

They entered the reception area to cheers of congratulations from all of the employees, including Lois, who had been joined by Maggie, Emma, Luke, Nora, Jarrett, Justin, Jessie, Ava, and Elle.

Danny smiled hugely. "I'd like to introduce the new owners of Dan's Designs!"

Lois had already handed out mimosas to the group. She handed three more to Danny and his sons.

She slapped each of them on the back. "Good for you!"

Danny made a toast to his sons. "May your ambition be the path to your success. Congratulations, boys!"

UNITY

The room cleared out once the drinks were finished. Each member of their family took turns shaking Dave's and Mike's hands and hugging them before leaving.

Mike and Dave couldn't wipe the smiles off their faces. They went out to the warehouse to start their day of work.

Their girlfriends invited the family to Mike and Emma's home for dinner.

The family arrived with armloads of snacks and coolers full of beer.

The pizza was delivered, and was devoured immediately.

The evening was fun and loud. So loud that none of them heard the doorbell ring.

Grace appeared at the patio door.

Jessie looked up from digging in his cooler when the space turned dead silent.

"Mom? What are you doing here?" Mike demanded.

"Looks like I've interrupted a party. What are we celebrating?"

"Uh, nothing. Just a family get together."

"I see. Can I speak with you and Dave for a moment, please?"

"Sure." Both men stood and walked through the patio door to the kitchen.

"What's up?" Dave asked.

"I've come to tell you that I'm leaving. I'm going back to Europe. There's nothing here for me, and it's time to go."

Dave nodded. "See ya. Thanks for stopping by." He left the kitchen and went to join his family.

Mike stood where he was. "Why'd you bother coming back at all?"

"To be honest, I was hoping to reconcile with your father and build a relationship with you and Dave. It's not happening, so I'm leaving."

"Safe travels." Mike left her standing alone in the kitchen as he went to join his brother.

Danny walked in. "I hear you're leaving."

"I am. Unless you'd rather I stay." She said it a little too sweetly.

Elle came in behind Danny and placed her hand in his.

"No, that's okay. We're good here," Elle said.

Grace scowled. "Then I'll be off."

"I'd say it was a pleasure meeting you but, I'd be lying," Elle said.

"Same here. Goodbye." Grace retrieved her purse from the counter and stomped out the door.

"Good riddance," Danny said, as he ran his hands through his hair. He bent to kiss his wife. "The good news just keeps coming today!"

They went back to the party.

Dave and Mike had sobered a bit after seeing their mother.

"Why didn't you tell her that you'd just bought the company?" asked Jessie.

"Because she wouldn't care. She's too damn selfish."

Mike agreed as he reached for his beer. He held it up and said, "Cheers to the amazing people in my life."

The group joined in on the toast and smiled.

"To family," Danny said.

The mood picked up again as the drinks flowed, and Grace was forgotten.

It turned into a late night once again.

The following morning, Danny walked into the warehouse with his hands behind his back.

Mike looked at him and said, "If you have a hammer, I'm going to fire you."

Danny laughed. He brought his hands out front holding two strong black coffees for his sons.

"Thank-you," they said gratefully.

"That was fun last night!"

"It sure was," Mike answered.

"So, did you want to talk about your mother?"

"Nope."

"Me neither."

"Okay. I'm here if you want to talk."

"Yeah, we know. Thanks, Dad. And thanks for the coffee."

"I was thinking we should all head up to the cottages on Thursday night to help out with the final details for the wedding."

"Sounds good. We'll make sure everything here is done before we leave."

Danny smiled. "The first rule of owning a business is to delegate. You are the bosses now. Give some of the workload to the others."

Both boys nodded. That would take some getting used to.

Danny went back to his office to make some calls. He wanted to contact his customers and contacts to let them know that they would be dealing with Mike and Dave soon. He was congratulated by each person he reached out to. The majority of their customers had dealt with both Mike and Dave in the past, and were not worried about the changeover.

He felt good about his decision to retire. He'd have to find a hobby.

Danny arrived home in the early afternoon to find Elle digging through their closet.

She looked up and smiled at him. "You're home early!"

"Yep. You'd better get used to me be around a whole lot more." He smiled back at her.

"Sounds good to me." She stood and kissed him.

"What are you looking for?"

"I'm trying to find some of my nicer sandals to bring up to the cottage for the wedding weekend."

"Need help?"

"No. They're not in here. Want a beer?"

"You bet."

They moved out to the deck. "So, we'll go up to the lake Thursday afternoon?" Danny played with her hair as he posed the question.

"Yep. I think all the kids will be up around the same time. Dave and Mike and the girls, too, right?"

"That's their plan. I spoke with the boys this morning."

"And how were they feeling?"

"Hungover." Danny smiled about the fact they were going to fire him if he'd had a hammer in his hands. He told the story to Elle.

"I don't know how they all do it! I can drink my share, but not like that!"

They shared a leisurely afternoon and a light dinner. Elle laid out the clothes they would need for the weekend, while Danny worked in the garage.

UNITY

Nora was franticly going over her list of things to bring with her. She had just gotten Jarrett and Justin to bed. She would normally spend quiet evenings with Luke, but they were both busy working on last-minute projects for the upcoming weekend. Neither seemed nervous—just a little overwhelmed.

Luke came up the stairs from the basement. "Need help with anything, babe?"

"No, thanks. I'm just double checking my list." She bent her head to go over the list once more.

Luke came up behind her and wrapped her in a hug. He rested his chin on the top of her head.

"No wedding is ever perfect. If we miss something, well, we miss something. It's going to be a beautiful day just being surrounded by our family and friends." He released her enough to turn her around. The sad look in her eyes cracked his heart. "You still haven't heard back from your parents, have you?"

She shook her head in answer.

"Okay. Don't you worry about it any longer. I'll figure it out."

"Thanks, Luke. I'm not so sure there's much you can do, though."

He tilted his head and smiled. He touched the tip of her nose. "I've got this." He left the room and went to the nursery to look in on his sons.

He let Nora know that the kids were fine and that he was going for a shower. He called Jessie as soon as he reached the bedroom.

"Hey, Luke. Nervous yet?" He chuckled into the phone.

"Not about the wedding. Nora's parents haven't responded to the invitation yet."

"Man, that sucks. What are you going to do?"

"I'm not too sure. I have a few more days to figure something out."

"Mom and Danny could walk her down the aisle."

"Hey! Yeah, they could." Luke smiled at his brother's solution. "Oh, but they were going to bring the kids up the aisle."

"No worries. Ava and I will do that."

Luke frowned. "You kinda have another job that day. Like standing beside me."

"Listen, Luke; you don't need this headache right now. Leave it with Ava and me. We'll figure it out. Every person attending is your friend. It won't be hard to have someone step up and help out."

"Yeah, you're right. Okay, I'll leave it with you."

"Good. Gotta go. Ava and I have work to do." He chuckled again and disconnected.

Luke had his shower and made his way back down the stairs. Nora was packing up items she felt she would need for the twins over the weekend.

He rubbed her back with one hand as he set his other over her busy ones. "Coming to bed?"

"In a minute."

"You need your rest, babe. Come on." He led her from the family room and into their bedroom.

"Your hot bath is waiting for you." He opened the door to the en-suite. He had lit candles and filled the tub with scented beads.

Nora sighed at his sweetness. She stood on her tiptoes to kiss his lips gently. "You're too good to me."

"Never." He kissed her back and gently pushed her into the room. "Now, go and relax."

CHAPTER 24

ON WEDNESDAY EVENING, LUKE AND NORA'S LANEWAY FILLED WITH TRUCKS. Every family member showed up to load their vehicles with whatever Luke and Nora handed them.

Nora hadn't wanted a wedding planner, so she and Luke had to bring and set up everything she wanted on her special day.

Luke installed Jarrett and Justin's car seats in Elle's SUV. She and Danny would keep the boys overnight and bring them to the cottages the following morning. They wanted Luke and Nora to concentrate on the wedding and not worry about the children.

Danny and Elle left shortly after arriving, with the vehicle loaded down with every imaginable thing that the kids could need. The rest of the gang stayed to help Luke and Nora.

Danny and Elle thoroughly enjoyed their time alone with their grandchildren. Elle was happy to be babysitting and not lugging stuff to her truck!

Thursday morning arrived with a few rain showers, but that didn't deter anyone.

"Let it rain now and be sunny on Saturday!" Ava said.

The convoy of trucks was on the road by ten o'clock in the morning. Everyone was in good spirits as they pulled away. Luke reached across the console to hold his soon-to-be wife's hand. "Doin' okay?"

She nodded and smiled. "You?"

"Absolutely! In two days, I'll be a married man and off the market."

Nora gave him a swat as she laughed.

Elle and Danny greeted everyone as they pulled in the laneway of the cottages. They each pushed a stroller. They couldn't keep the grins off their faces.

Nora reached them first, with many thanks for the babysitting. She then kissed each of her sons and tickled their bellies. "You two look like you had fun!" The boys cooed back at her.

"Okay. We'll take care of the boys while you all do the heavy lifting." Elle called out the remark as she turned to continue her walk with her husband and grandchildren.

Jessie smirked, jerked his head, and turned to Ava. "Why the fuck didn't we offer to babysit?"

Ava swatted him and started carrying the lightweight items while Jessie grumbled half-heartedly. They actually had fun joking around with everyone involved in the process. After a couple of hours, Luke opened his cooler and offered beer to the guys and wine to the women.

They thankfully accepted and sat to rest for a few moments.

Danny and Elle came back from their walk just as they had sat down.

"Slackers!" Danny joked.

UNITY

"Must be nice to just wander around the woods while we work our asses off!" Jessie retorted as he twisted the cap off his beer.

"Sure is!" Danny chuckled and reached for one of the beers in the cooler.

"Lunch is ready when you are." Elle had prepared a platter of sandwiches. "We've got beef on the grill for dinner. So, start with this." She set it on the picnic table and watched the food disappear.

It didn't take long to unload the rest of the supplies from the truck. The next day would be for setting up tables, chairs, tarps, and the simple altar that Luke had made from the cedar trees in the woods.

The evening had been spent around the fire after the wonderful meal Elle and Danny had prepared. The boys had been settled in their crib in Danny and Elle's cabin. They would spend the weekend with Grandma and Grandpa.

The evening was an early one. They all knew that there was a lot of work ahead of them the next day.

Maggie and Emma made a huge breakfast of pancakes for the crew. Working on full bellies made everything go quite smoothly.

By late afternoon, the tarps had been strung from trees, with little white lights spread atop them. Enough round tables and chairs had been set up to accommodate the guests. The centerpieces Ava had made would be placed on the tables the following morning. They were bundles of cedar with tall, slender candles nestled in the center.

The men hauled out the benches that Dave and Mike had built for the guests to sit on during the ceremony. They had been lacquered to a high gloss. The men had done a beautiful job of them. Luke, Danny, and Jessie assembled the cedar altar while Nora intertwined lights through it.

When Elle came out of the cabin with the twins, she was shocked at how much had been accomplished. She didn't remember falling asleep with the boys.

"This looks amazing!" She took it all in with a smile on her face. Nora stepped forward to relieve her of Jarrett and Justin.

"Thank-you so much for taking caring of these two." She kissed each of her sons.

"You're welcome, honey." She turned her attention to the crew. "Who wants to cool off in the lake?"

Everyone dropped their tools and raced to the water. After an hour of floating around, they each dried off and headed back up to search the coolers for something cold to drink.

Danny had made burgers for dinner. Elle had prepared the salads and had bought pies for dessert.

"So, are you happy with the progress, Nora?" Luke asked around a mouthful of food.

"Yes! Thank-you, everyone, for all your hard work."

Luke raised his beer bottle and said, "To tomorrow!"

All bottles and glasses were raised to cheer.

"Where are you sleeping tonight, Luke?" Jessie asked.

"In my cabin. Why?"

"You're not supposed to see the bride the night before the wedding."

Luke glanced at his sons and then rolled his eyes at his brother. "I think we can do away with traditions."

Jessie smiled, tilted his bottle, and drank deeply.

UNITY

Once the table had been cleared, Danny was surprised to see everyone head off to bed so early. The fire hadn't even been lit.

Jessie walked up to Danny and his mom once Nora had gone to her cabin for the night.

"So, we're all set for the plan tomorrow?"

"Yep!"

"Perfect. See you in the morning." He shook Danny's hand and kissed his mother's cheek.

They smiled and walked into their own cabin. The twins were softly snoring as they held each other's hand in sleep.

The clouds had rolled in during the night. The day was a little gray, but rain was not in the forecast.

Everyone made their breakfast and ate in their own cabins. They greeted each other by the picnic table shortly after.

"Happy wedding day!" Emma hugged Nora and then Luke.

Maggie repeated the sentiment and hugged them as well.

Jessie stepped forward. He kissed Nora on the cheek. "You sure you want to marry this loser?" He jerked his thumb at Luke.

Nora laughed and hugged him tightly. "It's the only way I'll get to see you all the time!"

Jessie threw his head back and laughed. Luke rolled his eyes.

Elle and Danny came out with the twins and wished Luke and Nora a fabulous day. They were hugged and kissed once again.

"Okay. Enough already! We've got shit to do!" Dave said loudly as he made his way to the couple.

Mike and the rest laughed at his remark.

Nora kissed her children before she was hauled off to her cabin for a shower, hair, and makeup. The girls surrounded her with love and care.

Elle would join them later. She would be with the children until it was her time to get ready.

Some of the guests came early to set up tents for the night. They were tucked in among the trees so they couldn't be seen during the ceremony. Help was given to spread the sand out smoothly, pick up branches, and any other debris that lay around. Elle sent them all to the showers with a warning to hurry up and get dressed.

The remaining guests began to arrive just as the women had finished their final touches. Emma had done a wonderful job of their hair and makeup.

Before Nora would let them leave, she handed them each a little black velvet box. As the women opened them, she said to each of them, "Thank-you for being my rock."

Their eyes widened when they saw the half-carat diamond earrings nestled in the boxes. They quickly set them in their earlobes.

Nora was hugged, kissed, and thanked before she gently pushed them toward the door.

The photographers had taken hundreds of photos of the women as they dressed, and the same of the men. Jarrett and Justin proved to be quite photogenic in their little black suits.

Luke handed each of his groomsmen a black ball cap with their names embroidered across the back and then dark sunglasses to wear during the wedding.

"Cool!" Jessie remarked as he slid both on.

UNITY

The photographer snapped a beautiful photo of Nora as she held the curtain back on the window and looked out at the guests. No one but Elle was aware of the fact that she was hoping to see her parents.

The men made their way out of Jessie's cabin to the altar. They smiled at the guests. It was so nice to see Hank sitting there in the back row. Was that Jillian with him? Jesus!

Danny held back to wait for Elle. They were to walk up the aisle with Jarrett and Justin in their decorated strollers, but plans had changed since Nora's parents had decided not to show up. Elle was extremely disappointed in them.

Danny's jaw dropped when he saw her. Her beauty never ceased to amaze him. He walked toward her with his natural swagger. He reached her and ran his thumb across her bottom lip.

"You are absolutely beautiful." He kissed her and then whispered, "Do we have the grandkids tonight?"

"I'll try to convince Emma or Maggie to take them." She smiled sweetly.

He groaned and took her by the hand.

Once the women had made their way up the sandy path to join the others, Elle and Danny quietly walked up behind Nora and offered her their arms. Nora's eyes grew wide and filled with tears.

"It would be our honor to walk you up the aisle to meet Luke."

"I thought I'd have to walk alone."

"Not on our watch," Danny said.

Nora simply nodded and hooked her arms in theirs.

"We love you, Nora," Elle whispered.

"And I love you guys. Thank-you."

The trio slowly made their way to the door.

Nora stopped. "Jarrett and Justin?"

"Are being escorted up the aisle as we speak." Danny smiled and opened the door.

Nora peaked out and watched Luke's band members wheel the two strollers past her. Their smiles were blinding.

The little sign hanging on the front of Jarrett's stroller read, "Daddy ... here comes our girl!"

The little sign hanging on the front of Justin's stroller read, "And she's beautiful!"

Nora smiled at the handiwork of Danny. "I love that!"

"Good! Shall we go?"

The band wheeled the twins up the aisle as they hummed their version of "Here Comes the Bride."

"Aww," could be heard from every guest. Luke smiled proudly.

The strollers were parked off to the side. Two of the band members, Grayson and Adam, pulled the boys free and set them on their laps.

With Danny and Elle flanking her, Nora smiled brilliantly and walked toward the love of her life.

Luke was floored by Nora's beauty. Her elegance as she floated up the aisle shook him to the core. The look on his face had Jessie patting his back. Luke and Nora locked eyes and didn't let go.

Danny and Elle kissed her cheeks before releasing her and taking their seats. There wasn't a dry eye in the crowd.

Luke stepped closer to take her by the hand. "My God, you are beautiful." She smiled sweetly.

UNITY

The minister grinned and asked the guests to take their seats.

"Before we get started, I have got to say that those two little boys are absolutely adorable." The crowd laughed and clapped.

Nora and Luke glanced at their sons and smiled proudly.

"Okay. Here we go." The minister said a few words, and then asked Nora to go ahead and say her vows.

She delicately cleared her throat.

"Luke. My Luke. I love you with all of my heart. I could not imagine my life without you and our sons. You make my world complete. I promise to spend the rest of my days being the best wife and mother I can be. I love you."

Luke's eyes filled as he held her hands.

"Nora. You have just said the exact words that describe yourself to me. I love that we have this beautiful, crazy life together, and I wouldn't change a thing. You, Jarrett, and Justin are my world. I love each of you to the moon and back."

Nora squeezed his hands.

The minister sniffed and swiped at her eyes. She turned to Jessie to ask for the rings. He nodded and reached into his front pocket.

Luke expected Jessie to pull some sort of stunt, but was surprised when he gladly handed the rings to the minister without mishap.

They exchanged rings and kissed with a flourish.

The minister looked at Jessie again. He shot Grayson and Adam a quick glance. They both stood and carried Jarrett and Justin to the altar. They handed the children to their parents. The boys were snuggled instantly.

"I now pronounce you husband and wife ... and the sweetest little family I have ever seen." The minister smiled broadly as the twins were hoisted in the air. The cheers from the guests echoed off the surrounding forest.

The bride and groom made their way back down the aisle, with their boys bouncing on their hips.

After spending a few moments with their guests, the family of four walked down to the water's edge for more photos. The rest of the guests joined them within twenty minutes. Nora had wanted pictures of everyone together.

The photographer stood as high on the hill as she could, and took photos of the entire group on the sandy beach.

The caterers had set the tables and poured champagne while the group was being photographed. The sun had just started to set. Jessie flipped the switch for the tiny lights. The atmosphere changed instantly to feel as though they were under a blanket of stars.

A few speeches were given during the meal.

Jessie stood. "I would like to make a toast." All eyes turned to him. He cleared his throat before he spoke.

"Nora, you are breathtakingly beautiful in your wedding gown. Now that you share our last name, you are responsible for Luke. I've had enough of babysitting this guy!" He jerked his thumb toward his brother. Luke rolled his eyes as the crowd erupted into laughter.

"Just kidding. Luke, I am so happy for you today. You finally got the girl of your dreams to say yes!" He adjusted his ball cap as the guests laughed again. Nora smirked at him. "Now for the big news. Your wedding party thought long and hard about what to give you for a wedding gift. We

UNITY

didn't come up with anything." He shrugged his shoulders. Luke shook his head at his jokester of a brother. Jessie smiled. "We've decided to send you on a two-week long river cruise!"

Nora covered her mouth with her hands in surprise. Luke smiled and thanked them.

From one of the tables, Elle shouted out, "Babysitting services included!" She and Danny were bouncing the boys on their laps.

Nora and Luke smiled and nodded as the crowd giggled.

Luke rose and hugged his brother. He took Nora by the hand before he spoke.

"Thank-you to everyone for being here with us today. It means the world to us to have our family and friends here to celebrate." Nora gave him a nudge, signally that she had something to add. "I would also like to thank you all. We had perfect weather, didn't we?" The guests cheered. "I want to say a special thank-you to Danny and Elle for walking me up the aisle today. I love you both so much." Her eyes filled with tears as did Danny and Elle's. Nora and Luke walked toward them and hugged them each tightly.

"Best parents ever." Danny was shocked to be called his parent. He'd never heard the words from Elle's kids, and it meant the world to him. Elle could feel her heart swell in her chest with happiness.

The evening proceeded with dancing to the band playing. Luke even joined them for a few of the songs.

Ava approached Elle. "I'm really tired, so I think I'll head off to bed."

"Okay, honey. Are you feeling okay?" She rested her hand on Ava's growing belly.

"Oh, yeah. No worries. I'll take Jarrett and Justin with me if you like. I think they've had enough for one day." She smiled as she saw them nodding off in their strollers.

"Are you sure?"

"Yep. I could use the company and the quiet."

They helped her with settling the kids before returning to the party.

Elle approached Hank and Jillian.

"So, this is the man you've been seeing?"

Jillian smiled. "It is. This is Hank."

"Yes, I know. We purchased this property from him."

Jillian looked at Hank. "You used to own this?"

Hank nodded. "Great place isn't it?"

Elle asked Hank if he would excuse herself and Jillian for a moment. Jillian touched his hand and promised to be right back. She walked away with Elle.

"I'm glad you and Hank have found each other."

"Thank-you. He's such a nice man."

"I'm a little concerned that Chase will now know where my family comes on weekends, though."

Jillian tilted her head slightly. "I would never purposely put your family in harm's way."

"I know that but, how do you plan to keep it from him?"

"I hadn't really thought of it, Elle. I was just looking for some happiness."

"And I am happy for you, Jillian, but my children and grandchildren's lives have already been in dangerous situations because of him."

"Are you telling me to stop seeing Hank?"

"No. But you have to promise me that Chase will never find out about this place. It's bad enough that he knows our home addresses."

"You have my word. I'll speak to Hank about it as well."

"Thank-you."

Jillian made her way back to Hank with a heavy heart. When would Chase stop taking her happiness from her?

CHAPTER 25

THE WEEKS PASSED BY IN A BLUR. THE WEDDING HAD BEEN A HUGE SUCCESS.
The bonus had been great weather. Jessie's tarps had provided the much-needed shade from the sun.

Ava had been exhausted since the week before the wedding. She had hoped to be feeling better and more rested after the party, but she still battled fatigue.

Jessie was getting concerned. He took it into his own hands to contact her doctor and make an appointment. Maybe it was time for her to be off of work for the remainder of her pregnancy.

They arrived at the doctor's office the following morning. Once the tests were run, and results returned, their doctor frowned. Jessie moved right into panic mode.

"What is it? What's wrong?"

"It looks like Ava has anemia."

"What the hell is that? Will she be okay? Will the baby be okay?"

The doctor smiled patiently while he ranted. "Everything will be fine." She turned her attention to Ava. "I want you to start taking iron pills, and I'm also writing a letter to your employer. You are off work as of today. I want you to get plenty of bed rest, take the pills, and relax."

Jessie sighed. "Done." He held Ava's hand as he spoke.

Ava squeezed his hand and smiled.

The doctor left the room for a few minutes, then returned with the prescription and letter.

"You'll be fine, Ava. Just do as I ask. Okay?"

Ava nodded. "Thank-you."

They left the building, hand in hand. "So, we'll go to the pharmacy and then to your office to hand in the letter."

"Okay."

"The doctor said you'd be fine. What's wrong?"

"I'll drive myself crazy being at home for six weeks before this little one arrives." She gently rubbed her belly.

"The time will go quickly."

"I hope so."

Ava's boss had been very understanding when she spoke with him and handed him the letter. Jessie stood beside her. If her boss had a problem with Ava leaving work early, he would tell him to shove his job up his ass, and storm out the door with Ava in tow. It wasn't necessary.

They stopped for a nice lunch before going home. Ava was ordered to bed. She didn't bother putting up a fuss. She was just so damn tired.

Once Jessie had been sure she had fallen asleep, he called Elle.

"Hi, Jessie! How was Ava's appointment?"

He relayed the conversation. The worry in his voice broke Elle's heart.

UNITY

"It's quite common for pregnant women to be anemic. I was anemic with both of you boys."

"Really?"

"Yep. And it all worked out just fine. Don't worry."

"Thanks, Mom. That gives me hope."

"Tell Ava that I'll be over in the morning to spend some time with her."

"Okay. Thanks. Talk to you later."

Elle set her drawings aside. She needed to work on a few more before her showing, but her family came first. The drawings would have to wait.

Danny arrived home early in the afternoon to find Elle preparing dinner. She wore short shorts, a tank top, and her feet were bare.

"Just what I like to see. My woman barefoot and in the kitchen."

She turned and smiled. "You're lucky you didn't say barefoot and pregnant in the kitchen."

He smiled back. "I'm brave, but not that brave."

"Speaking of pregnant, Ava is off work now because she anemic."

"Will she be okay?"

"Yes. I was too when I was pregnant. She just needs to follow the doctor's orders."

Danny chuckled. "You and Jessie will make sure she does."

Elle smiled knowingly. "I'm going to spend more time with her over the next few weeks."

He tapped her nose with a finger. "Of course, you will. What's for dinner?" He peeked over her shoulder.

"Stuffed salmon."

"Perfect. I'm gonna jump in the shower." He kissed her before he left the room. She watched him walk away and shook her head at her luck.

Jessie called in a panic an hour later.

"Mom?"

"Jessie, what's wrong?"

"It's Ava. We're at the hospital."

"What happened?"

"She woke up from her nap, we had dinner, and then when she stood up, she hit the floor."

"Is she okay?"

"They're going to induce the baby!"

"We're on our way!" She disconnected.

"Danny!"

They loaded into Danny's truck and raced to the County Hospital. Elle called Luke.

"Luke. Meet us at the hospital. Ava's going to have the baby tonight."

"I'm already on my way. Jessie just called."

"The kids?"

"Maggie and Dave are on their way. Nora will meet us later."

"Okay." She disconnected and starting wringing her hands.

Danny reached across the console to settle her down.

"She's in good hands, babe."

"I know but, the baby is six weeks early."

"The doctors wouldn't deliver the baby unless they were confident in their choice."

Elle nodded and held onto his hand tightly.

UNITY

They pushed through the emergency doors a few minutes before Luke. They had been told to have a seat in the waiting room. Nora arrived an hour later. The foursome sat there for at least three hours before Jessie entered the room, wearing his green scrubs. His smile was magnificent.

"Would you all like to meet the newest Chase?"

Elle jumped up and ran to him. "How's Ava?"

"She's doing great. She would love to see you!"

Luke shook his brother's hand. "Congratulations! Which name hat would you like? Boy or girl?"

Jessie shook his hand, smiled, and turned to lead them down the hall. Payback was a bitch. No way would he reveal the sex to his brother until the final second.

Nora smiled. She knew exactly what Jessie was doing. It was working, too. Luke's scowl said it all.

Danny chuckled as he followed the group. This smartass family killed him.

Ava sat up in her bed, cradling her newborn child. Her eyes shone with tears. She smiled when Jessie opened the door.

"Hi. Ready for some company?"

She nodded happily.

Elle was the first to enter. She made her way over to the bed to greet her newest grandchild. She ran her hand over Ava's hair. "Beautiful," she whispered and then bent to kiss the top of her head.

Luke stood holding two child-sized ball caps. One pink and the other blue. He tapped his foot impatiently. Nora laughed at him as she went to Ava.

"Which hat do you want?" Luke asked.

"Huh?" Jessie responded.

"Okay, okay. I get it. For Christ's sake, do I have a niece or a nephew?"

Jessie walked to him and slung an arm across his shoulder. He looked at both hats. "Well ... it seems we need ..." His finger went back and forth over both hats.

Luke rolled his eyes. "C'mon!"

Jessie chose the blue hat and slapped his brother on the back.

Luke cheered, "A boy!" He handed the blue hat over and went to Ava.

"Congratulations, Ava! Your husband is a jerk!"

"I know." She smiled back at him.

"What's the little guy's name?" Danny asked.

"We just need to pick one out of this hat," Jessie answered.

At the raised eyebrows of Danny and Elle, Nora went on to explain how she and Luke were responsible for naming the baby.

Elle laughed at the ridiculousness.

"Go ahead, Jessie. Pick a name for our boy." Ava could hardly contain her excitement.

Jessie closed his eyes and reached into the blue ball cap. He shuffled the papers around before he picked one folded piece of paper. He brought it to his wife so they could open it together.

Ava took a deep breath as Jessie unfolded it. They smiled when they read the name.

"Well, which name did you get?" Luke asked desperately. He and Nora had spent many sleepless nights trying to decide on three boy names and three girl names.

"Jaxson."

"That's one of my choices!" Luke announced.

"Do you like it?" Nora asked.

"We love it! Thank-you."

Luke let out a sigh of relief. "Thank God. Next time, you name your own child. That was way too stressful for me."

Elle and Danny laughed at the four.

"Well, hello there, Jaxson," Danny said as he moved in to get a closer look at the little guy. "He's so tiny."

"He only weighs four pounds and three ounces. The doctor said he's as healthy as can be, though."

"I'm sure he is. Can I hold him?" Elle asked

"Of course. Here you go, Grandma." She handed Jaxson to her.

"Hi, handsome." Elle kissed his tiny cheek and placed her hand over his heart. "You gave us quite a scare, little man." She pulled the receiving blanket back slightly to get a peek at his hair. Just as blond as his cousins.

Jessie dug into the hat to see what the other name choices had been. Luke tried to snag it from him. "You picked one. You don't get to see the others!"

Jessie pulled the ball cap out of his reach. "What does it matter now? We love the name Jaxson."

Luke shrugged and let him read the other names.

Jessie smiled when he opened one. "Jay. Seriously? Jay?"

"You said it had to start with the letter J. It seemed easy."

Nora laughed from where she stood beside Elle. "Another name he chose."

Jessie chose the last piece of folded paper. "Jed. That's a good one, too."

"What were the girl names?" Ava asked.

Luke unfolded the papers and handed them to her. "Jacqueline, Justine, and Jemma."

"Those are all beautiful." Her eyes filled with tears again.

Jaxson was passed around until it was time for the family to leave. Ava needed her rest. She and Jaxson would spend a few days in the hospital so he could be monitored.

Nora and Luke wanted to get home to Jarrett and Justin to relieve Dave and Maggie. They came home to find their sons and babysitters sound asleep on the couch. Dave lay on his back, cradling a sleeping Jarrett against his chest. Maggie was the mirror image of Dave over on the loveseat. Nora smiled at them and quietly walked toward Maggie. She gently touched her shoulder to wake her. Nora smiled when Maggie tightened her grip on Justin as she snapped her eyes open.

"Hi," Nora spoke softly.

"Hi." She glanced at Dave, who was also in the process of waking up. "I guess we dozed off."

Nora smiled sweetly. "It happens. How were they?"

Maggie smoothly sat up without loosening her grip on Justin. "These two boys are adorable, Nora!" She reluctantly handed Justin over. "How's Ava? Do we have a niece or a nephew?"

Luke answered proudly. "It's a boy, and they picked one of my names! Jaxson!"

Dave lay where he was, still holding Jarrett and smiled. "Cool name!"

"Right?" answered Luke. Nora rolled her eyes.

"Let's get these two little ones to bed and have a drink." Maggie stood and scooped Jarrett from Dave's arms to follow Nora.

UNITY

Dave sat up and then stood to stretch. "Comfy couch."

"It gets lots of use! C'mon, let's grab a beer and celebrate."

Elle and Danny were celebrating with a drink at home as well. The smile on Elle's face made Danny smile.

"Three grandsons!"

"Isn't it amazing!" Elle sighed as she touched her wine glass to Danny's beer bottle.

Jessie stayed with Ava until she was ready for sleep. He kissed her lips gently and said good night before he left the hospital room. "I love you."

"I love you too, babe. See you in the morning." She rolled over and instantly fell into a deep sleep.

Jessie smiled as he left. He drove straight to Luke's. He wanted a beer, and was pretty confident his brother would have one waiting for him.

He arrived twenty minutes later to find his family gathered around the kitchen table, talking happily about the newest addition.

Maggie gave him a huge hug. Dave shook his hand and slapped him on the back. "Congratulations!"

"Thanks! I'm glad the birth is over."

"Yes, because it's so hard on the man." Nora rolled her eyes and laughed as she said the words.

Jessie couldn't help but laugh.

Luke opened the fridge and returned to the table with a beer for his brother. They tapped the bottle necks together and nodded to each other. Words were not always needed between Luke and Jessie.

CHAPTER 26

JESSIE ARRIVED AT THE HOSPITAL BRIGHT AND EARLY THE FOLLOWING morning. He quietly opened the door to Ava's room to find her sleeping. He closed the door and strolled down the hall to the nursery. He wanted to see his son. He searched the little beds through the glass window, but couldn't see Jaxson. Jessie frowned as he made his way to the nurses' station.

"Excuse me. Can you tell me where Jaxson Chase is?"

The nurse smiled and checked her charts. He's in the room with Ava."

"No. He's not. I was just there. Ava is asleep, and Jaxson is not with her. I went to the nursery, but I didn't see him there, either."

The nurse frowned at the news and checked her charts again.

Jessie placed his hands on the counter. "Instead of checking your charts, why don't you get up and find my son." He was losing his temper.

The nurse picked up the phone and talked to one of the nurses in the nursery. "Gladys? It's Brenda. Do you have baby

Jaxson with you in the nursery?" She nodded into the phone and replaced the receiver.

She looked up at Jessie and said, "Your son is in the nursery now. He was being fed and changed when you were there looking for him."

"Thank-you. I'm sorry for being rude."

"New dads are like that." She lowered her head and continued with her work.

Jessie marched back to the nursery, and, sure enough, there was Jaxson, being placed back into his little bed. Jessie's sigh of relief was enormous. He tapped on the window. The nurse looked up and signaled for him to enter.

"Good morning."

"Good morning," Jessie replied.

"Would you like to take Jaxson back to Ava now?"

"Yes, please. She was still sleeping when I arrived, but I could sit in the chair with him until she wakes."

"Of course." She carefully handed him his son.

Jessie proudly walked back down the hall, whispering to Jaxson about how he had scared the hell out of him.

He sat in the chair, chattering away to him, when Ava woke. She smiled at the story her husband was telling their son.

"... so anyway, the moral of the story is that as you get older, you have to tell us where you are at all times. Even if you're somewhere that you shouldn't be, we will always be there for you. I'll drop whatever I'm doing to come and get you." He bent his head to kiss Jaxson's little cheek.

"It might be a little early in his life for sneaking out of the house." Ava smiled as she spoke.

"Good morning ... and it's never too early." He stood and went to hand Jaxson to her. He kissed her lips. "Did you sleep well?"

"Like a rock." She accepted Jaxson and kissed him.

Jessie went on to tell her of the misunderstanding with the nurses.

Ava scowled. "You didn't yell at anyone, did you?"

"Yell? No, but I was rude." He held up his hand. "I already apologized."

Ava laughed as Elle and Danny arrived at the door.

"Well, that's a lovely sound to hear! How's the little family doing?" Elle asked.

"Just great!" Ava answered.

Elle moved closer to stroke Ava's hair and kiss the top of her head. She rested her hand on Jaxson's beating heart.

Ava lifted him a little higher so Elle could scoop him up. He was immediately smothered in kisses. "Good morning, little man!"

Danny shook Jessie's hand and then went to kiss Ava's cheek. "Have they said yet when you can go home?"

"Hopefully tomorrow," Ava replied with a smile.

Elle had moved to the recently vacated chair to cuddle Jaxson. She looked up at Jessie. "He's just so precious."

Jessie moved closer and draped an arm around her shoulders.

The rest of the family arrived, full of excitement and with armloads of gifts.

Elle grudgingly gave up Jaxson so he could be passed around. Ava chatted happily with her family for the next hour. She couldn't hold back her yawns. Elle smiled sweetly at her and began to herd everyone out the door. Jessie took Jaxson from Emma and moved to Ava's bedside.

They thanked everyone for the visit as the group made their way out the door.

Before each of them headed back to work, Danny suggested that they all have breakfast together. He went on to complain that Elle had rushed him out the door before he'd had a chance to eat. He'd barely had time to drink his coffee.

Elle looped her arm through his. "Poor baby. I hope I can make it up to you somehow." She pouted and batted her eyelashes at him.

He raised his brows and then looked over his shoulder to his family. "Never mind breakfast. I'm not that hungry, after all."

"What?" Mike said, as he threw up his hands.

Elle laughed out loud. "He's kidding. Let's go."

Danny bent and whispered to Elle, "You are an evil woman."

"I know." She squeezed his hand and led him to her truck.

Jessie spent the majority of the day with Ava and Jaxson. He simply couldn't get enough of either of them. They went through the checklist of what he needed to do at home before she and Jaxson arrived. It wasn't much of a list. Ava was incredibly organized. He would call Nora to double-check, though. He wanted everything to be perfect. They weren't quite prepared for Jaxson to arrive as early as he did.

He finally left her side when she could no longer control her yawning.

Jessie made the call to Nora and was informed that she and Luke had checked on everything they could think of while dropping off the gifts that had previously been delivered to the hospital. He was told to relax, and they would see him at home the following day.

Jessie chuckled as he hung up. He figured they were old hands at this game. Now, what would he do with himself until morning? He decided to swing by Mike and Emma's for a beer. He visited with them for a couple of hours, then finally went home.

The following morning, he checked on a couple of his job sites and happily accepted congratulations from his crew. He would be stopping by at least once a day in case of questions or problems, but he had full confidence in his employees.

He stopped at the florist before going to the hospital. He strolled up to the nurse he had been abrupt with the day before, with a huge smile on his face.

"Good morning," he said.

She looked up and smiled warily. "Good morning."

He brought the flowers out from behind his back. "I would like to apologize properly for my rudeness yesterday." He handed her the bouquet and said, "I'm sorry."

Her eyes filled with tears. "This is so nice of you. Nobody ever brings me flowers."

"Well, I'm sure you don't deal with idiots like me very often."

"Actually, I do."

"Really? I'm so sorry to hear that!"

She shrugged her shoulders slightly. "It comes with the job. New parents are awfully stressed."

Jessie nodded and tapped his finger on her desk. "I hope you have a nice day, Brenda."

"Thank-you." She left her desk momentarily to search for a makeshift vase.

Ava could hear the exchange of words between Jessie and Brenda. She smiled when he entered her room. "That was really sweet of you, babe."

He approached the bed to kiss her and then his son. "She deserves to be treated with more respect than I showed her."

Ava nodded. "Doctor Evans will be in shortly to let us know if we're going home today." She nuzzled Jaxson. "Right, buddy?"

"It's pretty lonely at home without you."

"It's pretty lonely here, too." She handed Jaxson to Jessie's outstretched arms. Her son looked incredibly small in Jessie's big arms.

The doctor arrived during the handoff.

"Good morning. How are you feeling?"

"Hi. I feel great!" Jessie exclaimed.

"I think she was talking to me, Jessie." Ava laughed.

Doctor Evans smiled and chuckled. "I'm glad to hear that you feel great. Can I take a look at this little guy?"

Jessie handed him over and then moved closer to Ava again.

She shook her head at him as he took her by the hand.

Jaxson was taken to the little side bed and examined thoroughly.

"It seems to me that Jaxson is good to go home. I'd like to take your vitals now please, Ava."

Jessie took Jaxson and sat in the chair to wait for Ava's results.

Ava's examination impressed Dr. Evans, as well.

"Okay. So, I'd say you are both good to go home, Ava."

"Oh. Thank-you!"

"I want you to get as much rest as you can, though."

Jessie piped up. "I'll make sure she does."

"I'm sure you will." Dr. Evans smiled at him as she turned to leave the room. "Oh, and Jessie, the flowers you gave to Nurse Brenda are beautiful and very thoughtful.

He smiled back and said, "She deserves them."

Ava lay Jaxson in his bed so she could get herself dressed. Jessie gathered up her belongings. He called Elle and then Luke to let them know that they would be home within the hour.

They arrived home to find Elle and Nora waiting for them. The twins were napping in Jaxson's crib. Luke, Danny, and the rest of the family would be over to the house once they finished work for the day.

The table had been filled with snacks and the living room floor with gifts. Elle smiled when they entered the house. She scooped up Jaxson from his car seat while Nora led them to the pile of presents.

"This is crazy!" exclaimed Ava.

"It's so much fun to open them, too!" remarked Nora.

Elle settled in the rocking chair, while the girls opened the generous pile of gifts that friends had dropped off.

Jessie made a pot of coffee and joined the women.

Danny and Luke arrived in time for lunch. Mike, Dave, Emma, and Maggie would be coming after dinner.

Luke carried in a ride-on tractor for his nephew. Jessie jumped up from his seat to check it out. Danny was right behind him with a rocking horse he had made a few weeks earlier. He said hello to everyone and then went directly to Elle to relieve her of Jaxson. He earned himself a scowl for his effort.

Elle rose to finish setting the table to serve lunch to everyone.

Once all the gifts had been opened and oohed and aahed over, the rest of the family sat down to eat together.

Dave, Mike, Emma, and Maggie surprised everyone an hour later by showing up earlier than expected. They came in with their arms loaded down with more gifts. Mike returned to his truck and came back in with loads of food and drinks.

CHAPTER 27

ELLE SPENT THE MAJORITY OF HER DAYS RUNNING BETWEEN NORA AND AVA. She enjoyed spending time with the girls and her grandsons, but knew she was wearing herself out. She was exhausted most nights by the time she arrived home.

Danny watched her cover a yawn during dinner. "Are you not feeling well, babe?"

"Just tired."

"I think you need to slow down a bit with helping the girls so much."

She covered another yawn. "I think you're right."

His eyebrows shot up. "Seriously?"

Elle smiled and nodded. "It's time for the girls to be mothers and me to be a grandma. I'd like to spend more time with you here and at the cottage."

"Thank God!" He came around the table and hugged her. "And thank-you."

Elle giggled at him. "Let's pack for the cottage and get the hell out of here."

"On it!" He went to the bedroom to pack some clothes while she cleared the table.

Danny sent out a group text to all of the kids.

Leaving in the next hour for the cottage. Have a good week.

Each answered within seconds of each other.

Luke: Okay. Have fun.

Emma: Enjoy!

Dave: See you Friday night

Jessie: Everything okay?

Luke: Mom probably needs a break from you!

Jessie: Fuck you

Ava: LOL

Maggie: LOL, I'm bringing dinner for Saturday night

Nora: I'll supply Sunday morning breakfast :)

Ava: I'll bring Sunday lunch

Mike: Must be nice to be semi-retired. Oh, and I'll bring beer

Jessie: cooler full of beer here, too

Dave: beer here too

Ava: Who's bringing the wine? I'm ready for it!

Luke: We'll bring beer and wine

Danny: Jesus! See you all on the weekend

Danny left the room, carrying two duffle bags, with a smile on his face.

"What are you smiling about?"

He shook his head. "I just sent out a text to the kids. You should see their replies!"

"I can only imagine. Ready to go?"

"Yep."

Danny cranked up the tunes in his truck and threw it into gear.

UNITY

After an easy two-hour drive, they arrived at their cottage on Giggling Creek. Elle sighed and slid from the truck. She hefted the duffle bags while Danny grabbed the grocery bags. He set his on the kitchen island, and she headed up the stairs with hers.

Danny didn't know what the bags contained, but he stuffed them in the fridge. He caught up to Elle before she took too many stairs. He relieved her of the bags and then followed her up the rest of the steps.

She flopped on the bed in exhaustion. Danny smiled and lay beside her. He pulled her close to tuck her head into his shoulder. "Good night, babe."

"Mm-hmm."

Danny woke, fully dressed, at six the following morning. He quietly left the bed and tiptoed down the staircase. He wanted Elle to sleep. Once coffee had been made, he moved out to the porch to enjoy the quiet of his surroundings. Two cups of coffee later, he crept back up the stairs to check on his wife. She lay curled into his pillow, snoring softly.

Danny smiled at his sleeping beauty and made his way back downstairs again. He was glad she had decided to slow down with the grandkids. He knew they meant the world to her, but she needed some time to enjoy a few other things in life. He had packed her drawing supplies, and was hoping she would take the time to use them. Her talent still amazed him.

For now, he would prepare her breakfast and bring it up to her. He sliced up fresh fruit and set a bagel in the toaster. He pulled a tray from the cabinets and set it on the counter. The plate and cutlery sat, waiting for the food. He just needed one more thing. He grabbed a glass from the cupboard and jogged down to the beach.

He had only been gone a few minutes, but heard Elle moving around in their king-size bed when he returned. He pushed the bagels down for toasting, poured a cup of coffee, and climbed the flight of stairs. He whistled a tune on his way.

"Good morning, sunshine!"

"Good morning to you! What's all this?"

"Breakfast in bed." He smiled as he lay the tray across her lap.

"It looks great!" She picked up the sand-filled glass with dandelions jammed in the center of it. "And this?" She tilted her head.

"My shot at a bouquet."

"So sweet. Thank-you."

He bent to kiss her, and sat on the edge of the bed.

"Did you sleep well?"

"I did. What time is it, anyway?" she asked around a mouthful of fruit. She forked a piece of orange and fed it to him.

"Close to ten o'clock."

"Holy shit!"

"It's okay. We don't need to be anywhere." He ran his hand down her hair. "We can spend the day floating on the water. We can go for a walk. We can crawl under these sheets." He waggled his eyebrows at her.

Elle's eyes lit up. "All of the above, please."

Danny tried to remove her tray from her lap.

"Can I finish eating first? I may need the energy."

"You can eat later," he growled as he proceeded to lift the tray. He set it on the nightstand and scooted around the bed. He stripped down to nothing before climbing under the sheets. He ran his hand over her breast, and encountered material.

Elle laughed out loud. "Guess I never took the time to undress last night."

His eyes softened. "Let me help you now."

She sat up a little so he could pull her top over her head. Next, his hands wandered down her smooth stomach to remove her shorts. He unbuttoned them and slid the zipper down. Before he pulled her shorts off, he slid his fingers into her. Elle responded immediately. It wasn't long before they were both beyond the point of return.

The afternoon was spent in the canoe and then walking along the trails. They ate a meal of grilled chicken while sipping wine and beer. Relaxation mode felt good. Danny could see the stress leave Elle's face. He took her by the hand and squeezed.

"Are you enjoying your time away?"

"Absolutely. I love it up here, Danny!"

"Good. Let's enjoy the week before we get bombarded with the kids." He smiled and winked at her.

"I'm looking forward to the rest, but I'm also looking forward to seeing all the kids on the weekend."

"I know it. I am too, but I'm more looking forward to time alone with you. I feel as though we don't get enough of it right now." He held up his free hand. "I'm grateful for every minute of it. I love you, Elle." He released her hand and moved in closer to rub her bottom lip with his thumb.

Elle smiled. "Keep that up, and you'll get plenty of alone time right here on the porch." He rubbed a little harder.

As the sun was setting, they could hear gravel crunching in the laneway.

Danny stood. "I wonder who that could be. We didn't tell anyone except for the kids that we'd be here."

Headlights of a car shone on them and the cabin. It stopped and quickly backed out of the lane.

"What the fuck?" Danny stomped into the cabin for his truck keys. He came back out to find Elle sitting in the passenger seat.

"You're not coming," he said angrily.

"You're wasting time." She crossed her arms across her chest in stubbornness.

"Dammit." Danny climbed in and slammed his door. He started the truck and threw it into drive. Gravel flew as he hit the gas. It fishtailed a bit before he got it under control again. Within a few minutes, they had caught up to the only other vehicle on the road. Danny thrust ahead of the car and slowed. He blocked the road so it couldn't pass him. He set his truck in park while keeping an eye on the rearview mirror. There was no movement from the car. He stepped from the truck, reached into the box for a length of lumber, and stalked toward the car. Elle began to open her door.

"Get back in the damn truck, Elle! No arguments!"

He reached the car and wrenched on the door handle. Of course, it was locked. He tapped the windshield with the lumber.

"Open the door before I bust this fucking window!"

He heard the click of the locks, and the window rolled down.

"It's me. Don't hit me!"

Danny's jaw dropped when he realized it was Jillian sitting in the car.

"What the fuck were you doing at the cabin?"

She lowered her head without answering.

"Get out of the car, Jillian." He turned to signal for Elle to come over. She cautiously walked to the car and came face to face with the driver.

"Jillian? What are you doing?"

"It was stupid of me to come here." She started to wring her hands.

Elle grabbed her by the arm. "Tell me. Now!"

Jillian looked up and said, "Chase forced me to come here."

Elle scowled. "How can he force you to come here if he's in prison?"

"He threatened to hurt Hank and me once he's released if I didn't give him the lay of the land."

Danny shook his head. "This will never end, will it?"

"Dammit, Jillian. I told you not to tell him about Hank!" Elle yelled. "Now, do you see what you've done? What the hell does he want to know about the property?"

Jillian's eyes filled with tears. "How far it is from Hank's, what the roads are like, and if there's only one way in or two." She ran her hands through her hair. "I don't know what he plans to do, but I don't want him to hurt Hank."

"No. You'd rather he be our fucking problem again! Fuck!" Elle kicked the stones at her feet.

Danny pulled his phone from his pocket and called his police buddy, Jake. He explained the situation and the worry that came with it. Jake would be up to the cabin the following morning to speak with them and Jillian. Next, he dialed Hank's number. He would be over shortly.

Danny drove Jillian's car back to the cabin, with her sitting shotgun. Elle followed in the truck. Within minutes, Hank stood on the porch.

"What's the problem? Are you okay, Jillian?" She moved to stand beside him.

Danny explained the history between themselves, Jillian, and Chase. Hank could hardly believe what he was hearing. He turned to address Jillian.

"Why didn't you come to me with this threat? We could have taken care of the situation in a completely different manner."

Elle spoke up. "Jillian, are you helping Chase to come after us?"

Her eyes grew wide. "No! Of course not!"

"Then why are you doing this for him?"

"Because he terrifies me. We all know what he's capable of. I don't want myself or Hank to be on the receiving end of it."

The discussion continued for a bit longer before Danny decided to call it a night. They would all meet at the cabin in the morning with Jake.

Elle and Danny spent a restless evening with worry on their minds. They would speak with Jake in the morning and then relay the details to their family. They both hoped Jake would come up with a solution.

The group assembled around the kitchen table. Elle served coffee while Jillian told Jake exactly what Chase had wanted from her and about the threats he had used against her and Hank. "He told me that he has people on the outside." She hung her head.

Hank sat quietly, listening and shaking his head at the nonsense.

Jake listened intently and took notes. "Okay, so I'll speak to the county judge about this and see what can be done. I would assume that more time would be added to his sentence. The group nodded. Hank and Jillian left with instructions to contact Jake if any further contact was made. Jillian was told to tell Chase that she hadn't been to the property yet.

Jake hung back to speak privately with Elle and Danny.

"I can either go through the legal channels that I spoke of, or I can make arrangements for Chase to be taken care of for good." He held his hand up before they could question the second part of his statement. "I am not a dirty cop, but I can tell you that I have had just about enough of this fucking guy. Holding a gun on Jessie is one thing, but trying to kidnap innocent children is another. He's already taken a few beatings in jail for the latter. I've seen situations like this before, and they never end well. I'd be happy to reach out and have this problem go away. I think your only other option is to give him the money he's after, but I'd be afraid he'd just keep coming back for more."

Danny and Elle were speechless. Danny and Jake had been friends since childhood. It had never crossed his mind that Jake would have these types of connections at his disposal.

Elle spoke first. "Thank-you for your honesty. I want the son of a bitch out of our lives for good, but I will not have you or your job jeopardized."

Danny nodded in agreement. "I'm with Elle on this, Jake. There cannot be any repercussions for you."

"Don't worry about it. I have a lot of people that owe me a lot of favors. This is an easy one. From what I hear, he's been nothing but a pain in the ass and a disturbance for the staff and prisoners."

"So, how do you seeing this going down?"

"I won't discuss that with you. The less you know, the better it is for all of us. I will say that it will not happen until the timing is right. If it were to take place in the next few months, it would be suspicious to his mother and Hank."

Elle and Danny nodded. They ended the discussion and took a walk around the property. It would not be spoken of again.

CHAPTER 28

ELLE AND DANNY HAD DECIDED THAT THEIR CONVERSATIONS WITH JAKE, Jillian, and Hank would not be repeated. Danny had contacted both Hank and Jillian to tell them that he did not want their kids to know about the threats. He didn't want them living in fear of when the hammer would drop. Both swore to keep it to themselves.

They moved Chase to the back of their minds and enjoyed the rest of the week at Giggling Creek. They thoroughly enjoyed their time with their children and grandchildren on the weekend. Jaxson, Jarrett, and Justin had been scooped up by Elle the instant the trucks were parked. Danny had the strollers ready and waiting for when they arrived. They took the "Three Jays" for a stroll around the property while their parents unpacked and relaxed with a drink. Elle had missed her grandchildren desperately, and was as happy as could be to be spending some quiet time with Danny and the boys. By the time they arrived back at the cottage, the campfire had been lit, a beer opened for Danny, and a glass of wine poured for Elle.

"So, what have you guys been up to all week?" asked Luke.

"We don't need details!" Jessie interjected.

Ava gave him a swat with one hand while the other held Jaxson.

Nora rolled her eyes as she played with Jarrett and Justin.

Elle laughed at Jessie. "We just went in the canoes, walked, and slept."

"Yeah, let's go with 'slept,'" Danny said, as he hung an arm over her shoulder.

"See what you've started, Luke? Jesus!" Jessie shook his head.

"I only asked a question." Pointing a finger at Danny, he said, "He gave the answer he knew would drive you crazy."

Mike and Dave laughed at their comradery. Maggie and Emma smiled at the sound of laughter as they placed platters of food on the table for all to enjoy.

"Wow! This looks amazing, girls. Thank-you," Elle remarked.

"No problem. Enjoy." Maggie smiled and bent to take Jaxson from Ava's arms. Emma made her way to Jarrett and Justin's stroller to play with them.

"I'm glad you guys enjoyed your week up here," Ava said, as she reached for a cracker and began to add meat and cheese to it.

Jessie rolled his eyes. "Please don't start this conversation again."

Elle smiled. "We have had a great time, and I think we may start spending more time up here!"

"Good for you guys! Now that Dad's almost retired, you might as well," Dave said.

"Yep." Danny grinned and reached for a snack.

UNITY

The conversation continued for another hour before Ava and Nora announced that it was bedtime for the kids. Elle and Danny took turns kissing the little ones before they headed off for their beds.

Everyone moved closer to the fire for a few more drinks. Luke had brought out his guitar, and the singing went on for hours. It ended up being a very late evening. The next day was going to be hot and sunny, so the plan was to relax and enjoy the day by the water.

The only ones up early were Jarrett, Justin, Jaxson, and their moms. The rest of the family slowly exited their cabins a couple of hours later. Wine glasses and beer cans had been replaced with large coffee mugs. Groans of headaches could be heard from everyone.

The majority of the day was spent by the water. After a light lunch in the cottages, only a few came back out to enjoy the weather. The rest of the crew were napping.

Ava and Nora smiled to their husbands as they handed off their sons to them.

"Have a nice afternoon with Jaxson, honey. I'm off to have a nap." Ava laughed at the look on Jessie's face. He was extremely hungover and had planned on having a nap himself down by the water. Plans change in a hurry when you're a parent.

Nora smiled at Luke. "Ditto."

Luke groaned and grudgingly took the twins into his arms. He glanced at Jessie and said, "Might as well make the best of it."

They laid out a blanket on the sand by the river and covered it with toys to amuse the children. Jessie jammed an umbrella in the sand to protect them from the sun, while Luke headed back up to the cottages for drinking water.

"If you leave me here alone with these three, I'll hunt you down like the dog you are!"

Luke laughed, flipped him the bird, and continued walking.

"Your daddy thinks he's funny. But, you'll find out in time that he's not as funny as he thinks he is." He bent to kiss his nephews and smiled at their gurgling reaction. "I, on the other hand, am hilarious." He bent to kiss Jaxson. "Right, buddy?"

Luke came back a few minutes later and settled on the blanket with Jessie and the kids.

"These little guys are gonna love it up here as they get older."

"Yep. They'll wear out the four-wheelers, tip over the canoes, build forts, and get into lots of trouble. They'll have the world by the tail," Jessie replied.

"I'm looking forward to the teenage years, too. God, I hope they don't drive us crazy like we did to Mom and Dad." Luke smiled at the memories.

"They will definitely drive us crazy and worry their moms sick. Ava and Nora have no idea what's coming their way!" Jessie laughed out loud. Their wives didn't grow up with brothers, so this was going to be a whole new experience for them.

The two brothers were still chatting of the future an hour later when Nora and Ava arrived at the path's edge. They sat quietly beside each other a short distance away to listen in. They finally approached their husbands with tears of joy in their eyes.

UNITY

Nora hugged Luke and said, "I don't care how much trouble our sons get into. I only hope they have the same strong relationship that you two have."

Ava spoke up and said, "Me too." She hugged Jessie and then scooped up Jaxson. "Promise me that you won't worry me too much, okay?" She snuggled his chubby cheek and kissed him soundly.

"We can take over if you guys want to rest before dinner," Nora commented.

"I'm good right here, but thanks."

"Yep. Me too," Jessie added.

The four of them sat on the blanket with their children and enjoyed each other's company.

"Mind if we join in?"

The foursome turned to see the rest of their family coming toward them.

"Not at all. Have a seat," Jessie replied.

Mike and Dave carried a cooler between them.

Luke groaned when he saw it, but reached in for a beer when the lid opened.

Once everyone had a cold drink in their hands, Elle said, "Cheers to another wonderful summer together at Giggling Creek. May the laughter and giggles continue for eternity."

Each family member smiled broadly as they raised their drinks.

"Cheers to that!"

"Well said, Elle." Danny ran his thumb over her bottom lip before he took a sip of his beer.

"Enough!" Jessie groaned.

The laughter of the Chase and Jackson families could be heard floating across the water and dancing deep into the forest.

EPILOGUE

LIFE FOR ELLE AND DANNY SMOOTHLY MOVED INTO RETIREMENT MODE. THEY could come and go as they pleased to the cottage, or breeze into their children's homes for visits. Their kids took turns cooking meals for them and supplying all the beer and wine Danny and Elle could consume. How the tables had turned! Every now and then, they would whisk the grandkids away for the weekend.

Luke's company, Chase Your Dreams Construction, had taken off like a rocket. His schedule had been filled for the next two years. He still worked twelve hours a day, but when he arrived home in the evenings, his world revolved around his wife and children.

Nora couldn't be happier raising her twin boys. Yes, they kept her busy with their shenanigans, but she loved every minute of it. Jarrett and Justin kept her on her toes. She still dreamed of owning that little boutique. Time would tell.

Jessie could barely keep up with the jobs that poured in. He hired a few extra men to join his crew. He continued to work like a Trojan on the sites, and was nothing less than a loving father and husband to Ava and Jaxson. His nephews thought he was hilarious.

Ava filled not one but two walls with framed photos of Jaxson. He was her pride and joy. She had slipped in a few of herself and Jessie as well. Elle's artwork hung over Jaxson's crib. It was part of her "new beginnings" collection. More hung over Jarrett and Justin's cribs. Ava never did return to her accounting job. She thrived at her photography.

Dave and Mike continued to make a success of their father's company. Dan's Designs flourished. They didn't feel the need to change the name; it was, after all, their father's legacy.

Maggie wasn't as keen about being part of the administration team at the hospital, so she resumed her old position as a full-time nurse. She had missed seeing her patients and co-workers, and they had missed seeing her. Her return had been welcomed with open arms.

Emma's idea of wedding hair and makeup had done well with the shop. Once word had spread, she ended up spending more time at the bride's home instead of the shop. Her Saturdays were busy, but she was able to join Mike for Saturday evenings and Sundays at the cottages with the family. She reserved Friday nights for her girlfriends.

Lois continued to work for Dave and Mike. She kept them in line just as she had done with Danny. They loved her for it.

Kim and Tony certainly enjoyed the new guest cottage when they visited. Their tent had never been used, and while Kim still wanted to burn it, Tony decided to donate it to Elle and Danny for overflow guests.

Jillian and Hank had quietly married on a beautiful Friday evening. They had found happiness in each other's company.

UNITY

Their only guests were Elle and Danny. Jillian had burst into tears when Elle handed her their wedding gift—an envelope containing a cheque for five hundred thousand dollars. It was for her to do with as she pleased. She certainly deserved to spoil herself. Her son would not have the opportunity to spend it.

Chase did not attend the wedding. He had met his demise during a gang fight while serving his time in prison. The doctors could not save him.

Jake Riley did not have any part of it. His record as a clean cop had never encountered a single smear.

Elle continued to draw, write music, dote on her children and grandchildren.

Danny kept himself busy with wood projects. Creating wooden toys for his grandchildren turned into his new pastime. The garage overflowed with finished projects for the next babies that would come along.

Elle and Danny continue to be grateful for reuniting after so many years. He never stopped rubbing her bottom lip with his thumb.

As for those Chase boys, they may have stirred up a little trouble over the years, but turned out to be wonderful, fun-loving men, just like their dads.

DAR PETERSEN

THE BOYS

What in the world did I do to deserve two boys like you
It's so simple and true my heart aches from my love for you
It's a mother's right to worry every day and every night
Yeah, and it's God's job to keep you in his sights

I would lay down my life in a single beat of my heart
That's the deal he and I made right from the start
I wouldn't question it, no I wouldn't say a word
That's how it is when your kids are your world

Your laughter on the air and the sun in your blond hair
Young and full of life, living it without a care
Oh, all those crazy parties that went on all night
While I just sat and waited to see your headlights

From tiny arms reaching up high to be carried
To two grown men, one about to be married
Brothers side by side, that's just how it's always been
Grandpa smiling down as you hand off the ring

I smile as I see you shake your brother's hand
He's just the proudest to be your best man
You guys steal my heart away when you hug me and say
I love you Mom and thank God for you every day

What in the world did I do to deserve two boys like you
It's so simple and true, my heart aches from my love for you
It's a mother's right to worry every day and every night
Yeah, and it's God's job to keep you in his sights

May 4, 2015
Written by Darlene Petersen